Paul's Pursuit:
Dragon Lords of Valdier Book 6

By S.E. Smith

## Acknowledgments

I would like to thank my husband Steve for believing in me and being proud enough of me to give me the courage to follow my dream. I would also like to give a special thank you to my sister and best friend Linda, who not only encouraged me to write but who also read the manuscript. Also to my other friends who believe in me: Julie, Jackie, Lisa, Sally and Narelle. The girls that keep me going!

—S.E. Smith

Montana Publishing
Science Fiction Romance
PAUL'S PURSUIT: DRAGON LORDS OF VALDIER
BOOK 6
Copyright © 2013 by Susan E. Smith
First E-Book Publication June 2013
Cover Design by Melody Simmons

Summary: Paul's missing daughter suddenly appears with a warrior from another world, and he realizes he has has to return with her to her new home or lose her forever.

ISBN: 978-1-942562-41-2
ISBN: 978-1-942562-05-4 (eBook)

Published in the United States by Montana Publishing.

{1. Science Fiction Romance. – Fiction. 2. Science Fiction – Fiction. 3. Paranormal – Fiction. 4. Romance – Fiction.}

www.montanapublishinghouse.com

## Synopsis

Paul Grove loves two things in the world more than anything else: his daughter, Trisha, and roaming the mountains and forests of Wyoming. One he would kill for, the other is who he is. He has spent his life devoted to his 'little' girl, even though she isn't so little anymore.

When she disappears, he focuses all of his hunting and tracking skills on finding her. The tracks he has found make no sense, the clues left behind unlike any he has ever seen before, and the disappearance of Trisha and her friends a mystery he is determined to solve. When his daughter unexpectedly returns with a warrior from another world, he realizes he has no choice but to return with her to her new home or lose her forever.

Morian Reykill is a High Priestess for the golden symbiots of their world known as The Gods Blood. She is their protector and a member of the Royal House of Valdier. When her first mate is killed, she is devastated, for while he was not her true mate, they loved each other very much.

She thought to join her mate in the next life, but something told her it was not yet her time. She believes it is because of her five sons, all Princes of Valdier devoted to protecting their people and the Hive, the birthplace of the symbiots. When her sons and her people are threatened, she will do whatever she has to in order to protect them.

Paul Grove finds love in the beautiful alien woman who takes his breath away. For the first time since his wife died when Trisha was a baby, Paul wants someone of his own to hold. When a madman threatens his new family and takes the woman he is determined to claim, he will use all of his skills in hunting, tracking, and guerilla warfare to get her safely back by his side.

Morian discovers that the alien male who has claimed her is the true mate she has always hoped of having but thought an impossible dream. Will she be able to save him before a powerful Valdier Royal kills him as he did her first mate, or will she lose not only her true mate but her entire family to a man obsessed with gaining control of the Hive and the people of Valdier?

She is willing to sacrifice anything, including her life, to protect them. What she does not know is that Paul is the ultimate predator when his family is in danger. For when he is in pursuit of an enemy, his prey never gets away.

# Contents

## Prologue

**Twenty-six years earlier**

Paul Grove stood tall and proud as the cold breeze swirled around him. There was the promise of the first snow dancing in it, but he already felt a numbness that not even the cold weather could touch. He was a huge bear of a man, even though he was only twenty-one years old. He had always been big for his age and years of hard work on his parent's ranch had sculptured his muscles early, giving him an even more formidable appearance.

He wore his black hair short simply because it was easier to maintain. At six and a half feet, he had lost the gangly limbs of just a few years earlier. His deeply tanned face reflected the hours he spent outside working in the wilds of Wyoming. Today, it was not his height or build that captured the attention of those standing around; it was the grief reflected in his dark brown eyes and the small bundle wrapped protectively in his arms.

His arms tightened around the tiny body pressed up against him. Tears clouded his vision, but he refused to let them fall. He focused on the small, sweet warmth he held close to his heart. It was all he had left of Evelyn, his beautiful young wife who died less than a week ago from a brain aneurysm. A part of him wanted to rage at God for taking something so precious, so beautiful, far too early. Her beautiful brown eyes shining with love and laughter shimmered in his mind. The way she would dance around their little house with a laugh and a song on her lips still a vivid memory.

He had loved her forever, it seemed. When her family moved to town when she was in first grade and he was a big third grader, he swore that he would love her forever and take care of her. He remembered her parents kneeling down next to her curly head and promising that she would be fine. He had walked over and introduced himself. Ten minutes later, he was holding her small hand in his and walking her to class as her parents watched with worried eyes.

"I'm so sorry, Paul," another one of their former classmates from school said. "If there is anything I can do...."

Paul nodded automatically, his arms drawing his tiny daughter closer as if to shield her from the looks of worry, sadness, and pity. He knew what many were thinking. That he was too young to be raising a little girl on his own. He had already had several offers to take his baby girl from him, to let others raise her. Hell, even Evelyn's mom tried to insist she take Trisha and raise her. She tried to tell him it would be best if another woman raised his little girl. He had turned her down with barely restrained politeness.

"Paul," Evelyn's mom, Rosalie, walked over to him. "Let me take her."

Paul turned his grief-stricken eyes on the woman who had changed over the last few years from a pleasant, if strict mother, into a first class bitch when it had come to her own daughter.

Rosalie had changed when Evelyn's dad left her and Evelyn when Evelyn was in sixth grade. Paul had listened as Evelyn cried as she told him that nothing she did was good enough for her mother. He had doctored the bruises and welts on Evelyn's delicate skin from the times her mother had gotten drunk and hit her over some small infraction.

He had even gone and warned Evelyn's mother that if she ever hit her daughter again, he would show her no mercy. Her mother had tried to keep them apart, but he would have fought the entire world for his beautiful wife. He would do no less for his precious baby girl.

"No," Paul said shortly, looking into eyes that would have reminded him of his wife if not for the anger and bitterness in them. "She is fine. She's sleeping," he added in a gentler tone.

"Give her to me," Rosalie begged. "Haven't you taken enough from me? Haven't I lost enough? Let me raise my granddaughter. You are young. You can find another girl, marry, have more children. I'll never have another Evelyn. I'll never have another chance."

Paul felt the rage building inside him as he listened to Rosalie. "You never appreciated the beautiful daughter you had. What makes you think I would ever let you take mine?" He asked in a cold, barely controlled voice. "I loved your daughter more than life itself, Rosalie. I love our daughter just as much. She is my life now. I am her father and I will always be her father. I will be there for her. I will be the one to teach her, guide her, and love her with every fiber of my being."

Rosalie's eyes grew as cold and bitter as the wind blowing through the graveyard. "We'll see about that. I have money. I will fight for my daughter's child. I will take her and raise her if it is the last thing I ever do. She will be mine!"

Paul felt a calm resolve course through him as Trisha shifted and raised her curly little head. She pulled her tiny thumb out of her mouth and looked up into his eyes. A small, innocent smile curved her tiny, pink lips and her dark brown eyes lit up with love and trust.

"Dada," she giggled, leaning forward to hide her cold nose against his smooth cheek.

Paul looked at Rosalie with a new determination and maturity not often found in a twenty-one year old. He had discovered the painful lesson that life was not fair this past week. Perhaps fate had stepped in, knowing it was important for he and Evelyn to marry young. Evelyn might not have lived long, but she had given him something very precious in her short life; the knowledge of what it was to love and be loved and a beautiful daughter.

His hand moved up and cupped the back of Trisha's curly head. He buried his nose in the wild curls; breathing in the fresh scent of the strawberry shampoo he had used on her hair earlier that morning. He refused to let anyone take his reason for living away from him without a fight. Right now, Trisha was the only thing keeping him moving forward through the grief and heartache threatening to consume and tear him apart. When he turned his eyes back to Rosalie, they were almost black with quiet rage.

Rosalie took a step back, her hand going to her throat as she recognized that she had just pushed her son-in-law too far. Subconsciously, she had always known that Paul would be a formidable opponent if cornered or provoked. A shiver coursed through her at the knowledge that he could also be a deadly one.

Paul shifted Trisha again and looked down at Evelyn's mother with a cold, grim expression on his face. "I can promise you will never get your hands on my daughter, Rosalie," Paul said before he turned and walked away without a backward look.

* * *

**Twenty-one years before:**

"What is this?" Paul asked quietly, kneeling down along the narrow animal trail.

A small bundle of long curls fell forward almost touching the ground as the tiny figure next to him squatted down. Small fingers reached out and barely touched the soft imprint in the moist soil. Trisha focused on the shape, picturing in her mind all the different animals that lived in the region and what their footprints looked like. She curled her hand around the small bow her dad had made for her before she looked up and around her with dark, serious eyes.

"Mountain lion," she whispered with wide eyes. "It is an old one from the size of the print. Do you think it is close?"

"You tell me," Paul asked quietly smiling down proudly into her intense face. "How old do you think the track is?"

Trisha looked down at the track again before her eyes moved to the next one. "Not old. See how the leaves are pressed down into the print? It is still damp and firm. Maybe this morning," she murmured.

"Good job, baby girl," Paul said standing. "We need to get back to camp. Ariel and Carmen are going to camp out with us tonight."

Trisha grinned excitedly up at her dad. "Is their daddy coming too?"

Paul laughed as he swung the large pack up onto his shoulder. "Yes. Their mom has gone to visit her sister so he figured it would be a nice break for the girls from his cooking."

Trisha laughed as she skipped down the narrow animal trail. "Will we still get to talk to mommy tonight?"

Paul's chest tightened at the innocent delight. Every night they would lie outside when the weather permitted and look up at the brilliant stars in the sky. And each night, he would pick a different one where his beautiful Evelyn would be looking down on them. He thanked her each and every night for giving him the precious gift that was skipping in front of him. It was only when he was out in the wilds with his baby girl or lying under the stars talking to his beautiful wife that he felt a sense of peace. His eyes drifted up to the clear, blue skies. He wondered if he would always feel that nagging feeling that there was someone else out there for him. He had searched but none of the women he had met so far calmed the restlessness in his soul.

His eyes jerked down suddenly as his ears picked up the changes in the forest. Trisha recognized the changes at the same time, her little body freezing into perfect stillness. The hair on the back of Paul's neck stood up in warning.

"Trisha, come to me, baby girl," he said quietly.

Trisha immediately stepped backwards, scanning the forest for whatever had caused both of them to realize that danger was near. Paul raised his rifle to his shoulder and widened his stance so that whatever came at them would have to go through him first.

"Trisha, get in the trees now," he hissed out quietly. "Don't come down until I tell you."

He listened as Trisha scrambled over to a low tree branch and started climbing. He didn't turn around to watch her. He let his ears guide him in knowing when his precious daughter was safe.

Out of the woods to his left, he heard a crack before the old mountain lion burst out in a rush of speed at him. Paul held his stance until he knew he had a clear shot. He held himself motionless, waiting. If he missed, it could leave the animal wounded, making it even more dangerous. He took his shot as it leaped. The force of the blast cut through the mountain lion's heart, knocking it to the side where it rolled and disappeared into the high ferns covering the forest floor. Paul pulled the bolt back, releasing the spent shell and loaded another shell into the chamber with a calm efficiency built from years of training.

"Daddy," Trisha whispered. "I can see it. It is the mountain lion. It's not moving."

"Stay there, baby girl. I need to make sure it is dead," Paul said, walking slowly forward.

Paul moved through the ferns until he was next to the mountain lion. It had been a clean kill. It was unusual for one to be this far down the mountain. He knelt down next to the huge, old cat and did a quick inventory of it. It was very thin. He pulled back its upper lip and saw that its teeth were in bad shape. He looked down at its paws and could see the left back paw had a deep cut that was infected.

"It is time to seek the next life, old friend," Paul said quietly as he rested his palm on the head of the old cat for a moment. "May the Earth take your body and keep it to nurture others."

Paul stood and walked back to the tree where Trisha was standing on a limb watching him. "Come on down, baby girl. There is nothing we can do for him."

He kept his eyes glued on Trisha as she climbed down, reaching up and swinging her down when she was close enough. He smiled down as the wild curls swirled around her as she clung to him for a moment. He was going to have a time brushing out the knots tonight.

He looked up one last time at the clear blue sky and thanked his beautiful wife for looking out for them. His heart lightened as if he could feel her smiling down on them.

*One day,* he thought, *one day I am going to find the one woman who can fill my heart the way you did.*

# Chapter 1

**Present day:**

Paul ran his finger along the burn marks. He had been here a dozen times over the past six months. He refused to give up. He had been the one to find the cabin five miles beyond where the road ended. He was the one who had found the first of four bodies buried around it.

His stomach churned at the memory. When Trisha failed to show up when she promised, he had called. She always answered his calls if she could. If they missed each other, they would call the moment they got back no matter what time of the day or night.

Two days later, he had received a call from the California State Police. Trisha and several other women were missing. She had failed to return on a flight for Boswell International. The experimental business jet was still on the runway in Shelby, California.

He had driven through the night to get there. A new security system showed what happened in the dimly lit parking lot. The local sheriff had kidnapped Abby Tanner, an artist that his daughter and her childhood friend, Ariel, had been returning home from New York.

The FBI and State Police had taken over the investigation when it looked like one of their own was involved. Paul had pulled some strings and was given permission to help with the search due to his expertise in wilderness tracking.

It took three days to locate Abby and the sheriff's trucks. The motorcycle his surrogate daughter, Carmen Walker, had delivered before they landed was lying on the ground behind it, dark skid marks evidence that Carmen had laid the bike down in a hurry. During those three days Paul discovered things about the local sheriff, Clay Thomas, that chilled his blood.

Thomas was discharged from the Marines under suspicion of murdering women outside the base he had been assigned to in the Middle East. There was no proof because none of the women's bodies were ever located. Paul called in more favors and received a copy of all the reports. He reviewed each report carefully and was able to piece together a chilling account of a man who enjoyed hurting others, women in particular.

Each family that was interviewed talked about how Thomas had stalked their wives, sisters, or daughters. They reported him to the local authorities, but nothing was ever done, even after their loved ones mysteriously disappeared. Thomas always had an alibi for where he was and was careful about making sure he wasn't followed when he left the base.

When Paul found the cabin, he knew they were dealing with a serial killer. The inside of the cabin held a wide variety of instruments designed to inflict the maximum amount of pain. Dried blood pooled between the wooden floor planks.

Paul had circled the property as investigators poured into the area. He needed to 'see' the area before all the 'experts' destroyed the evidence. He had expanded his circle until he came to the first grave. The body of the female had been dismembered before being wrapped in plastic and covered in a shallow grave. He found three more bodies before he felt sure there were no more.

A part of him died with each find. His biggest fear that Trisha, Ariel, or Carmen was one of the discarded females ate at him. It had taken two long months before the results showed none of the women were from the plane. He had traveled back and forth between his ranch in Wyoming and Shelby, California once a month since then revisiting the sites for more clues.

Now, he stood looking down at the burn marks on the trees. The fire investigator's report was inconclusive. They could find no chemical residues and no explanations as to how or what could cause a fire that would burn hot enough to reduce a small section to ash without touching anything else.

The marks were extremely precise, as if they were directed from a source that could be fired. He had shown photos of the damage to experts in the military, but even they were baffled. One report stated no known source on Earth could have created a fire hot enough to cause that damage without igniting the forest around it.

Paul stood and looked at the spot where a very fine pile of ash was discovered by one young investigator. The analysis suggested it was human remains, but not even cremation could reduce a body to that fine an ash. He reached up and pulled a small, folded tissue from his pocket.

He opened it and looked down at the silver dollar size scale lying against the white tissue. He had found it tucked in between the bark of a tree near where the pile of ash had been discovered. It was dark red with a trace of dark green and gold along the edges. He had an analysis done on it at Wyoming State University. Hugh Little was a friend of his from high school and worked in the Bio-research department. A shiver ran down his spine as he remembered Hugh's late night call.

"Hey Paul," Hugh had said excitedly. "I, uh, listen I need you to call me as soon as you get back. That scale you sent me. I really need to talk to you about it." Hugh had been so excited Paul had driven the extra two hundred and fifty miles to the campus where Hugh was a faculty member.

Hugh had greeted him with a pent-up excitement that Paul had never seen in the normally placid man. He had taken Paul back to his lab and began explaining his findings. Paul had listened carefully, but it was the images that held him captivated.

"The scale came from some type of live creature. I have no doubt about that. At first I thought it might be reptilian, but now I don't think it is. It is unlike anything I have ever seen before. It isn't just the chemical makeup of the scale or even the size, but look at the scale when it is magnified," Hugh explained.

Paul watched as the blurred image of the scale cleared and a very intricate pattern came into view. The edge was perfectly curved with a thin line of gold etched with dark green oblique lines cut along the edges. The red glowed with swirling colors, making it look like it was on fire. In the center of the scale was a symbol that looked like a spear. Paul walked closer, looking carefully at the pattern.

"Is it real?" He had asked Hugh in a quiet, thoughtful tone.

"Oh, it's real alright. Do you see those swirling colors? I tried to take a small sample of it. It destroyed every needle I used. When I tried to cut through the scale, it melted my cutter," Hugh replied. "I don't know where you got this from but I'll tell you one thing, I've never seen anything like it on Earth before."

A cold wave of dread swept through Paul as he stared at the swirling red. That was the third time someone had said that same thing. He had retrieved the scale under protest from Hugh that he still needed to do more tests on it. Paul explained it was needed for the investigation for now, perhaps after Trisha was found he could send it back to him. For now, he needed it.

Paul tilted his head up to look at the overcast sky. It was going to rain soon. He could smell it in the air. Walking back to his truck, he looked around one more time, deep in thought, before sliding into the driver's seat. He had one more person to visit before he returned home again. He had only discovered the name a couple of days ago. None of the investigators had thought the old woman who was a friend of the artist important enough to interview.

Paul pulled the clipboard off the dash and looked down at the address. Edna Grey, age sixty-six, family friend of Abby Tanner. Grey had known Abby's grandparents who had raised her. She had worked with them in the entertainment field before retiring.

Abby often watched her animals when Grey visited her children, according to some of the leads he had talked to. Paul laid the clipboard down on the seat next to him and started the big Ford 250 diesel. He backed up, making a three-point turn so he could head back down the mountain.

Turning onto the highway, he turned his windshield wipers on as the rain began to fall. He hoped to God that this Edna Grey could give him some information he could use. He was running out of leads.

He rubbed his chest over his heart. He knew his baby girl was still alive. He could feel her. It wasn't like when Evelyn died.

Then, he knew she was gone. He could feel the emptiness in his heart. He had known something had happened before he received the phone call from his mom who had been visiting when Evelyn collapsed.

No, Trisha was still alive. He could feel her calling to him. It was almost as strong as the other feeling he had been having lately. That his life was about to change. He felt restless, as if something called to him, telling him that the emptiness he had felt for so long was about to be filled to overflowing.

Paul turned his blinker on and slowed to make the narrow turn onto the long, gravel driveway. He could see a large, two story house at the end of the drive through the rain-smeared windshield. A large wraparound porch seemed to welcome visitors to sit and stay for a while.

He pulled up along the curved drive in front of the steps and shut off the engine. Opening the door, he pulled his large Stetson down lower to protect his face from the cold drizzle. He strode over to the front steps of the porch, taking them two at a time.

A low barking sounded on the other side of the door. Before he could even raise his hand to knock, the door opened to reveal the soft face of a woman in her mid-sixties. She had her long, dark gray hair in a braid down her back and was dressed in a pair of well-worn jeans with a solid blue button up shirt tucked in at the waist. She didn't say anything for a moment before she smiled and opened the screen door. A large golden retriever stood beside her with a lime green tennis ball in its mouth, its long tail wagging back and forth.

"Ms. Grey, my name is Paul Grove," Paul said removing his hat and holding it between his hands nervously. "My daughter is Trisha Grove. She was the pilot of the plane returning your friend Abby Tanner."

Edna nodded as tears filled her eyes. "Come in. I've been expecting someone to come."

Paul bowed his head in acknowledgement as he walked on silent feet into the house. He looked around as his eyes adjusted to the dim interior. His eyes noticed everything in one sweep. He saw the photos of famous singers and actors mixed in with pictures of Edna's family along one wall, before his eyes swept over the display case filled with awards.

"Follow me," Edna said, moving toward the back of the house.

Paul glanced up the stairs, noting the worn but polished wood on the steps. His eyes moved to take in the formal sitting room before he passed by it. He followed Edna through the narrow hallway until they came into a bright, very modern kitchen. Large windows lined the back, letting in plenty of natural lighting. Edna waved him to sit at the worn, white table near the window while she put some water on to boil.

"I'm going to tell you a tale, Paul Grove. You are probably going to think I am a senile old woman who is living in a fantasy world. I'm not," Edna said, looking pointedly at Paul with a firm, but reassuring smile. "Whether you want to believe me or not is up to you. I can only tell you what I know and what I suspect."

"Is my daughter alive?" Paul asked in a deep, rough voice.

Edna smiled as the water boiled, not looking at Paul at first, but at the steam coming out of the top of the kettle. "Let me tell you my tale and then I will ask you that question."

Edna poured the boiling water into two cups. She reached up and opened a cabinet and pulled out a couple of tea bags and placed them in the cups. Placing each cup on a saucer, she picked them up and carried them over to the table, setting one in front of Paul and the other in front of her seat before she sat down. The golden retriever came into the room and curled up at her feet, dropping the ball between his front paws before resting his chin on it with a small whine.

"Bo misses Abby," Edna said before she blew on her tea and took a sip. "So do I but she is in a better place. At least, I believe she is."

"Where do you think she is?" Paul asked, wrapping his cold hands around the cup, but not drinking any of the fragrant brew.

Edna released a sigh before she looked at Paul with clear, intelligent eyes. "Six months ago I dropped my dog, Bo, and my mule, Gloria, off at Abby's place up in the mountains. Abby inherited the cabin from her grandparents. She was born and raised there and never planned to leave," Edna explained, pausing to take a sip of her drink.

Paul didn't say a word. He just waited until Edna was ready to continue. He found that if he waited and listened long enough, he would learn more than trying to rush a person's story.

Edna nodded and smiled at Paul. "Abby would like you. You are a patient man, Paul Grove. Abby had been working on a fancy stain glass piece for the

Boswells. Your daughter, Trisha, was the pilot on the flight I understand."

"As well as three other women who I care about very much," Paul agreed. "Trisha was the pilot. Two of her childhood friends were also on board as well as another young girl my daughter and Ariel had adopted under their care."

"Yes, I read about them in the paper. It is what was not in the paper that you need to know," Edna said leaning forward. "When I returned to pick up Bo and Gloria after visiting my son and daughter-in-law, I found Abby was no longer alone. There was a man there. He was unlike anything I had ever seen before. There was a wildness, a power to him that was not.... normal."

Paul's face tightened into an unmoving mask. "Do you think he hurt Abby?"

Edna shook her head and leaned back in her chair. "Just the opposite. I think he saved Abby…. and your daughter and the other women."

"Why do you think that?" Paul asked stiffly. "You admit there was something off about him. What was different?"

The smile on Edna's face faded as her eyes darkened with memories. "Because he loved her and swore that he would do everything in his power to protect her and make her happy. I believed him. You see, his name was Zoran Reykill and he was an alien from another world," Edna said carefully.

Paul's mouth tightened as he returned Edna's unwavering stare. "You expect me to believe my daughter was kidnapped by aliens?" He asked in a deep, unemotional voice.

"Not kidnapped so much as rescued," Edna responded lightly, taking a sip of her tea. "I told you I was concerned when I saw a strange man with Abby. You have to understand, Abby is a very quiet, reserved person. She does not open herself up to others very easily. She was perfectly happy being alone on her mountain. This man was extremely large, even bigger than you. He had black hair that hung down his back and solid gold eyes with elongated pupils. He understood what I was saying, but I was unable to understand him until….," her voice faded as she remembered the golden ship in the high meadow.

"Until…." Paul encouraged quietly.

"Until he took me to his spaceship," Edna replied lightly. "Zoran took me up to the high meadow not far from the cabin. There was nothing there at first then out of nowhere a huge, golden spaceship appeared. It was floating above the ground by several feet. It was alive. I could see the swirling colors and it shivered as I approached it. Zoran touched it and a doorway with steps suddenly appeared. He took me inside. Seats of gold formed under us and a panel appeared. I could understand what he was saying while we were inside the golden ship." Edna looked up at Paul with determination reflected in her eyes. "He told me he crashed on our world and Abby found him. She cared for him and he knew she was his true mate. He told me he was going to take her with him when he left. I'm not making this up. I have no proof, but what I have told you. Whether you want to believe me or not is up to you. Can you explain some of the things you've found? You are not the only one who has done your research, Mr. Grove. I know what evidence was left and I know what your background is. What have your findings suggested?" Edna pressed.

Paul tore his gaze from Edna's to look out the window. He could see the barn where an old mule stood outside in the light rain. His eyes moved to the mountains in the distance before he turned his gaze back to the woman sitting across from him.

"That something not from this Earth was there," he responded quietly.

Edna nodded slowly. "Now, I'll ask you the question that you asked me. Is your daughter alive?" She asked quietly, laying her hand gently on top of his.

Paul looked down at his untouched cup of tea and swallowed over the lump in his throat. Tears burned the back of his eyes as he pictured his beautiful baby girl. He wondered if she was happy. If she was safe. If she missed him as much as he missed her. Paul looked up before he finally nodded.

"Yes, she is still alive. But, I don't know what to do now. How can I bring her home if she was taken to another world?" Paul asked, voicing his fear to this woman who gave him the only answers that were beginning to make sense.

Edna sat back. "Something tells me she won't be any happier being away from you than you are from her. If she is even half as tenacious as you are, it wouldn't surprise me if the aliens return. When that time comes, perhaps it will not be for you to bring her home but for her to take you with her."

Paul looked at Edna for several long moments. For the first time in six months, he felt hope beginning to build inside him. He spent the next hour with Edna. He asked her question after question trying to learn everything he could about this Zoran Reykill and his golden ship. He politely declined dinner telling Edna he had a lot of things to think about on the long drive home.

He nodded his head to Edna and Bo as he pulled away, heading back to his ranch. He made a series of calls on the long drive home. He had a lot of things to settle. If his baby girl had gone to the stars like she had always promised she was going to then he had a few things to set in place. He had promised her if she ever went he would be going with her.

## Chapter 2

Morian Reykill released a sigh as she carefully touched the new plant she had just transplanted. She looked over the atrium she had created in the hopes of finding a place where she could find a measure of peace. She smiled and shook her head. It was ridiculous to feel so lonely. Her life was filled to overflowing if she would just accept what she had been given.

All five of her sons had found their true mates. There were still things that needed to be smoothed out, but they would find their way. She just might need to help a little. The beautiful creatures they had returned with were unlike anything she had ever encountered before…. and very stubborn.

A chuckle escaped as the little bloom opened up briefly only to close up tight as if mad about being moved from where it had been to a new home. The women were much like this little plant. They were not sure this is where they wanted to be either. In time, they would stretch out their roots and find their way, making a new home in this strange new world they had been brought to.

So much had happened in the past few months. Morian closed her eyes as pain flared inside her as she thought of her mate. That his own brother had taken his life tore at her heart. She had always been thankful when she had been joined with Jalo.

He had been a gentle, kind, and intelligent male who had won her heart with his tenderness. He had been patient with her, getting to know her before they had come together. His dragon had tolerated her because she was a priestess for the Hive.

His symbiot respected her for the same reason, but they did not have the burning passion that the man had for her. She had known she was not Jalo's true mate and had even accepted that if he should ever find his true mate that she might be cast to the side, loving him from a distance. But, he had not found another female that was accepted by the three parts that made the man. In fact, he appeared content to be with her despite the hunger she knew burned deep inside him.

It had been Raffvin's idea to go hunting the week Jalo died. The reports that came back said it was an accident. His dragon had been crushed under a sudden rock fall. Raffvin had supposedly been killed as well, but his body was never found. Morian knew why now. He had murdered his brother and tried to murder her sons as well while hiding behind his own faked death.

Morian's hands trembled when she thought of losing any more of her family. She didn't think she could survive another loss like that. It had devastated her when Zoran had disappeared.

His return had been a blessing, for he had returned with a species that was accepted by both their symbiots and their dragons. Females were rare on Valdier. The few that were of age had already been mated.

Unfortunately, few females were being born. Their scientists believed it was a combination of their male's dominant personalities and the need for warriors during the Great War. But, even though the Great War between the Sarafin, the Curizans and the Valdier had ended over a hundred years before, few females continued to be born.

The need for mates for the adult males was reaching a critical level. Many Valdier warriors were looking to the Sarafin and Curizans for mates now. The biggest issue was finding a female all three parts of the male would accept. If the male was lucky, he might find one the three parts tolerated at best. Over time, the need and hunger of his dragon and the unhappiness of his symbiot would eventually rip the couple apart if they were not careful. At worse, one or both parts of him might not accept the female and would try to kill her.

Morian was thankful her sons would not face this issue any longer. Now, they just needed to learn to understand and accept their mates for the independent, strong-willed women that they were.

Personally, Morian appreciated their free will. She had often gotten in trouble for her own wayward behavior. Jalo had tolerated it, but as a young girl, she had often been disciplined for doing things a female was not supposed to do.

She was fortunate as a priestess to the Hive and the Queen Mother to the Dragon Lords she was given more freedom than other women on Valdier. Most women were closely guarded by their mates and not allowed to travel freely in the way she did now that she was unmated.

"Morian," Abby's voice called out from the door of the Atrium.

Morian smiled as she thought of her beautiful, quiet new daughter. Abby was her oldest son Zoran's true mate. Her gentle touch and quiet manner hid a strength that had already proven she was no delicate flower to be hidden away.

The sound of a baby's laugh had Morian washing her hands anxiously. Abby had recently given birth to a baby boy. Her first great child. Cara, Trelon's mate, had delivered twin babies shortly after Abby. They were the first girls born to the royal house in centuries and were already proving they were going to be a replica of their mother. They were just a few months old and already turning over and trying to scoot.

"Abby," Morian called out in delight, holding her arms out for her new great son who screeched with joy when he saw her. "How is my wonderful baby boy?" Morian cooed softly.

"Oh, he is doing great," Abby said with a tired sigh. "I am not so sure about your oldest son though. He is about to drive me up the wall!"

Morian's chuckle filled the atrium and drew another gurgle of laughter out of Zohar. "What has he done now?"

Abby moved over to sit down on the bench near the center fountain. She pushed her heavy length of dark brown hair back and relaxed. A smile playing on her lips as she watched her son try to pull some of Morian's hair free from the twist she kept it in. That was why her hair was down. Zohar screamed whenever she put it up and he couldn't grab it. Zoran had insisted it remain free so his son could touch it whenever he pleased.

"He won't let me put my hair up for one thing. If I try, he takes it down because he says Zohar doesn't like it up. I think he is just as bad. I threatened to cut it off once, but he…." Abby blushed as she remembered what Zoran had threatened to do to her if she even thought of cutting her hair.

Morian's eyes glittered with humor as she looked over at Abby. "His father was the same way. I was going to cut my hair once. I even had the shears in my hand when he came in and caught me," Morian chuckled as her own face turned a rosy color. "He kept me tied to the bed for three days."

"Three days?" Abby gasped in disbelief. "What did you do?"

"I enjoyed it so much I threatened to cut my hair at least once a month after that until…." Morian's voice faded as her eyes grew sad. "Until he was murdered."

Abby stood up and walked over to where Morian was sitting on the edge of the fountain with Zohar. "I'm so sorry, Morian," Abby said, placing her hand on Morian's shoulder.

Morian looked up and shook her head. "It has been many years, but I still miss him. He was a good mate. I miss the way we used to just talk," she admitted softly. With another shake of her head, she smiled. "So, how were you able to sneak out without Zoran knowing?"

"She didn't," a deep voice growled out from the shadowed path leading up to the fountain.

Abby rolled her eyes and sat down next to Morian. "Hi sweetheart."

"Don't you 'Hi sweetheart' me," he growled out as he walked up to her. "I thought I told you to stay in our rooms. You need to rest. Zohar woke you a half dozen times last night," he said, pulling Abby to her feet and into his arms.

Abby relaxed against Zoran's chest, enjoying his warm skin against her cheek. "He wasn't the only one," she muttered darkly.

This time it was Zoran who turned a little red. "Yes, well, you smelled extremely sweet," he whispered flickering a glance at his mother who raised her eyebrow at him. "Well, she did. The milk she produces for Zohar is.....," he started to add defensively.

Abby groaned cutting him off as she hid her hot face in his chest. "That is more information than your mother needed to know," she groaned out.

"Yes, it is," Morian chuckled. "But like I said before, he is like his father."

Zoran's mouth dropped open before snapping shut and he shook his head. "That's it. Time to go back to our rooms. Come here, little warrior. Let's go put you down for a nap. I think your *Dola* needs a nap as well."

Morian chuckled when Zohar glared mutinously at his father before scrunching his face up and letting out a loud wail when Zoran carefully untangled his little fingers from the hair he had pulled loose. Zoran grimaced at the high pitched cry and looked at Abby, desperation clearly written on his face. Abby raised her eyebrow and shook her head as she reached out and scooped Zohar back into her arms. The minute his little fingers wrapped around her long, dark strands he gave a little hiccup and quieted down, a soft sigh escaping him as he buried his face in her neck.

"This is why you must never cut your hair," Zoran said stubbornly. "I do not like it when he cries. It hurts my ears."

Morian chuckled as she listened to Abby and Zoran walk away, arguing about how Zohar needed to learn he could not always have his way just to keep him from crying. She remembered having the same arguments with Jalo. She hoped Abby had more luck than she did. Jalo loved his sons and she knew they got into more mischief than they should have because they had him wrapped around their fingers.

She turned on the cool stone seat and gazed out over the atrium that was her sanctuary. She dipped her fingers into the clear water of the center tranquility pool, swirling the water around absently as the silence grew to the point that instead of being comforting, it was almost suffocating her. She let her eyes drop down to gaze at the ripples she had made in the water. She couldn't help but think her life was like the rippling water.

"What is wrong with me?" She whispered to herself. "Why do I feel so restless? Why do I feel this growing hunger inside me?"

She turned her head when she heard the sound of leaves rustling in the thick ferns on the left side of the pool. A huge golden shape emerged from the shadows. Jalo's symbiot had become her constant companion since his death.

She had been stunned when it refused to leave her after Jalo's death to return to the Hive. She had even taken it down to the Hive herself. When Jalo's symbiot had re-emerged from the river of the Gods, it had immersed her smaller symbiot into its form to become even stronger; both in strength and in binding with the essence of her dragon and her. That was something it hadn't been able to do before. Since that time, it was seldom more than a few feet from her.

"What is it?" Morian asked softly, puzzled, but the rapidly shimmering colors swirling over its body. "You feel it too, don't you? As if something is about to happen," she said looking around again. She closed her eyes, seeking deep inside her for what could cause the feeling.

*Mate, our mate is coming,* her dragon stirred for the first time in a long time. *I can feel him.*

Morian's eyes snapped open in shock. She pulled her trembling hand from the water. She didn't even feel the dampness of the water on her fingers as she pushed back the strand of black hair that Zohar had pulled free.

*A mate*, she choked out to her dragon. *That is impossible. I have no mate. Jalo is gone.*

*Not Jalo*, her dragon growled out, raising her head and tilting her head upward toward the clear glass dome. *Our true mate comes. He comes to protect us.*

*No*, Morian said fiercely. *No, I won't let myself care for another male again. I won't take the chance of losing him. You will listen to me on this!* She demanded as she felt the snort of her dragon.

Morian stomped her feet in frustration when her dragon just turned with a grunt and settled down with a contented sigh. The blasted thing was not going to listen to her, she just knew it. The damn thing had gotten her into more trouble than she could count when she was younger. It had settled down a bit when she mated with Jalo and had the boys, but she could feel that same sense of expectation which ALWAYS meant trouble.

"You know I've worked hard to behave myself," she hissed out loud. "Don't you ignore me, you trouble-making leather winged bandit. The boys have no idea of the mischief I used to get into. I am not about to let them know," she added defiantly. "You better behave yourself!"

Her eyes grew huge when she saw the image the golden symbiot sent to her. "Oh for crying out loud! Not you too!" She snapped, tossing her head, then cursing under her breath as her dark hair cascaded down her back as the clip holding it up finally broke free from where Zohar had tugged on it.

"Argh!" She growled as she bent and snatched up the fallen clip.

She would show her dragon and Jalo's symbiot that she was nothing like the young girl she had been. She was mature. She was a priestess for the Hive. She was too old to be someone's mate! No, she would keep her distance at the first sign of her dragon being interested. She would show any male her dragon looked at that she was above such feelings. She would…. Morian looked down at her trembling hands and closed them into a fist around the colorful, jeweled clip in anguish.

*Please,* she begged silently to the Gods. *I don't want to be hurt again.*

## Chapter 3

Paul ran his hand down his face and looked tiredly into the bathroom mirror. He didn't get home until almost two o'clock this morning. He had a full day of work ahead of him even though he had cancelled all of his survival trainings until further notice. He didn't need the money. His folks had done well in their investments and he had continued it. He was a multi-millionaire several times over, but money had never meant much to him except as a means of providing for him and Trisha.

At forty-seven, he had just the first hint of gray sprinkled through his dark hair. Most of it had come on over the past six months since his baby girl disappeared. He leaned forward and gripped the edge of the sink with both hands as he fought the fear gnawing at his gut. The muscles along his shoulders rippled as he breathed deeply, trying to calm the fear. His eyes returned to the mirror where they stared with steely determination back at him. He would find her. Someway, somehow he would find his little girl.

Shoving away from the sink, he grabbed a dark blue long sleeve button up shirt hanging on the back of the door. He quickly slipped it on and tucked it into the waist of his jeans before fastening the dark brown leather belt around his narrow hips. Striding into his bedroom, he pulled his boots on before grabbing his hat off the hook next to the door as he exited the room.

He ran down the stairs on light feet, jumping when he came to the last three steps. His hand slid into his pocket to pull his truck keys out even as his other hand reached for the doorknob.

He was going to drive into town and talk with Annalisa Hollins, one of the deputies there. She had been a detective in Miami before moving to Wyoming. She didn't tell him what happened there and he didn't ask, but he knew it was enough to scare her which is something he didn't think happened very often.

He knew she was a good person and that was all that mattered to him. She had been a huge help to him over the last few months getting information on the case, especially when the State Police refused to share it at first. In fact, she was the one who had suggested he talk to Edna Grey.

He pulled open the door and stepped out, not bothering to lock it after him. Samara, a young local girl he had hired a couple of years ago, would be here soon to look after the horses if she wasn't already. Besides, he lived far enough off the beaten track he didn't have to worry about thieves.

His mind was already running back over the information Edna had given him. He wanted to ask Annalisa if there had been any unusual sightings reported over in Shelby, California about six months ago.

He jogged down the steps and was just rounding the corner of his truck when he heard a familiar cry. His head snapped up in astonishment. For a moment, he wondered if he was hearing things but even as that thought crossed his mind it was replaced by a surge of overwhelming relief and happiness as his eyes locked on the sound of the sweetest voice he had ever heard.

"Daddy!" Trisha cried out excitedly.

Paul's heart pounded as he saw Trisha breaking out of the small hammock of trees. He watched as she broke into an awkward run. Even from this distance he could see the sheen of tears in her eyes. He took first one step, then another before he broke into a run. His arms opened wide as Trisha threw herself at him. He pulled her close to his huge body, burying his face in her wild curls as he closed his eyes and wrapped his arms around her in relief.

"Baby girl," he whispered softly, trembling with emotion.

He pulled back far enough so he could stare down into her beautiful tear-filled eyes. Unable to believe she was really here, back in his arms, he hugged her close again. His breath caught in his throat when he felt the telltale roundness of her stomach. His eyes jerked downward and he drew in a breath of shock before his eyes moved back to hers in concern.

"What...?" He asked uncertainly.

Fear threatened to choke him again. He knew what the doctors had said about how dangerous; if not impossible, it would be for Trisha to have children. She didn't know that he knew. He had made it his business to know everything about her after she had almost been killed.

The doctors had told him that it wouldn't be safe for her to have children after the helicopter she was traveling in crashed coming home from a training mission. She had been the only survivor. He had led the search as part of the rescue team because of the remoteness of where the helicopter went down. After they got her out of the mountains, he had sat by her bedside for two weeks as she struggled between life and death. It had taken almost a dozen surgeries and a year of physical therapy before she learned to walk again.

That was the first time he almost lost her. The second time was when her no-good loser of an ex-husband let her think she was no longer a whole woman. She had sunken into such a deep depression he had feared she wouldn't be able to find her way out again. He had paid a visit to the bastard when he found out the asshole thought to blackmail Trisha after his career went to hell when his commanders discovered his infidelity. He had no problem letting Peter know that he could make him disappear and no one would ever know what happened to him if he ever came near Trisha again.

He opened his mouth to ask her where she had been when a movement out of the corner of his eye drew his attention to the figure that had been standing in the shadows. His gaze fastened on the shape of a huge, dark-haired man standing near the woods. Paul put a protective arm around Trisha, trying to turn his body so she would be behind him.

The predator in him came out as the need to protect his family washed over him. His eyes narrowed in challenge as the man stepped out into the early morning light. Trisha glanced over her shoulder and smiled at Kelan Reykill, her mate and the alien who had changed her life. She held out her hand for him to come closer.

"I tagged him, Daddy. He's mine," Trisha said, referring to the game they played when they were training soldiers in guerilla warfare. She turned to look up at him and smiled.

Paul stared down into the beautiful face of his only daughter. There was something different about her—a wholeness that she never seemed to have before. Her face glowed with a sense of peace he never thought to see. She was in love.

He turned his attention to the man walking toward him. He was taller than him by a couple of inches, but not much broader. He quickly processed everything about the other male. The fact that he walked with an air of confidence spoke of leadership and power. There was a quietness in his step that told Paul he could be swift on his feet - dangerous.

He could see the muscle definition and grace with which he moved, showing he would be skilled at hand-to-hand combat. He also noticed that the male was heavily armed judging by the weapons he had on his hips and back. Paul instinctively knew the male would have others hidden on his body.

Paul's eyes narrowed, focusing on every detail. The man's hair was almost as long as Trisha's but black as night and straight with two long braids in the front. He wore boots that reached just below his knees and was dressed all in black.

Paul took a step back, drawing Trisha with him, as he looked back up into the man's eyes. There was no way in hell they were human. Deep, dark gold with black elongated pupils, almost like a cat, gazed back cautiously at him. It took a moment for him to realize Trisha was trying to get his attention. He finally forced his gaze away from the man/creature/alien, whatever in the hell he was, and back to his precious daughter.

"Daddy, this is Kelan. He is my true mate…. My husband," Trisha said hesitantly as Kelan came to stand by her.

Paul studied the male silently, noting when he gently reached out and clasped Trisha's slender fingers in his large hand. He watched as the male's eyes softened when he looked at her and how protective he was as he slid his other hand to lay it over Trisha's swollen stomach.

"Daddy," Trisha said softly, waiting until he looked down at her again. "I love him. He took me to the stars and made me whole, just like you said momma made you feel."

Paul's throat tightened at the mention of Evelyn. Even after all these years, he could still picture her beautiful face in his mind. She would forever be in his heart.

Looking down at Trisha, he could see Evelyn looking back at him, almost as if reassuring him that everything would be alright. His throat worked up and down as he realized that his baby girl no longer needed him as much as he needed her. If he wanted to be a part of her and his grandbaby's life, he would have to accept the man she chose.

He cleared his throat and gave Kelan a small smile. "Well, son, my daughter once promised me if she ever went to the stars she would take me with her. When do we leave?" He asked gruffly.

"Oh, Daddy," Trisha breathed out, looking up at him with a huge, relieved smile.

"How about we go into the house?" Paul asked hesitantly. "I could use a cup of coffee and you can tell me about what happened."

* * *

Paul sat back in his chair and sipped his tepid coffee. After they had returned to the house, Trisha had explained that Kelan would need to insert a translator behind each of his ears so he could communicate with him. Paul had sat perfectly still, his fists clenched as Kelan pulled out a slender metal tube and pressed it behind each ear.

"Can you understand what I am saying?" Kelan asked quietly.

Paul's eyes jerked around, narrowing as the deep, slightly accented voice washed over him. He knew the words coming out of the other male's mouth were not English, but in his mind, he could understand him. He gave a short, curt nod before clearing his throat. His eyes went back to Trisha when she reached over and squeezed his hand.

"What happened?" He asked huskily. "When I found out you were missing, I joined the search. I found the cabin the Shelby Sheriff, Clay Thomas, used. He had killed four other women. When...." He paused to draw in a deep breath. "When I found the first grave I was terrified it was you. With each grave...." He broke off again as the memory washed through him.

"Cara, Ariel, and Carmen are fine," Trisha assured him. "Cara and Carmen saw the Sheriff kidnap Abby. Carmen took off on her motorcycle after them while Cara hotwired Abby's truck so we could follow. The Sheriff stabbed Carmen when she tried to stop him." Trisha's voice broke as she remembered Carmen's battered body lying on the muddy road.

Kelan immediately placed his hands on Trisha's shoulders in support before looking down at Paul. "My brothers and I were also in pursuit of the male. Abby is my brother Zoran's mate. He felt her pain and fear. We arrived, but not before Carmen was mortally wounded. We had no other choice but to transport all of the women to our warship. Zoran would not have left without Abby and the other women had seen too much." He looked down tenderly at Trisha and smiled. "My dragon and I knew the moment we saw Trisha that she was our mate. I would not have left without her either once I saw her. I could not."

"Your dragon?" Paul asked, his eyes narrowing in disbelief before he remembered the scale tucked safely in the front pocket of his shirt. He reached up and drew it out, carefully unwrapping it. "Is this yours?"

Trisha bit her bottom lip as she looked back and forth between her father and Kelan. She felt Kelan squeeze her shoulders in reassurance. He nodded briefly before letting her continue.

"Kelan is a dragon shifter," Trisha began hesitantly. "He, and now I, can transform into dragons."

"The scale you have belongs to my brother Zoran. He is the leader of the Valdier since the murder of our father," Kelan added.

Paul's throat worked up and down as he stared back and forth between his daughter and the male standing protectively behind her. His mind worked through all the information he had gathered during his investigation. The unusual scale that appeared to belong to an unknown creature, the heat and precision of the fire that burned the body of Clay Thomas and the trees, the tracks that he had not shown to the investigators, and what Edna Grey had told him were all adding up to a clearer picture.

He looked down at his empty coffee cup before looking back up at Trisha. "Are you happy with him?" Paul asked, staring intently into his daughter's dark brown eyes. "Are you sure you want to stay with him?"

A low growl escaped Kelan at Paul's questions. His eyes narrowed dangerously as his dragon and he sensed that the big male across from him would not hesitate to fight him if Trisha wanted to remain on her world. The gold symbiot on his and Trisha's arms moved restlessly as the tension mounted. Kelan sent a command to his symbiot to come. He wouldn't kill the male because he knew that would hurt his mate, but he would not let him take Trisha away from them either.

"Kelan," Trisha murmured softly in rebuke before turning back to her dad. "I'm very happy with him. I told you, he makes me feel complete – whole. I can't remember ever feeling this way except when you and I are out in the mountains. Even then, it is nothing like what I feel now. And yes, I do want to stay with him. I love him very much."

Paul relaxed back into his seat with a nod. His eyes swept over Trisha, stopping on her rounded stomach again as the fear for her health came back. "The baby?" He asked, looking at her before turning his eyes to Kelan. "The doctors told me it would be too dangerous for her to have children. That it could kill her and the child."

Kelan was about to respond when the back door to the kitchen snapped open sharply, hitting the wall and a huge, golden creature pushed part way through the entrance. Paul rose fluidly out of his chair and swirled around to face the door and the unusual intruder. His hand was wrapped around the huge knife he kept in a sheath at his waist. He made sure he placed his body between the creature and Trisha.

"Bio!" Trisha called out sharply, standing up behind her dad. "Be nice! This is my daddy. You are not to hurt him," she said firmly, placing her hand on Paul's back.

The huge golden symbiot, in the shape of a Were Bear, shivered for a moment before it pulled back its lips to reveal sharp, golden teeth as a warning to Paul. Paul slowly stood up straight, a look of amusement on his face as he studied the creature standing in the middle of his kitchen door.

"She named you, did she?" Paul asked the symbiot warily. "If she named you, you've been claimed."

Bio snorted and pushed the rest of its large body through the door, lumbering up to Paul and rubbing absently against his leg before circling around to where Trisha had sat back down in her chair. It put its massive head as far as it could on her lap and purred as she gently stroked its head.

Kelan's lips twisted in amusement before he looked at Paul who had turned silently around to watch the display of affection. "She has my symbiot wrapped around her fingers. Even I cannot get close to her if I upset her without it protecting her. My symbiot has the ability to heal me and my mate. There is no danger to Trisha or our son," Kelan reassured Paul. "I apologize for the surprise."

Paul sighed heavily as he picked his empty coffee cup up and walked over to the counter to pour more into it. He turned, leaning back against the counter and watched as Kelan moved to sit down at the table next to Trisha. He smothered a grin when the male picked up Trisha's other hand and threaded his fingers through her slender ones. Since he met him,

Kelan seemed unable to go more than a few minutes without touching Trisha.

"It looks like I have a lot to learn," Paul admitted. "When do you plan on leaving? How is it you are able to visit our world without the military being all over you? How far and how long will it take to get back to your planet? And what in the hell did you mean, your brother is now the ruler since your father was murdered?" He shot out. "Have you caught the bastard who did it and is my little girl in any danger from him?"

Kelan's eyebrow rose at the last question. Everything in him wanted to deny that Trisha was in danger, but he knew couldn't. He looked at his mate with worried eyes before turning his head back to Paul.

"The man who murdered my father is still at large. He is very dangerous. Before we traveled here, he had kidnapped Trisha and planned to murder her. To kill the mate of one is to kill the other," Kelan replied honestly.

Paul's face tightened in concern as he looked at Trisha who had drawn Kelan's hand to her lips and pressed a kiss to the back of it. "What happened?" He asked tightly.

Kelan stared tenderly into his mate's eyes for a moment before replying. "My uncle underestimated the training of my mate," he said lightly before looking at Paul with amusement. "It would appear her father trained her well. She killed three of the men holding her and helped two others who were with her survive on a planet most could not have until I arrived. She is a very skilled warrior."

Paul couldn't contain the chuckle as he watched Trisha's cheeks turn rosy with embarrassment at Kelan's compliment. "You couldn't ask for anyone better to be by your side," he admitted. "You said your uncle was responsible?" He asked as he moved to sit back down at the kitchen table.

Paul, Kelan and Trisha spent the next several hours discussing everything that happened. They went over from the first moment Trisha picked Abby up until their arrival into Earth's orbit several days before. Paul fixed them all a quick bite to eat while they talked.

At one point, he had to excuse himself to take care of a few matters when Samara came to let him know a new foal had been born and his ranch manager, Mason Andrews, came by to go over a few things. Trisha, Kelan and Bio took the time to go upstairs. Trisha wanted to show Kelan some of the things she had saved when she was growing up and start packing items she wanted to take back to Valdier with her.

* * *

"Your father has surprised me with his acceptance of what has happened," Kelan admitted reluctantly as he looked around the small bedroom. "I had expected him to resist more."

He walked over to pick up a picture of Trisha when she was twelve. She was standing in front of a large group of men dressed in varying shades of green and black. He could tell they must be warriors of her world. She was holding a large bowed weapon in her hands and was dressed just the same as the men. She had a huge smile on her young face, while most of the men looked back at the camera with pained expressions on theirs.

He sat down on the bed and pulled another book with a picture on the front onto his lap. He opened it and began slowly, looking through the images. Each one was of Trisha at different stages in her life. In all of them, she appeared to be the happiest when she was dressed in the dark green and brown clothing and surrounded by thick forests. Trisha smiled over at Kelan where he sat on the edge of her old, full size bed looking through her picture album.

"My dad loves me," she said simply. "He has always supported me in my decisions, even when he didn't think they were the right ones." She turned back to the box of stuff her dad had moved from her apartment after her disappearance.

"Does he think you are making the wrong decision now?" Kelan asked tentatively, looking up at his mate with darkened eyes. His blood heated every time she bent over.

Trisha looked over her shoulder at Kelan in surprise. "No, he likes and respects you. I can tell from the way he talked to you. He never had any respect for Peter. He was always polite but he never opened up to him the way he did with you in the four years I was married."

Kelan's lip pulled back in a snarl at the mention of Trisha's ex-husband. "I want to find this man who hurt you," he growled out in a deep voice.

Trisha stood up and turned around with her hands on her hips. "You will most certainly not go find him. He is history and doesn't deserve a second thought," she said in exasperation. "He lost the power to hurt me a long time ago," she added.

"That is not true," Kelan said setting the photo album back on the nightstand. "I saw your fear when I first wanted to claim you. I saw the hurt in your eyes," he growled out. "I just want to kill him, that is all," he said with a persuasive grin.

Trisha tried to keep from laughing at his obvious enjoyment at the thought of terrorizing Peter before he killed him. She couldn't quite hold back the chuckle because at that moment he looked like a little boy hoping to get to play with his favorite toy. She just shook her head and walked over to him.

"You can't kill him," she said, laughing softly. "But I have to admit it is kind of fun thinking about scaring the shit out of him."

Kelan wrapped his hands around her expanded waist and looked at the opened door to her bedroom. "How long do you think your father will be?" He asked huskily.

Trisha slid her hands up Kelan's chest, shivering with desire when it began to vibrate with his and his dragon's purr. "I think if the door is closed he'll think I needed to rest for a bit," she whispered, reaching up to run her tongue along the seam of his lips.

"Pregnant women need lots and lots of rest," she murmured.

Kelan picked her up in his arms, turned and laid her gently on the bed. He pulled away long enough to hurry over to the door where he closed and locked it. He turned back around; reaching for the weapons on his hips and began loosening the clasp that held them there. His eyes burned with gold flames as he slowly stalked toward her with a grin on his face.

"I think I need to make sure you get plenty of rest," he said, letting the strap holding his laser pistols slide from around his waist.

"Oh my," Trisha breathed, growing hotter by the minute. "Have I ever told you how sexy you are when you take off your weapons?" She asked with a giggle before their lips met. That was the last coherent thought she had for quite some time.

## Chapter 4

Paul looked up later that evening as Kelan came quietly back down the stairs. He had spent most of the afternoon talking with Chad Morrison, his childhood friend and attorney. He had also met with Mason.

He hadn't known Mason as long as he had Chad but they had become good friends when Mason had trained with him almost fifteen years ago. Mason had retired from the Special Forces five years ago after taking a bullet to the back that almost killed him. He decided to call it quits after that. He realized that there was more to life than dying young. He wanted to be there for his wife, Ann Marie, and he wanted to be there to watch his two teenage daughters grow up.

He had debated if he should tell the two men the truth or not and finally decided if what he and Kelan had talked about this afternoon while Trisha slept was to come to fruition, then he was going to have to bring a few trusted 'humans' into the secret. Kelan had reluctantly agreed that the ranch would make the perfect 'home' base of operations. Paul had listened carefully, asking questions, and making notes as Kelan explained in detail to him the need to find females for Valdier. Kelan swore that only those who were true mates would be taken back to his world and only if they agreed.

"You realize that if anyone finds out about you, even suspects what you are, there will be hell to pay?" He had asked Kelan.

"We are aware of the risks," Kelan responded softly. "It is one we are willing to take. I have already spoken with my brothers. If there is a chance other warriors can find their true mates how can we deny them? To do so would be to sentence them to a life of increasing pain and torment."

"I'll do what I can to set everything up so the ranch is a safe haven for your people to come to," Paul said. "It is going to take me at least a week to get everything organized, maybe two. Will that be a problem?"

Kelan smiled as he sat back in the soft leather cushion of the chair he had settled in. "No, it will not be a problem," he replied, pausing for a moment before deciding on what he wanted to say. "I need your help. I have something I wish to take care of while I am here," Kelan suddenly said with a small twist of his lips.

"What do you need?" Paul asked, puzzled.

"The location of the one called Peter who hurt my mate," Kelan had responded with a sharp tooth grin.

Paul's own face slowly broke into an amused grin. The asshole who had hurt his daughter had actually had the gall to call him several times over the past six months demanding to know if Trisha was alive or dead. Paul had found out his ex-son-in-law had taken out a huge life insurance policy on Trisha and was hoping to cash it in. He had already planned to visit Peter after he found Trisha. The idea of having Kelan visit the bastard with him made the planned trip even better.

"I'll do you one better," Paul said with his own devious smile. "I'll take you to the bastard."

\* \* \*

Two days later, Trisha stood glaring at her father, Kelan, Mason, and Chad. "Why do I have to stay here?" She demanded. "Where are you two going and why can't I go with you?

Kelan reached out to soothe his irate mate, but she stopped him short with a growl. "Trisha, *mi elila*, we will not be gone long, just a couple of hours. Mason and Chad will stay to make sure you are safe."

"Why are you taking Bio?" She asked suspiciously. "Daddy, what are you doing?"

Paul grinned at Trisha and raised his eyebrow. When she turned 'the look' on him and talked to him in that tone she sounded just like Evelyn used to when she knew he was up to something he didn't want her to know about. Hell, he felt like a teenager again getting drilled for trying to sneak out.

"Honey, Kelan just wants to get a good look at the ranch," Paul lied smoothly. "I was hoping you could keep an eye on the new foal. Samara could use a hand with feeding it since its mother is refusing to."

Trisha's eyes widened in concern. "The mare is refusing to nurse it?" She asked worriedly.

Paul nodded in relief, knowing his daughter couldn't resist a baby animal in need. She was almost, not quite, but almost as bad as Ariel when it came to animals. He knew the minute her shoulders relaxed that they would be able to escape for the few hours they needed to take care of Peter.

"If you are sure," she asked doubtfully. "I would love to see the foal," she admitted grudgingly.

"I think that is a wonderful thing," Kelan said, moving to rub his hands up and down her arms. "Promise me you will not over do it while I am gone. I have made your father's friends promise they will protect you with their life. Kor and Palto are here as well. They will not leave your side."

"Okay," she agreed reluctantly. "You two are just going to check out the ranch, right?"

"Of course, baby girl," Paul assured her with a wink. "I just want to share a little bit of the beauty of the place with him."

Trisha sighed and nodded. "I'll go see how the foal and Samara are doing. I can't wait to see her. She can fill me in on all the good gossip that has been happening in town. Her older brother is always getting into trouble."

Paul and Kelan waited until the door closed behind Trisha before they turned to grin at each other. Mason and Chad looked at them and shook their heads. Mason had a grin on his face while Chad had a worried look. Both men had taken the news of Kelan and aliens better than he expected.

Oh, they had been shocked and maybe a little scared at first, but after Kelan swore that he and his people meant no harm to anyone on their planet and had no desire to invade it or anything else, they had relaxed – a little. Kelan even went so far as to take Paul, Mason, and Chad up to the warship for a tour before returning them safely back to the ranch.

It had taken two long days to finally get through most of their questions and rest their doubts. Paul had to admit it had been the human women who had finally set the men's minds to rest. They had talked to Abby, Cara, Ariel, and even Carmen before sitting down to a long dinner with Trisha. She had been honest, answering all their questions.

The fact that both men had known Trisha for years helped as she didn't act any differently than she always had. Well, except for one big difference that Paul could see - she was happier than he had ever seen her. Paul came back to the present when he heard Chad's deep voice asking him a question.

"You two aren't going to need legal counsel for whatever you are about to do, are you?" Chad asked drily. "If so, I don't want to know about it ahead of time. I think ignorance as your attorney is going to be best."

Paul laughed and slapped Chad on the shoulder. "Ignorance is definitely going to be best in this case. We aren't going to kill anyone but that doesn't mean the person we are going to see will know that."

"No, but it will be very tempting," Kelan said, letting his hand shift slightly to reveal his dragon's claw.

"Oh shit!" Chad whispered hoarsely while the other two men stared wide-eyed at the jade and silver claw.

* * *

Paul leaned forward, looking down as Kelan's symbiot glided over the tall buildings of Seattle,

Washington. He had been fascinated as he watched the golden creature shift and expand until it became a sleek spaceship. He had been a little apprehensive when the side had opened up and Kelan had walked in. He had followed, motivated more by curiosity than desire. As soon as he was inside, the door disappeared and a gold chair formed. He sat gingerly on the edge until they lifted off the ground.

"This thing is incredible," Paul said, glancing sideways at Kelan. His eyes narrowed on the twin golden bands that were wrapped around Kelan's wrist and melded into the chair as well. "Are you sure no one can see this thing?"

Kelan looked at Paul with a look of amusement. "I'm sure. My symbiot knows we must remain unseen. It has the ability to let its body reflect the environment around it. Almost like a three dimensional reflection. Because of that, it appears invisible to the eye. It is pure energy. It uses that energy as a propulsion system so it is silent as well."

"How are you controlling it?" Paul asked curiously.

Kelan laughed. "I simply let it know what I want and it takes me there. I have never really thought about it much. Our symbiot and dragon are an extension of ourselves," he admitted humorously. "I don't distinguish it as being a separate part of me. The gold bands know what I think or feel and in return do as I ask."

Paul nodded, not sure he understood. He ran the palms of his hands over the smooth, silky surface and was surprised when he felt a wave of warmth and an image of enjoyment from it. He looked up at Kelan who just glanced at him with a small smile.

"There!" Paul said, pointing to a small, suburban area on the outskirts of the city. "Do you think you can land us in the backyard? His house is the one on the end of the cul-de-sac."

"Do you think he is home?" Kelan asked, feeling the anger beginning to burn deep inside him at the male who thought to take advantage of his mate, even in the case of her death.

*Burn him,* his dragon snarled, pacing deep inside him. *Gut him first and let me cook his entrails as he dies.*

*You are feeling even more bloodthirsty than I am,* Kelan chuckled. *I promised our mate I would not kill him. I did not promise not to make him wish he was dead.*

*She not know what he did,* his dragon snapped back impatiently. *He want her dead!*

*Patience, my friend,* Kelan said tightly. *He will not wish it ever again by the time we are done with him. Even our mate's father is in agreement with this.*

Kelan grimaced as his dragon raked at him again in frustration. He would have to be very, very careful to keep his dragon under control or Peter Mullins could very well end up dead. He ignored his dragon's grunt of glee at the thought.

"I don't see his car yet, but he should be here soon," Paul replied as the golden symbiot spaceship landed deftly in the backyard behind Peter's small, brick home. "Let's go make ourselves at home."

Kelan sent a message to his symbiot to remain invisible at all times and to be prepared to leave immediately in case of an emergency. He stood up and followed Paul out the door the symbiot created. Paul moved silently over the thin spread of grass.

Kelan couldn't help, but take a moment to observe the huge man as he moved. He could appreciate how Trisha's father carried himself. From everything he had heard and seen so far, he could imagine the male would be a fierce warrior.

He had already seen how protective he was of Trisha and his friends. Kelan's eyes glimmered with a hint of amusement as he wondered how Paul would fit in on Valdier. He also couldn't help but wonder if the other male would find his mother attractive.

*Where in the hell did that thought come from?* He wondered vaguely as he watched Paul slide a tool into the lock of the back door and open it.

* * *

Paul looked around the kitchen as he stepped in. He had scanned the house just a few days before Trisha's return and noticed that while Peter had a sign in his yard stating he had a security system, he really didn't.

Paul moved silently from room to room. His face twisted with disgust when he saw the paperwork lying on a desk in the back bedroom along with news articles of Trisha and the other women's disappearance and rumors they had been murdered by a serial killer. He gently picked up the life insurance policy, noting that it was worth over half a million dollars.

He laid it down and picked up the yellow legal sized notepad that Peter was using to take notes. Peter had listed several questions on it placing an asterisk by several. The first question was how long it took to have someone declared dead. The list continued with his wanting to know how long would it take for him to receive the money from the policy, did he have to supply the death certificate or could the insurance company request one, so on.

"What is that?" Kelan asked, nodding to the yellow legal pad that Paul was clutching tightly in his hand.

Paul glanced up at Kelan with a grim expression. "It's Peter's death sentence. The bastard thinks he is going to profit off of my daughter's supposed death," he growled out in a low voice. "I warned him about ever trying to use Trisha again. I don't give second warnings."

Both men turned when they heard the sound of a car door slamming. They moved down the hallway and into the living room where Peter would have to enter to go to any other part of the small two-bedroom house. Kelan nodded and took up a position near the living room windows.

The room was cast in shadows due to the late afternoon cloud cover that had moved in and the fact that Peter kept the blinds drawn. Paul leaned casually up against the doorframe leading between the living room and the kitchen. Once Peter came in, he would be trapped between the two men.

\* \* \*

The front door opened and closed and the echo of a heavy case being dropped on the tile sounded loud in the quiet house. Peter pulled his tie loose with a muttered oath and dropped his car keys in the dish on the small foyer table. He was tired of working in a dead-end job for little pay and even less gratification.

"Why can't they just declare the bitch dead," he muttered under his breath. "At least then I could get out of this shit hole and live a decent life."

He walked into the living room, switching on one of the small table lamps with one hand while he unbuttoned the top buttons on his shirt with the other. All he wanted was a stiff drink and to see if anything new had been discovered in the last forty-five minutes since he checked the Internet for updates on the case. A strangled oath escaped him when he saw the huge shadow leading into the kitchen straighten.

"Hello Peter," Paul said with a sardonic twist of his lips. "I got your messages asking about Trisha."

"P.... Paul," Peter stuttered jerking to a stop and looking wildly at him. "I.... What are you doing here? How did you get into my house?"

Paul stared intently at Peter. "If you want to advertise you have a security system, I suggest you really have one," Paul replied, pulling his hands out of his pockets and spreading them wide. "You might want to think about getting better locks for the back door as well," he added with a jerk of his head to the door behind him. "Very flimsy."

Peter nodded his head nervously. "Thanks for the advice. I'll be sure and take care of that tomorrow," Peter breathed out. "You know it is against the law to just break into someone's house. You could get into a lot of trouble."

Paul chuckled and shook his head back and forth. "Peter..... Peter..... Peter.....," Paul said in a low voice. "What did I tell you the last time you tried to use my daughter for your personal gain? Do you really have such a short memory?" He asked, tilting his head to the side and staring at Peter with cold brown eyes. "Or do you have a death wish?"

Peter gave a nervous laugh and backed up a few steps. "I was just worried about Trisha when I heard what happened," he said licking his lips. "I mean.... I was her husband for four years. That has to count for something. Have.... Have they found her body yet?" He asked, unable to keep the note of hope out of his voice.

Paul looked over Peter's shoulder and smiled. *That isn't a nice smile*, Peter thought vaguely in the back of his mind. He glanced over his shoulder briefly, but didn't see anything. He turned back and looked at his ex-father-in-law, feeling a little stronger at the thought that the man may not like him but surely he wouldn't really hurt or kill him.

"Yes, Trisha has been found," Paul answered softly.

"She has?" Peter said in relief before he realized he needed to act the grieving ex. "I'm so sorry for your loss, Paul. I heard they knew who killed her. She was a very beautiful woman."

"Yes," Paul answered calmly, stepping so close to Peter that the man tripped on the corner of the coffee table and fell backwards onto the couch. "I didn't believe she could be any more beautiful than she already was, but I have to say she positively glows now."

Peter frowned. "What do you mean? She's dead, isn't she?"

"No," Paul answered with a shake of his head. "In fact, she is not only alive, she has remarried and is expecting her first child. So you see, you won't be able to collect on that life insurance policy you took out on her – ever."

Peter stared at Paul in disbelief before his face flushed with anger. He rolled off the couch, making sure he kept the coffee table between him and Paul's larger frame. His mind was about to explode at the idea that all his hopes for the past six months were about to be swept away. He shook his head, refusing to believe it.

"No, no, no, no, no!" Peter ground out not caring that Paul was seeing his rage. "She's dead! That crazy sheriff killed her and those other two bitches. She has to be dead. She has to be!"

Paul's eyes narrowed and his face twisted in disgust, but that was not what had Peter turning around and almost shitting his pants. It was the dark, menacing growl that rumbled so low and long the walls of the small house actually shook. Peter tripped over his own feet, moving backwards and knocking into the end table near the chair, causing the matching table lamp to topple to the floor.

"What the fuck….?" Peter breathed out.

"Not what the fuck," Paul said, glancing over to where Kelan stepped out of the darkened shadows. "Peter, I'd like you to meet Trisha's mate, Kelan. He is an alien from another world," he added casually enjoying the expressions racing across Peter's face. "By the way, those other two bitches you were talking about happen to be his brother's mates – or wives if you please."

Peter glanced at Paul briefly before his eyes swiveled back to the huge male who had stepped out from the corner of the living room. Peter almost shit his pants when he saw the dark, dangerous flames burning in the guy's gold eyes. His heart actually skipped a beat when he realized that Paul hadn't been joking about the guy being an alien. There was no way in hell eyes like that could be human.

"Gold," he choked out hoarsely, turning pale.

Kelan smiled coldly, letting his face transform just enough that his teeth elongated and jade and silver scales rippled across his skin. He had enough of the other male thinking his mate was an easy target. He had also heard the male's comment when he walked in the door wishing Trisha was dead. The fact that this male had once meant something to her sent a wave of jealousy flooding through his body. It was almost impossible for him to control his dragon.

Peter scrambled back into the corner, pushing himself behind the overstuffed beige leather chair. His hand reached clumsily for the fire poker. He knocked the matching shovel and brush off the brass rack as he gripped the poker in front of him.

"Stay….stay back, damn you," Peter screeched in a high pitched voice. "Paul, you have to help me!"

"Why?" Paul snarled out, staring coldly at the man who had meant something to Trisha at one time. "You lousy piece of shit," he growled out in a low, menacing voice. "You took a life insurance policy out on my daughter in the hope that she had been murdered. You made her life a living piece of hell when she needed you the most then you had the nerve to try and blackmail her when she asked for her freedom. I warned you then if you ever –ever – tried to use her in any way again, you would rue the day you were ever born."

Peter was shaking so bad the fire poker in his hand weaved back and forth. He swallowed over the lump in his throat, trying to think of how he might get out of this situation alive. It had been stupid to call Paul and try and get information, but he didn't know what else to do. None of Trisha's old friends or coworkers would give him the time of day much less any information they might have heard.

He was in debt up to his eyeballs and had taken out the life insurance policy on her less than a month before she disappeared with the help of his brother-in-law who had forged a few documents so he could get it. He had figured with her injuries she would more than likely die young, preferably very young, and he would collect on it.

He could only afford the half a million dollar policy with the little extra his brother-in-law charged him to maintain it. He figured that would last until he could find another woman who was wealthy, or at least came from a wealthy family. That was why he had targeted Trisha in the first place. He liked having a certain standard of living, but since his divorce from Trisha that had been impossible. Now, it looked like he wouldn't live long enough to cash anything in.

"Paul, I'm sorry," Peter began, looking back and forth between Paul and Kelan. "I didn't mean anything by it. Life has been hard since Trisha left me. I got demoted and ended up as a shitty ass inventory clerk after she kicked me out."

Paul put his hand up to stop Kelan from reacting to Peter blaming Trisha for his life being miserable. "I don't give a damn about how miserable you have been. I warned you to never come into my daughter's life again. Now, you are going to learn what happens when you cross me. Kelan is very protective of Trisha. He is not very happy with you at all for the way you treated her then or now," Paul said with a cruel grin. "As much as I would like to be the one to deal out justice, he has asked me for my permission to do it. I think it only fitting that he shows you what happens when you cross a Valdier warrior by trying to use his mate. Kelan, he is all yours."

Peter was shaking his head back and forth and trembling uncontrollably as Kelan's face began to elongate and his body began to shift into the form of his dragon. He dropped the poker and slid down the wall, trying to curl into a little ball as he whimpered. Kelan reached out a long jade and silver claw and sunk his nails deep into the beige leather chair. With a flick of his wrist, the chair went flying across the room to crash next to the opening leading to the front door. Peter's whimpers turned to sobs as he hid his face in his hands.

"Please, I swear I'll never even think about her again," Peter sobbed loudly. "I swear! I promise! Please don't kill me, please don't kill me," he pleaded over and over.

* * *

Kelan turned his huge head and rolled his eyes at Paul, who was fighting back his laughter. From the strong smell of urine, Peter had pissed his pants. Paul hoped to God he didn't shit in them. If he did, he was leaving his sorry ass ex-son-in-law to Kelan.

Kelan turned his head back to look down on the shivering mass of wasted space. Even his dragon was having a hard time dealing with the blubbering human male. It was as disgusted by the human as he was. Kelan reached around with his tail and gingerly wrapped it around the male's feet, dragging him out of the corner and holding him upside down where he screamed hoarsely. Inhaling a deep breath, he let a burst of hot air surround the male who screeched even louder, hurting Kelan's ears.

"Kelan," Paul choked out. "You'd better decide if you are going to eat him, burn him to ash, or drop him on his head because I have got to tell you, he is giving me a damn headache with all his whining, crying, and screeching."

Kelan opened his mouth wide, showing off his razor-sharp teeth. Peter's eyes widened before they rolled back in his head as he fainted. Kelan snapped his jaws shut in disgust and dropped the limp figure onto the floor before shifting back into his two-legged form.

"You have got to be kidding me," Kelan said in disgust. "Please tell me what my mate ever saw in this spineless waste of living tissue?" He asked, placing his hands on his hips and looking down in revulsion at the unconscious male. "I hope he is not the standard of your warriors. If he is, your planet is going to need help if it is ever invaded," he added, looking over at Paul who was trying hard to contain his laughter.

"Some women find his good looks and smooth talking attractive," Paul said with a shake of his head. "I have to admit I was taken in by him at first, but it didn't take long to discover it was all bullshit. He was very good at hiding it from Trisha," he said. "Help me get him on the couch. I want him to watch you burn the insurance papers to a crisp when he comes to. We'll let him know that is what will happen to him if he ever tries to mess with my family again."

Kelan bent down and grabbed Peter's left arm while Paul grabbed his right. Neither wanted to get too close to him since he reeked of urine. Paul had to admit he was a little disappointed Peter hadn't fought or tried to make a run for it. He had been hoping he would just so he could watch the slimy bastard stew for a bit.

He glanced at Kelan and bit back a grin. This was the type of son he would have enjoyed having. He had found the Valdier warrior to be intelligent, caring, loyal and Paul enjoyed his wicked sense of humor. He had to admit as they settled Peter on the couch that Kelan's approval rating went through the ceiling when Kelan stated his desire for revenge. Kelan wanted justice for the hell Trisha had gone through because of her miserable ex-husband.

Kelan stood back from the couch and wiggled his nose in distaste. "He stinks," he growled out in annoyance.

Paul chuckled. "Yes, in more ways than just because he pissed his pants."

Kelan looked at Paul with a raised eyebrow. "By the way, neither I nor my dragon eat trash. I hope you didn't honestly think I would even consider putting my mouth on something this disgusting," he added.

Paul just chuckled and shook his head. "No, but Peter didn't know that. Keep an eye on him while I go get the insurance papers. After he comes to and you burn them, we need to get out of here. Trisha will get suspicious if we return too late. She'll know we were up to something."

Kelan grimaced. "I have a feeling she already does," he sighed. "She is very good at getting me to confess when I do things I don't want her to know about."

Paul laughed as he turned and headed down the hallway. *Yes,* he thought, *if I couldn't have a son, then at least I have a son-in-law that I know will take care of my baby girl.* He couldn't help but wish that Evelyn could have met Kelan. He knew she would have approved of him.

## Chapter 5

The next two weeks flew by as preparations were made for the return trip to Valdier. Peter had sent Paul a certified letter showing the cancellation of the insurance policy and his sworn promise that he would never even think of Trisha again. Paul felt certain that Peter would keep his word this time.

Mason and Chad had been by every day going over details for Paul's absence and how to handle any inquiries as well as the maintenance of the ranch and his assets. Mason would continue to manage everything. The big house would be reserved for their visitors. Ann Marie would make sure it remained clean and stocked. Chad would handle any legal issues as well as all the financial.

Jaguin and Gunner, two of Kelan's warriors from the *V'ager*, were staying behind to search for mates and help secure the area with additional security technology. Kor and Palto had found their true mates and had returned with them the night before.

Unfortunately from what Kelan had been able to get out of his two friends, neither one of the women were being very cooperative at the moment. Kor had returned early last night with a female over his shoulder while Palto had returned a little later with one that was cursing, scratching, and biting him. Kelan made sure that neither Paul nor Trisha saw his two friends. The last thing he needed was for Paul to decide they were invading the planet and stealing the women. While they were not doing the first, the latter could definitely be considered somewhere in the gray area according to Paul's attorney friend, Chad.

Kelan, Trisha, and Paul talked to Creon and Carmen late last night after they had departed Earth's orbit. It had been good to see his younger brother smiling and happy. They had talked about the attack on Mandra and how his uncle had changed his symbiot from positive to negative energy. Creon said Mandra, who had been seriously injured in the attack on his uncle's hidden base, would recover, but he and his symbiot needed to return to Valdier in order to do so. He also wanted Trelon and Cara to take a look at the red jewel that Ariel had been given.

Kelan turned as Paul walked onto the bridge of the *V'ager*. "We will be able to increase speed soon. It will take less time to return home. Cara has found a way to increase the speed with the use of our symbiots and different frequencies. I am ready to return. I am not sure Trisha will make it before our son is born though. She is due any day," he explained in a worried voice. "Kor returned with a female doctor from your world familiar with delivering babies. She will work with our own medical staff. I did not want to take any chances," Kelan said defiantly.

Paul raised his eyebrow at Kelan and waited. He almost grinned as Kelan shifted uncomfortably under his scrutiny. He could hear the hesitation in Kelan's voice and noticed the way his new son-in-law refused to meet his eyes after he explained about taking the human doctor. After the silence lengthened into minutes, Paul released a deep sigh.

"Let me guess," Paul said drily. "You took first, then asked if she wanted to come."

"Not me - Kor," Kelan said before glancing at Paul again and shrugging his shoulders. "I wanted the best for Trisha," he muttered defensively. "Besides, the female turned out to be Kor's mate anyway," he grumbled out in a low voice.

Paul sighed again. "Did she have any family?" He asked, worried about the girl.

Kelan shook his head. "Not that she talked about," he said in relief. "Kor believes she had not seen her family in many years and was not close to them."

"You promised that you wouldn't take any female without their understanding and acceptance," Paul reminded Kelan calmly. "Your men have to think of the woman and if she might have a family who will love and miss her."

Kelan rolled his shoulders and turned to look coldly at Paul. The look of compassion and understanding on Paul's face soon changed the look to regret. It was hard for him to be upset with Trisha's father. The human male reminded Kelan of his own father. He had the same keen intelligence and ability to understand combined with patience. Kelan knew he and his brothers were going to be in trouble if they thought to outsmart or bully this man.

"I will speak with them again. It is difficult," Kelan admitted ruefully. "Once our dragon and symbiot have accepted the female it is impossible for the man not to accept her as well. It is a dream come true for a warrior to discover their true mate. Given enough time, the three parts of ourselves will win the female over. It is difficult to do so on your world as we might be caught during the courtship," Kelan added with a mischievous grin.

Paul's lips twisted into a wry smile. "Nice try," he replied drily. "The men still need to ask first. As long as the woman says 'yes' then I consider it okay."

Kelan's eyes narrowed and his brain sped through the different conversations he'd had with Kor and Palto. He remembered both men saying the women said 'yes' at least once. It might not have been to leaving, but they had said the word so that meant they had satisfied Paul's requirements.

"I will ask both men, but I am sure they and the other women did say the word 'yes'," Kelan said with a satisfied grin.

Paul looked at Kelan suspiciously. "What do you mean…. and the other women?" he asked.

Kelan grinned and chuckled. "Let us just say it was a very good trip for many of the warriors."

Paul grumbled under his breath about feeling like he was stuck with a bunch of teenage boys on a field trip who have just discovered girls. He shook his head and decided he would go find a quiet spot with the information tablet that Palto had given him. He was just about to tell Kelan he would see him and Trisha later at dinner when medical buzzed to tell them Trisha had gone into labor.

Kelan swayed on his feet and his face turned pale before he clenched his teeth. "Let us go welcome my son into the world," he said hoarsely.

* * *

Morian looked over at the twins who were crawling across the floor trying to get to Zohar who was chewing on a toy while sitting on her lap. She bit her lip to keep from bursting out laughing when Amber charged as fast as she could on her hands and knees toward him with a gleam of delight in her eyes. Jade was not far behind her. Both girls had their mother's red hair minus the purple streaks that Cara liked. Jade sneezed suddenly and fell onto her stomach with a low growl of frustration before she started whimpering. Before the second whimper was out Trelon burst into the room looking frantically around.

"What's wrong?" He demanded. "Which one is hurt?"

Morian couldn't contain her laugh at Trelon's frazzled look and even more frazzled hair. "What happened to your hair?" She asked, not even trying to hide her amusement.

Trelon looked at her with bruised eyes. "Cara put the girls in bed with us last night because they wanted to play instead of sleep. She didn't realize I had given them some fruit earlier and their hands were still sticky from it," he grimaced as he tried to run his hand through the long strands but found it was too knotted to do anything but make it stand out even more. "I haven't had a chance to get a shower since Cara went out for a little while. I thought it would be good to give her a break. The girls have been very active," he said tiredly.

Morian searched her son's exhausted face. "Are you having difficulty sleeping, Trelon?" She asked in concern. "Cara asked if I would come watch the girls for a little while so you could get some sleep. She is worried about you. I thought they would like to come play with Zohar. I was able to talk Zoran into letting me take Zohar out for a little while."

Trelon walked over to sit on the edge of the chair where he could keep an eye on the girls. He set his sword down on the floor, then had to immediately pick it back up when Amber giggled and headed straight for it. He winced when he saw her little face scrunch up and a wail burst from her lips. Reaching down, he picked her up and settled her in his lap.

Amber giggled and reached for the sword on the arm of the chair with a squeal of delight. Trelon tried to shift her away from it, but she refused to be denied the prize that she wanted and grabbed a handful of his tangled sticky hair, forcing him to put the sword down again so he could untangle her little fingers from it.

"I have to protect them," he grumbled, grabbing his sword and moving it to the other side of him as Jade pulled herself up on the chair and reached for it. "I don't want any of the warriors getting ideas about them. I....," he stopped as Amber tried to crawl up over his shoulder while Jade started to make a beeline for the other side where the sword was balanced on the table until she discovered his booted foot. "I.... sweetheart, you can't have daddy's sword. No Jade, don't chew on my boot. Amber, honey, that is my ear you are biting," Trelon said gruffly as he tried to get one wet, slobbering mouth off his ear and the other off his boot.

Morian finally took pity on her exhausted son just as Cara came bouncing into the room with a big grin on her face. "Morian! Thank you for coming. Trelon, why is Jade chewing on your shoe? Amber, let go of daddy's sword, honey. You have to be a little older before you get one. Morian, I was down at the workshop and I made a baby monitor for the girls so we could keep a better eye on them," Cara said dropping the devices she was carrying on the couch as she hurried forward to pull Jade off of Trelon's boot where she was growling and shaking it back and forth.

Trelon looked at Cara in disbelief. "You said you were going to the market and maybe for a short flight," he growled out then winced when Amber bit down really hard as Cara took the handle of the sword out of her little fist. He winced again when Amber began crying in his tortured ear.

"Oh, I did that hours ago while the girls were sleeping," Cara grinned. "We need to get the girls in their own bedroom and until we can figure out how they keep getting out of their crib, I thought a video monitor with an escape alert would come in handy," she said holding Jade up and nibbling on her belly drawing giggles from her squirming daughter. "Yes, mommy taught you too well on how to escape, didn't she?" She teased, chuckling when Jade leaned into her and gave her a big, wet kiss.

Trelon wrapped his arm around Amber as he surged to his feet in aggravation. "They will not be out of our sight!" He snarled. "I will protect them with my life! No one will get near them."

Morian rose and set Zohar on the floor while Jade and Amber stared back and forth between their parents. "Trelon, give me Amber. Cara, give me Jade," she demanded.

Trelon held Amber who heard her Grand *Dola's* words and started squealing with delight. Jade was hanging upside down in Cara's arms where she was trying to get loose. Zohar was giggling and pounding his toy on the floor at all the excitement.

"What are you going to do?" Trelon asked as held the squirming little body as best he could.

"I am going to take the children to my living quarters until tomorrow and you….," Morian paused, looking pointedly at Trelon. "You are going to get some sleep. Cara, I expect you to totally exhaust my son so he can't keep his eyes open."

Cara looked at Trelon with a raised eyebrow, noticing the wild hair and the dark shadows under his eyes. "Why? He looks like he's about ready to crash as it is," she said. "How can I get him any more exhausted?" She asked looking at Morian.

Morian raised her eyebrows at Cara and grinned. "By fucking his brains out, of course. I wouldn't mind having more great children to chase after if you need another reason."

Cara's laughter drowned out Trelon's shocked hiss at his mother's words. Before he could say a word of protest, Cara had pulled an excited Amber out of his arms and tucked her safely into the carriage that Morian's symbiot had formed. Morian deposited Jade in next to her sister and scooped up a happy Zohar, who happily crawled in between them.

"Goodnight, Trelon," Morian said with a wave of her hand as she strolled out the door of their living quarters. "We'll see you tomorrow."

Trelon watched in shock as his mother walked out the door with his infant daughters. His mind was too dazed and tired to protest too much. He turned and looked at Cara, who was studying him with a critical eye, noting the lines of fatigue around his mouth and eyes.

"Did my mother just tell you to fuck my brains out?" He asked in shock.

Cara burst into laughter all over again. "I think she did," she murmured, pulling him toward their bedroom. "I think I'm going to give you a bath first. You smell like a fruit salad."

Trelon looked at Cara and his eyes turned a dark gold as she licked her lips. "How about you see if I taste like one?" He growled out, snatching her up in his arms with a low rumble as she squealed in delight.

\* \* \*

Morian walked back toward her living quarters cursing silently, a furious blush on her cheeks. She couldn't believe she just said that to Cara and Trelon. She fanned herself as her symbiot moved silently beside her, the three little ones wrestling with each other and giggling.

*What is wrong with me?* Morian asked herself silently. *I swear I'm reverting to my youth again! Goodness knows that should happen. I got in enough trouble the first time to know the heartache it can cause. I definitely don't need to go through it again.*

*Mate is closer,* her dragon purred. *I feel it. My true mate is coming.*

*Not that again!* Morian said in shock. *I thought you were over that!*

*Not over, just beginning,* her dragon purred.

Morian was saved from answering her dragon by Ariel, who was hurrying down the corridor toward her. "Morian! Trisha had her baby. Kelan wants to show you," she exclaimed excitedly. "Come on! Mandra is talking to him right now. The baby is adorable."

Morian felt her symbiot shiver with excitement. The three little ones playing must have felt it also because they began squealing even louder and rolling around. Poor Zohar was on the receiving end of the girls. One was lying across his belly while the other one was trying to grab his toes so she could chew on them. Morian chuckled when she realized it was Jade. That little one was always chewing on something. Morian picked up speed as she hurried after Ariel.

"When will they be home?" Morian asked anxiously as she walked through the door of their living quarters and over to the viewport that had been set up in the living area. "Mandra, should you be up yet?" She asked worriedly as she saw her second son sitting in front of it.

"I'm fine," he growled out. "Ariel has made sure I get plenty of rest."

Ariel blushed as she glared at him. "I haven't heard you complaining," she muttered under her breath. "Now scoot over so your mom can talk to Kelan and Paul and see the baby."

"Paul? Trisha's father?" Morian asked, horrified as her hand flew to her long, tangled hair. The first thing Zohar had done when she picked him up was pull her hair loose from where she had it pulled back. "I...." She didn't get any further before Ariel was pushing her down into the seat Mandra had just vacated.

"Kelan," Morian breathed out nervously. "How is Trisha?"

"She is fine. Paul, bring my son over," Kelan said smiling proudly. "He is very strong. Just like his mother," he boasted.

Morian's eyes widened when she saw the handsome male step closer to the viewscreen. Her hands started shaking and she felt faint as her breath caught in her throat. Her dragon snapped to attention and began purring. She could feel the damn thing rubbing against her skin wanting to get closer to the male.

*Oh shit!* She thought stunned. *He is my true mate.*

# Chapter 6

Paul's head jerked up from where he was smiling down at the tiny infant in his arms when he heard the husky voice of the woman on the other side of the viewscreen. His eyes narrowed as he took in her flushed cheeks and shy look as she stared back at him. A wave of unexpected need washed through him, surprising him and making him scowl at the fierce response.

The woman on the screen flushed even rosier. Paul was mesmerized by the classical beauty of the woman glaring back at him. Her gold eyes met his defiantly, almost challenging him. Her face was framed by long, thick black hair that hung in glossy waves over her shoulders and down her back.

His arms tightened around the baby cradled against him. His fingers itched to thread them through her thick hair. His eyes moved down to her lips when she spoke again. He desperately wanted to know what she tasted like. When his eyes moved back to hers, the heat in them must have warned her that he was not immune to what he saw as the words died on her lips and her eyes widened in alarm.

"*Dola?*" Kelan asked when she didn't respond to his answer. "Did you hear me? I said Trisha is doing well. She is tired. The healers have told me that is not uncommon. Bio is with her now, healing her body. We've named the baby Bálint."

"Oh," Morian replied vaguely, dragging her eyes away from Paul. "Tell her I cannot wait to see her again. " Her eyes shifted away from Kelan's face as he leaned over Paul's shoulder to gaze lovingly down at his son. "He is beautiful, Kelan," she said softly as her eyes gazed tenderly down at the small face of her newest great child. Now, only Carmen was expecting at this time.

"He is a miracle," Paul murmured, staring down at the bundle in his arms again. "When the doctors told me Trisha would never be able to have children it broke my heart for her," he said, looking up into Morian's eyes with a smile. "I knew the joy of having her in my life and knew how much Trisha wanted children. Your son has given me a priceless gift. He has given me back my baby girl and a beautiful grandson."

Morian blushed again as his eyes met hers and she knew without a doubt that it was desire burning brightly in them as they gazed back at her. She didn't even remember what else they discussed. Kelan finally signed off when Bálint started fussing. He gingerly took him out of Paul's arms with a quick apology that he needed to get back to Trisha.

"I look forward to meeting you," Paul's deep voice said as they said goodbye.

Morian's hand moved to her throat as she tried to swallow over the lump in it. "Yes," she muttered, before disconnecting the connection.

"Morian, are you okay?" Ariel asked, suddenly concerned. "You look a little flushed."

Morian's head jerked up and she forced a smile to her face. "Yes…. Yes, I'm fine. I think I'll take the little ones back to my living quarters and see if they are ready for a nap."

Mandra laughed as he looked down at his little nephew who was squirming, trying to get away from the two little girls who were looking at him as if he was their new favorite toy. Zohar was beginning to whimper as the girls tackled him again. Even the little creatures the symbiot was creating to distract them weren't working. The girls were both focused on their slightly bigger cousin.

"I think Zohar is going to need it after the twins get done with him," Mandra said, picking up a squirming Amber and tickling her stomach. The minute she squealed, Jade was trying to crawl out of the golden carriage. All three adults started laughing when Jade growled out at Mandra.

"I think Trelon is going to have his hands full with these two," Ariel said scooping Jade up into her arms. "I'll walk back with you to your living quarters and help you get them down. I think Zohar needs a break."

Morian's eyes turned to her oldest great-child and she chuckled as she saw he had already fallen half asleep now that he was safe. Her symbiot had formed a light layer to act as a cover and had wrapped it snugly around his little body. Zohar gave out a soft sigh, stuck his thumb in his mouth and was gently sucking on it as his eyelashes fluttered closed.

"Give me this little bundle of terror," Morian said, holding her arms out for Amber, who was busy rubbing slobber in Mandra's hair. "I would appreciate the help, Ariel. Mandra, get some rest. I'll return your mate to you soon."

Mandra stood up and wrapped his arm around Ariel pulling her and Jade into his arms. He whispered something into Ariel's ear that caused her to blush and smile up at him before they both caressed Jade's silky red hair. Morian watched for a moment before understanding dawned, and a small smile curved her lips. It looked like the royal house was about to get even fuller.

* * *

Paul stood in his living quarters on board the *V'ager* staring out into deep space. It still felt unreal that so much had happened in such a short time. He didn't regret one minute of his decision to leave everything he had ever known behind.

He had accepted a long time ago that life was too short to waste on regrets. His thoughts turned to the dark haired beauty he had seen earlier. The fact that she was Kelan's mother did not distract him from his interests. She was a very beautiful woman and there was something about her that called to him. He hadn't felt such an intense emotion since – Evelyn.

Paul frowned as he tried to understand how just hearing Morian's voice and seeing her on a viewscreen could have more impact on him than all the women he had met and known since his wife died. He hadn't been a saint during the years that had passed.

He was a healthy male with an even healthier appetite. It was just none of the women had stirred more than a passing fancy. Hell, the longest relationship he could remember had only lasted three months. That had ended the moment the woman started trying to show him dresses in the latest wedding magazines. He ran a hand over his face in aggravation. He might not be a young man anymore, but he still had the same hopes and desires, it would appear.

A calculating smile curved his lips. He would need to be careful. The last thing he wanted to do was to have an affair with his son-in-law's mother and end up in a sticky situation on a world where the men could roast his balls if he pissed them off.

*No*, he thought as his mind went through each scenario in an effort to determine the best possible move. *I'll have to wait until we meet to know for sure which course to take. Once I know if the feelings I felt are genuine or not, then I'll know what to do. Hell, it could be it's been a while and I just need a little companionship to ease the ache. But, if the feelings are genuine,* he thought with a wry smile, *if they are, I don't give a damn about what anyone says. I've waited for this moment for almost thirty years. If she fills the emptiness inside me, she is mine.*

Satisfied with his decision, Paul turned to go check one more time on Trisha and his grandson before he settled down for the night to go over the geography, demographics and cultural makeup of the Valdier world. He liked to be well informed and he still had a lot to learn before they arrived in a couple of weeks. The fact that it was an alien world where the men could turn into dragons and their weapons were advanced wasn't something he would ignore but he would not be intimidated by it either.

If he knew what he was up against he could overcome any obstacle. If this Raffvin was still on the loose, he was not going to let his guard down either. From what he had learned during his conversations with Kelan, the man was a threat to his family and as far as he was concerned, that was not acceptable.

* * *

The next few weeks flew by. Paul spent part of his day with Trisha and Bálint before meeting with either Kelan or some of the other warriors for training. He had become good friends with Palto and Kor and two other men who were Curizan, not Valdier. Jaron was a healer for his people and Terac was his best friend and an accomplished pilot. Both men spoke with a quiet respect as they described their awe at Trisha's abilities as both a warrior and her skill and knowledge at surviving in the wild.

Paul's heart swelled with pride at his baby girl's abilities. He was also thankful for being there to give her the knowledge she needed to survive. He had talked to her at length one afternoon while Bálint slept protectively in his arms. She blushed as she admitted that she had gotten frightened not long after Kelan had taken her to his world. She explained she had knocked out one of the guards and escaped into the forests. It had taken her five days and a long talk with her dragon to come to terms that she was not part of some weird government experiment.

She told him of her tagging the guys. She giggled when she later told him about how Kelan had to help her call forth her dragon and her dragon tossing him in the mud for his arrogant attitude. Paul watched as her face glowed with happiness as she talked about her mate. The whole time, the huge symbiot she had nicknamed Bio laid protectively next to her not letting its eyes move from her or the baby. Paul felt confident that while Kelan might be the most unexpected man he would have chosen for his daughter, he was the perfect one for her.

Late the next day, he finished packing for his trip down to the planet. They had arrived in orbit around Valdier a couple of hours ago and preparations for disembarkment and resupplying were well under way. He had to admit he was anxious to get down to the surface.

He had only talked to Morian on two other occasions during the past couple of weeks and each time made him want more. He had been shocked by the heat and need to touch her that increased whenever he heard her husky voice, saw the flush in her beautiful cheeks, or saw the shyness in her eyes. He had begun to wonder if he would explode from spontaneous combustion if he couldn't touch her to see if her skin was as silky as it looked and the thought of kissing her….

Paul looked up when the door of his living quarters chimed, jerking him out of his reverie. He shook his head in amusement at his own thoughts as the computer identified Terac was at the door. He called out the command giving Terac permission to enter.

Straightening up, he looked startled when he also saw Lodar standing in the corridor with a small female next to him. "Hey Terac, I was just finishing up," he said as he slung his duffle bag over his broad shoulder. "Who is the girl?"

Terac looked over his shoulder with a small smile. "Our mate," he replied, looking at Paul with cautious eyes. "Her name is Kei."

Kei's eyes flashed at Paul. "And she can speak for herself," she snapped out.

Terac grimaced, fighting back a growl of frustration when Kei glared up at him. "Hi Paul," Lodar sighed. "Do you need help with anything or are you ready to head to the transporter room?"

"I've got it," Paul replied, biting back a grin as Kei moved closer to Lodar when he walked out of the room. "Hello Kei, my name is Paul Grove," he said holding his hand out.

Kei hesitated a moment before she slipped her tiny hand into his larger one. Almost immediately, she pulled back and stepped back between the two men who towered over her. Paul studied the small female who shyly slid her hand into Lodar's larger one.

"I thought you only kidnapped women," Kei responded, looking between Terac and Lodar with a confused frown.

Paul's eyes jerked up to Terac who moved protectively in front of Kei as Lodar pulled her back against his tall frame. "What the hell?" He snapped out, looking at Terac with dark cold eyes. "Did you kidnap her? Are you holding her against her will?"

Terac's jaw clenched and he stared back at Paul. "This is between us," he said. "She is our mate."

Paul let the duffle bag on his shoulder slide down off his shoulder and drop to the floor. "I'm making it my business," he replied through clenched teeth. His eyes swung to Kei's beautiful dark brown eyes. "Are they holding you against your will?"

Kei's eyes softened as she felt the hard body behind her stiffen, waiting for her answer. A soft sigh escaped her slightly parted lips and she shook her head, sending waves of silky black hair swaying around her tiny head. She bit her lip before she looked up into Paul's thunderous eyes.

"No," she whispered. "They are not holding me against my will. We just have things we need to work out," she answered, her exotic eyes turning to gaze up at Terac's shuttered eyes. "I have a problem with holding my temper sometimes," she admitted. "When I get scared I sometimes say things I don't mean," she added before bowing her head and letting her hair cover her face.

Paul watched as Terac's face softened as he stared tenderly down at the small Asian-American female. "We will talk once we are on the surface. Lord Kelan has offered both of us accommodations and a position aboard the *V'ager*." Terac turned to look at Paul before continuing. "No harm will come to her, I swear this on my life," he said, looking Paul in the eye to let him know that he would also fight to the death if necessary to prevent anyone from taking Kei away from him.

Paul studied the three figures standing quietly before he gave a brief nod. "Good. I'd hate to have to kick your asses if you didn't," he added before bending down and grabbing his duffle bag. "Let's get off this flying boat. I'd like to see what in the hell I've gotten myself into," he added with a grin.

Terac and Lodar nodded silently. Both men led the way with the tiny female tucked between them. He fought back a grin when he watched the small woman slide her hand timidly into Terac's. This was going to be a very interesting experience. He had a feeling from what he had been reading that many of the different species, Valdier, Curizan, and Sarafin, were not accustomed to independent, outspoken females.

His thoughts turned to Morian. He had a hard time believing she would be the submissive type. The fire in her eyes that she tried to hide spoke of a passion that burned beneath the surface. He cursed as he felt his body harden for the hundredth time at the thought of having Morian in a submissive position under him.

*Damn it*, he thought as he fought the urge to adjust his cock that was rubbing painfully against the front of his jeans. *I hope to God she isn't as hot in person as she is on the viewscreen. If she is, there might be hell to pay with her sons because I'll be damned if my control is going to last long at the rate I'm going.*

## Chapter 7

Morian nervously ran her hand over her already smooth hair. She had pinned it up in the neatly controlled chignon that she normally wore. She stood to the side of the transporter waiting for Kelan, Trisha and Bálint to arrive. She refused to acknowledge that she was also waiting breathlessly for her first meeting with Paul Grove.

It didn't seem to matter how much she scolded herself, her dragon or her symbiot about not thinking about the huge human male it was an impossible endeavor to ignore her excitement, restlessness, and hope. She couldn't even sleep at night without dreaming about him. She swore it was a conspiracy between her dragon and her symbiot, though both acted innocent when she confronted them.

She wiped her hands on the slim folds of her gown. She had been tempted to wear something less formal, but thought she would appear more in control if she wore the royal gowns distinguishing her position as a Priestess. The long white gown flowed around her in shimmering waves, thin gold stitching catching the light and making it sparkle. The bodice of the gown was strapless and showed off the delicate curve of her shoulders.

She wore a gold pendant formed by her symbiot in the shape of her dragon. As a Priestess, she was one of the few females who had a symbiot of her own. It was necessary to protect her and her dragon at all times.

Morian let her fingers drop to touch the golden figure by her side. If she'd had any fear that her symbiot might not accept him it was fast dissipating. The symbiot had taken on the strange form of an animal from Earth known as a dog, much like Carmen and Creon's symbiot.

It had thought the form would be more welcoming to Paul. The damn thing had been spending time with Abby, Cara, and Ariel, sorting through one shape after another. Cara had laughingly called it Darwin's grab bag as it kept switching until Ariel had assured it that Paul absolutely loved dogs and it was much easier to have one of those around than a grizzly bear, horse, cow, or the other dozens of shapes it shifted into.

Now, the three of them stood waiting nervously for the man who had been an aggravating pain in her head and heart for weeks. A small smile curved her lips as her symbiot sent her a wave of nervous warmth. Even her dragon was shifting around inside her with nervous energy.

"He will accept us," she murmured as much to calm herself as her dragon and symbiot. "He has to accept us."

*He might not like dragons,* her dragon fretted. *He might not think me pretty.*

*He'll think you are beautiful,* Morian assured her dragon.

Her symbiot sent an image of him not wanting to touch it. Morian fought the urge to roll her eyes. Both of them were acting like this *NOW*?

She was the one who had finally come to terms with the idea that if the human male was her true mate that it would be ridiculous to fight it. Instead of fighting, she would control it. She would only let a small part of her open up to him. She could protect the rest of her.

Just because he might be her true mate didn't mean she had to really love him. She could just be affectionate toward him. She wouldn't have to open herself to the pain of loving and losing again. She could keep her heart safely locked away. Once she had decided to do that she had felt more confident that she could handle whatever the gods or goddesses threw at her. She really believed that – until the moment she saw him in person. Then she knew her heart would never be safe again.

* * *

Paul blinked as his eyes adjusted to the new location. A slight sense of disorientation stayed with him for a few seconds after the transporter beamed them down. It was weird to be on a warship in space one minute than in a strange room on the surface of an alien planet the next. His brain needed a moment to process the change in environment.

His eyes quickly scanned the area and categorized everything in the room. He knew where every male was, where a possible threat could come from, and how he would react if a threat did appear. Once he had assessed his current situation, he gave into the desire to return his eyes to the female standing regally near the console of the transporter. His eyes swept over her. Fire flamed inside him as he took in the neatly captured black tresses of her hair.

*That would have to go,* he thought immediately. *I want to be able to wrap my hands in it.*

He let his eyes roam over the smooth olive skin of her neck and shoulders, highlighted by the beautiful white gown. His gaze continued all the way down to the sleek gold slippers she wore on her feet before traveling back up again. He liked what he saw and he wasn't ashamed to show it.

He knew his eyes had darkened with desire and a small, triumphant smile curved his lips as he took in the rose color that highlighted her cheeks showing she was not immune to him either. His heart beat heavily as he felt his body react to finally being near the woman who had been a constant companion in his mind for weeks now.

It took every ounce of his self-control not to drop his duffle bag, march over to her and swing her up in his arms so he could find a quiet place to sate his hunger. He started forward, stepping down off the platform as he followed Kelan, Trisha, and Bálint over to where Morian stood.

"*Dola,*" Kelan said, releasing his touch on Trisha long enough to give his mother a kiss on her cheek. "May I present our son, Bálint," he said formally, turning back to Trisha who was holding the sleeping infant protectively in her arms.

"Oh Kelan, he is beautiful," Morian said, smiling down at the baby. She reached over and gently caressed his tiny cheek with her finger. "He will grow to be a strong young man. His matching has already been scheduled. Zoran is anxious that he be joined with his symbiot as soon as possible," she said referring to the ceremony where all warriors are matched with the symbiot that would grow with them and become a part of their life. "It will be done this evening."

Kelan nodded as he looked down with pride at his son. "I would like to see Zoran and Abby's son and Cara and Trelon's daughters. Has Trelon relaxed any since the girls were born or is he still trying to stand guard over them day and night?" Kelan asked in amusement.

Morian chuckled softly. "Cara has convinced him that the girls will be fine without him hovering over them all the time. Poor Trelon was on the verge of collapsing from exhaustion until he and Cara finally figured out how the girls were escaping their cradle. Cara designed a set of baby monitors and they found out the little ones were using their symbiots to help them. Symba now monitors them as well as Cara's invention. Those two take after their mother. They are very inquisitive."

Kelan laughed and shook his head. "I feel for Trelon if he has two girls like Cara. She is enough to wear him out. It will be interesting to see what happens when the girls get older."

"Kelan," Trisha interrupted softly. "Bálint is awake which means he's hungry," She smiled apologetically to Morian as Bálint woke with a slight whimper and began rooting around the front of her top. "If he doesn't get fed soon everyone is going to know about it. Daddy, perhaps Morian will give you a tour of the palace," Trisha suggested with a hopeful smile. "Ask her to show you her atrium. You'll love it," she added as Kelan placed his hand on her lower back and began guiding her toward the door.

Paul watched as his baby girl and Kelan left him alone with Morian in the transporter room. He had enjoyed watching her as she interacted with Kelan and Bálint. Each move she made was like a symphony conductor, graceful and fluid. When she chuckled huskily, it felt like a vice clutching at his stomach and damned if his cock didn't swell again at the sound.

He loved the furious blush that swept up into her cheeks again when she finally didn't have any excuse not to look at him. Shifting his duffle bag over his right shoulder, he held out his hand to her in greeting. He watched as she nervously ran hers along her hip before she reached to clasp his hand with her smaller one.

"Paul Grove," he said in a husky voice. "It is a pleasure to finally meet you in person."

"Yes…. Yes, I'm Morian," she responded shyly. "Of course, you know that," she added with another furious blush as she gazed up at him.

Paul grinned mischievously before he closed his hand around hers, trapping it in his warm grip and jerked just enough to pull her off balance. He sealed his lips to hers in a brief, but passionate kiss. Pulling back slowly, he looked down into her startled, flushed face.

A slight smile pulled at his lips. "Just as I suspected," he murmured.

Morian stared up at him for a moment before she blinked. "What…. What did you suspect?" She breathed out in confusion.

"That you taste even better than I imagined," Paul responded lightly before stepping back. "So, what about that tour?"

"Tour," Morian repeated before she pulled her shoulders back and drew in a deep breath. "Yes, I…. A tour, follow me and I'll show you to your living quarters first so you can put your things down. Anything else you have will be delivered there later this evening," she said, turning on trembling legs to exit the room.

She let her fingers brush against her symbiot even as she cautioned her dragon to sit the hell back down. She could feel the slight tingling on her skin and cursed the fact that she probably had scales rippling uncontrollably over her skin. His kiss, followed by the softly spoken words, had thrown her mind into chaos.

*Will you go lay down!* She snapped at her dragon as it pushed against her skin again.

*No,* her dragon growled back. *He kiss you. He taste good. I want to bite. I want mate! Now!*

*It was just a kiss, not an invitation to jump him. It is probably just a human's way of saying hello,* Morian responded silently in exasperation as she led the way down the maze of corridors.

She knew she should be giving Paul a brief history of the palace but she was too distracted by the kiss and her dragon to do anything but try to keep both of their libidos under control. It didn't help that her symbiot kept pushing her closer and closer until she was practically glued to his side. When Paul's hand moved to the center of her back and she felt his thumb rub back and forth against her, it became too much for her and her dragon. The moment they were in the long corridor leading to his living quarters her dragon pushed forward, snapping her slim control.

"Oh hell," she muttered before she swung around and wrapped her arms around Paul's neck, dragging him into a nearby alcove. "Kiss me again," she demanded breathlessly.

Paul didn't need a second invitation. He dropped his duffle bag onto the floor, kicking it to one side as he wrapped his arms around Morian's slender waist. His lips crushed down on hers again, meeting her halfway as they devoured each other.

His hungry groan echoed hers as he ground his hips against hers to let her know that he was just as affected as she was to the chemistry igniting between them. His left hand moved up her back until it reached her hair. With a few quick moves, it tumbled down her back in a silky wave. He wound his fingers through it preventing her from pulling away from him as he deepened the kiss.

Morian's throaty moans turned to gasps as his lips left hers to travel along her jaw, down to her neck. She cried out when he nipped her throat before running his tongue soothingly along it as she exposed more to him. Her fingers tangled frantically in his short hair trying to pull him closer.

"This is crazy," he breathed out. "From the first time I heard your voice I haven't been able to stop thinking about you," he growled out, pulling back to gaze down into her dazed eyes. "You've been in my thoughts, in my dreams, every fucking minute."

Morian reached up, sealing her lips to his in an answering kiss filled with pent up frustration and need. Her lips opened under his as he ran his tongue along the seam. He quickly took advantage, plundering deeper as his tongue battled with her own. He finally pulled back when he heard a soft threatening growl behind him. He thrust Morian behind him as he turned, slipping his hunting knife into his hand and positioning his body protectively in front of her.

"What do you think you are doing?" Zoran snarled as his teeth elongated and his skin rippled with red, green and gold scales. "You think to assault the Hive's Priestess and my *Dola*?"

Paul's eyes narrowed and he adjusted his weight so he was on the balls of his feet. He had been training with Kelan and many of the other warriors aboard the *V'ager* over the past few weeks in both their two-legged and four-legged form. He wanted to know what to expect if he should have to fight this Raffvin in his dragon form. He needed to know areas of weakness.

He had discovered more than he had shown the Dragon Warriors as he had come to think of them.

They were too confident in their dragons and their symbiots to save them. Trisha had quietly shared that same thought. She had expressed hope that perhaps he could show them where their weaknesses were and improve their guerilla tactics.

"Zoran, stop!" Morian's horrified voice called out in embarrassment. "It's not what you think!"

Zoran's blazing gold eyes turned to stare in disbelief at his normally serene mother. Her hair was flowing wildly down her back, tousled from the man's fingers, her lips were swollen from his kisses and her eyes.... Zoran pulled his dragon back as he stared into the glistening eyes as she looked at him with a look of pleading. She reached up a trembling hand and laid it gently on the human male's shoulder.

"It's not what you are thinking," she whispered.

Paul relaxed his stance enough to reach out to grab Morian's hand as it fell from his shoulder. He squeezed her fingers in an effort to give her comfort. He recognized the huge male as the leader of the Valdier Warriors and her oldest son. Paul refused to apologize for his behavior. Life was too short to apologize for taking what he wanted and he wanted Morian Reykill. Besides, from what Trisha had told him, none of her boys hesitated taking what they wanted or apologized for doing so.

"Zoran," Paul nodded warily to the huge Valdier warrior.

"Paul," Zoran acknowledged, still trying to come to terms with seeing his *Dola* looking more like a woman than his mother. "Can I ask you what you thought you were doing?"

Paul's lips twitched at the almost parental tone in the warrior's voice. "You can ask, but if I need to explain I think we are going to need more time than I have right now," he responded with a shrug, slipping his arm around Morian's waist and pulling her against his side when she tried to slide around him.

The tremble in her body was the only indication that she was unnerved by what happened between them. "I was showing Paul to his living quarters," she tried to explain in a quiet voice.

"That isn't what it looked like to me," Zoran pointed out gruffly. "It looked like he was more interested in showing you something."

Morian glared up at her older son. "I…. You…. We…..," her dragon growled out in frustration when she stumbled over the words she was trying to get out. "It is none of your business what he was interested in!" She finally retorted angrily before she jerked away from Paul, turning once she was far enough away he couldn't reach for her. "I'll let Zoran show you the rest of the way. I need to…." She drew in a deep, calming breath before finishing her sentence. "I need to see about dinner, if you will excuse me," she finished in a husky voice that sounded suspiciously close to tears.

Paul's mouth tightened into a grim line as he watched Morian turn and hurry down the corridor in the direction they had just come. After she disappeared, he turned a dark look on Zoran before he bent and picked up his discarded duffle bag. He slung it over his shoulder before he looked directly into the confused eyes of the Valdier leader.

"Your timing sucks," Paul drawled. "Has anyone ever told you that?"

Zoran had the grace to flush. "I never expected to find my brother's mate's father amusing himself with my mother," he growled.

Paul's eyes flashed in warning. "Let's get something straight. I don't amuse myself with women. Your mother is a beautiful woman. My woman. I'm letting you and your brothers know up front that I have every intention of courting her. If you don't like it, stay the hell out of my way," Paul said in a cold, calm voice. "Now are you going to show me to my living quarters or do I find them on my own?"

Zoran studied the man who was almost as tall and broad as he was standing his ground. Zoran knew of very few men who could do that. His face relaxed into a smile as he glanced back the way his mother had hurried off.

"Did she want you to kiss her?" Zoran asked curiously, turning to look back at Paul. "I don't want her hurt."

"Me either," Paul said, nodding his head in agreement. "She not only wanted it, she kissed me first," he replied with a grin before stepping around Zoran and heading down the hall, ignoring the way the big Valdier's mouth dropped open at his statement.

# Chapter 8

Paul had been in the atrium for almost an hour before Morian entered. He knew she had been avoiding him over the past two and a half weeks. The only time he had seen or talked to her was during the evening meals or when she came to visit with Trisha and Bálint. She always managed to slip away before he could get her alone.

*That is about to change,* he thought with grim determination as he watched and waited.

He had been in the training room earlier with Mandra when he discovered the information he needed to catch her alone. Mandra, who had finally received clearance from the healers that he could return to his normal schedule, was showing him how the Valdier used a laser sword in conflicts where they could not shift into their dragons. During the course of the training their conversation had turned to Raffvin and later to Morian.

"*Dola* has been very lonely since our father was killed," Mandra had said as he wiped the sweat from his face. He leaned back against the wall in the training room and looked intently at Paul. "We were all afraid she would choose to join him in death even though he was not her true mate."

Paul lowered the bottle of water he was drinking and stared through narrow eyes at Mandra. "What do you mean – follow him? As in die?" He asked harshly.

Mandra nodded. "If *Dola* would have been father's true mate, she would have. A woman can grieve and heal, possibly when her mate is gone, but not so a dragon. When a dragon's mate is killed, the dragon becomes inconsolable. Without the dragon, it is a half-life for the other two parts of ourselves. Soon our two-legged form joins the dragon and the symbiot cannot survive without the essence of our dragon and our two-legged form. It must return to the hive or perish as well," he explained.

"What do you mean when you say 'true mate'?" Paul asked, staring intently at Mandra.

Mandra's eyes softened in memory. "When I first saw Ariel I knew she was mine. My dragon wanted to claim her and my symbiot was all over her." He laughed as he remembered. "She did not feel the same way," he added with a twinkle in his eye. "I thought to scare her into submission with my dragon. Instead, she snared my heart with her touch before she broke my nose with her head. She demanded I change back."

Paul chuckled and shook his head. "Ariel was always, and I mean always, bringing home animals. I could tell you stories that would give you nightmares about some of them," he said. "Her mom wasn't much of an animal person, but her dad understood. He built her a barn so that she could have some place to house them all."

Mandra shuddered as he remembered some of the creatures Ariel still continued to bring home. They had a damn Pactor from the Antrox mines living out at his mountain estate. The damn thing was still growing and thought Ariel was his mommy! It followed her everywhere when they returned. He hoped it never decided to try eating her because he would roast the damn thing if it so much as put a scratch on her and that would really upset his mate.

Mandra jerked back to his musings when he heard Paul's quiet statement. "I feel the same way about your mother," Paul said quietly. "The first time I heard her voice it was like…." He paused and looked at Mandra. "I haven't felt this way since my first wife. Even then, this is different, stronger in a way. I loved Evelyn with every fiber of my being, don't get me wrong. I knew the moment I saw her, she was mine and I hoped that I'd find another woman one day who could make me feel just half of what she made me feel. But, the first time I heard Morian's voice." Paul's voice faded as he looked down at the mat for a moment before looking back up into Mandra's eye with a steely determination. "She's mine," he stated bluntly.

If Paul was expecting a negative response from Mandra he was going to be disappointed. The huge Valdier warrior threw his head back and laughed before he looked at Paul with a huge grin. He walked over to Paul and threw his arm around his broad shoulders.

"Good!" Mandra said. "She needs a male like you. She will be in her atrium in a little over an hour. I heard her telling Ariel that before I came to meet you. Just understand one thing, Paul," Mandra said as they walked toward the exit of the training room.

Paul looked up into the larger male's eyes. He had to admit that Mandra was a huge ass male even by Valdier standards. He wasn't in the least bit surprised that Ariel had fallen for the big male. She always did know how to handle larger than life creatures.

"What is that?" Paul asked as he pulled away to head back to his living quarters for a quick shower.

Mandra grinned, letting his teeth lengthen for effect. "If you hurt her, I will rip you apart."

Paul looked seriously at Mandra. "I will protect her with my life," he promised quietly, making sure the warrior knew he meant it.

"Good. I hope it never comes to that because I have seen the way she gazes at you," Mandra responded with a nod. "You are her true mate, whether you like it or not," he stated before turning and heading in the opposite direction.

Paul stood watching him go before he turned and walked slowly back to his rooms. A sense of serenity settled over him as he made up his mind. There would be no more hiding or avoiding him. It was time to let Morian know that she was his and he was not accepting anything less than all of her.

* * *

Now, Paul stood waiting in the shadows of the atrium for Morian to appear. When she did, he felt the breath leave him as it always did when he first saw her. She was breathtaking in her beauty and in the way she moved. He could watch her all day and never grow tired. He waited until she had turned her back to gaze down at the center pool before he came up silently behind her, sliding his arms around her and trapping her against his hard length.

"You've been avoiding me," Paul murmured gruffly. "I don't like that," he added as he pressed a kiss against the side of her neck. "I don't like it at all," he breathed out against her silky skin.

Morian gasped at the unexpected embrace. She had spent the last two and a half weeks doing everything in her power to stay away from Paul Grove and his explosive touch. The one blazing kiss in the corridors had shattered all her perceived concepts of keeping her heart safe. His touch ignited her until she was sure she glowed from the flaming embers of desire that she could barely contain.

"Paul," she whispered out, wanting to protest, but unable to say more than his name.

Paul turned her slowly in his arms. He kept her caged within them, unwilling to take the chance of her escaping from him again. Once she was facing him, he pulled her close against his body. He wanted her to know that he was not taking no for an answer this time.

"I want you," he said quietly, looking intently into her eyes to see her reaction to his claim. "I want to make love to you. I want to hold you in my arms. I crave it with a force that is driving me mad," he admitted ruefully. "I haven't felt this way since… since Evelyn."

Morian tilted her head back to look into his eyes. "Evelyn…. Trisha said she was your… true mate," she responded hesitantly.

She tried not to feel the hurt deep inside that came from knowing another man she loved could never feel the same way about her. Tears burned her eyes and she turned her head slightly and lowered her lashes to conceal the tears from him. Only through the self-discipline that she had worked so hard at developing over the past centuries was she able to hide her heartache. She was about to pull away when she felt his hand tenderly caress her jaw.

"She was my soul mate when I was but a boy back on Earth," he agreed before adding quietly to his statement. "But you….," he murmured tilting her head back so she had to look at him. "…. What I feel for you is much more. You consume me with the need of a man," he added before he claimed her lips in a passionate kiss of longing and need.

Morian felt not only her passion flare, but her dragon's. Neither one of them would be denied any longer. His words resonated through her, sending hope and desire crashing through the flimsy walls she had tried to erect around her heart. A low sob escaped her as she felt his answering response. Her head fell back as he threaded his fingers through the long tresses that he had unbound.

*He is worse than Zohar*, she thought fleetingly before all thoughts were consumed with claiming him as hers.

"Paul," she whispered hoarsely as she pulled back enough to expose her throat to his searching kisses. "I want you," she moaned.

"Come with me to my living quarters," he requested huskily.

Morian pulled back just far enough to smile up at him. "I have a better idea," she responded with a seductive smile.

She turned and looked at her symbiot briefly before giving it a jerky nod, a clear image that it was to protect the atrium from any intrusion. She wanted to make sure they were not disturbed - not for a very long time. It would bar the door to the atrium and make sure no one entered. She pulled out of Paul's arms, sliding her hand down to grasp his. The darkening of his eyes sent a wave of hot, furious desire coursing through her.

"You are mine, Morian," Paul whispered as he looked down at their clasped hands. His fingers tightened possessively on hers and he brought them to his lips. "You need to understand when I take you, there will be no more distance between us. There will be no more hiding from me. You will be mine. You will be by my side from now on."

Morian bit her lower lip and nodded. "I claim you, Paul Grove. You are my true mate – for now and for always," she swore out quietly. "Come with me," she said, pulling on his hand.

Paul let out a low growl at her words and swept her up into his arms. "Show me," he demanded hoarsely.

Morian wrapped one arm around his neck and buried her lips against his neck as she pointed with her other one toward the stairs leading up to her private sanctuary. Even as he carried her up the staircase, she felt her teeth elongating despite her attempts to hold back. She knew the males claimed their females through the dragon fire, but she and Jalo had never shared that experience as neither her dragon nor his cared passionately for each other the way their two-legged forms did. Their dragons had tolerated each other because it was expected for the sake of their people. In truth, their dragons had never even mated with each other.

Now, her dragon refused to hold back. She was determined to claim her mate. Morian fought against the desire to bite him, not wanting to hurt him, but her dragon had waited too long for this time. The moment he reached the top step, her dragon overwhelmed her control and sank her teeth into the vulnerable neck exposed to her.

"Shit!" Paul groaned fiercely as he felt a sudden sharp pain as Morian sank her teeth deep into the curve of his neck. "Morian…." He moaned as the pain turned almost immediately to hot waves of lava coursing through his blood straight to his cock.

When Morian began breathing the dragon's fire into his blood Paul stumbled and leaned against the doorframe for support. The initial wave burst over him with a ferocity that knocked him off balance. He didn't know what was going on but whatever in the hell it was, it was causing his body to explode with a powerful yearning. It took all of his self-control to focus on the large divan that was against the wall in order to keep from coming in his pants. He knew one thing, he was going to fuck Morian hard and fast this first time. His control was shot to hell from being denied for so long.

He barely made it to the long couch where he laid her gently down on the soft cushion. "Morian," he choked out through gritted teeth. "God woman, I have to have you!"

Morian slowly withdrew her teeth as the first wave of the dragon's fire finished pouring out of her. She gently licked the two puncture wounds on his neck, savoring the taste of his blood on her lips and tongue. Her dragon was panting and purring deep inside her as it sensed the burst of fire coursing through its mate.

It knew that its claim had begun, there would be no turning back. The thought of finally being sated by her true mate caused the dragon fire in her own body to ignite from the slow burn to a blazing inferno. The scorching heat only increased as Paul took a step back to gaze down at her as his hands reached for the bottoms of his shirt.

Her eyes followed the slow movement of his hands, darkening to a molten gold as he pulled his shirt over his head. The sight of his rippling muscles caused her nipples to swell and pucker to the point the thin fabric covering them became painful. Her eyes widened as she allowed her gaze to slide over his smooth shoulders and down over the dark hair that coated his chest. A purr escaped her as her eyes followed the line of hair as it narrowed and disappeared under the waistband of his jeans.

"Paul," she whispered as she reached out to touch his flat stomach with the tips of her fingers. "You are so beautiful."

* * *

Paul closed his eyes as he felt Morian's tentative touch along the smooth skin of his stomach. His fingers stilled on the buckle of his belt. He felt an unfamiliar heat building inside him, driving him with a primitive need that almost frightened him. His head dropped forward and he gritted his teeth as she continued to explore, her touch becoming more confident the longer he held still. He breathed in through his nose trying to stay focused on holding onto his fragile control. His eyes snapped open when he felt her fingers on top of his, loosening the buckle.

"Morian," he hissed in warning.

She looked up into his eyes even as her fingers undid the button on his jeans before pulling the zipper down. "I want to see you," she breathed. "Let me do this…. Please."

Paul's throat closed up at the innocent plea. All he could do was nod and clench his fists to keep from burying them in her hair. His eyes closed half way as he watched her grasp the sides of his jeans at his hips.

He drew in a swift breath as she slowly pulled them down, taking his boxers with them. A sense of masculine pride caused his lips to twitch at her gasp when his fully engorged cock sprang free. He was a big man - all over. He was also not shy about his desire for her. His cock jerked eagerly as she released his pants, which pooled around his ankles. He quickly toed off his shoes and kicked them and his pants to the side.

He reached out and gripped her wrist in warning. "Don't!" He growled out in a low voice when she reached up to touch his cock. "I won't last," he admitted ruefully when she started to touch it. "You have far too many clothes on," he muttered as he pulled her up to stand in front of him.

"No, I don't," she said, reaching up and releasing the clasp at her shoulder.

The gown she was wearing parted and slid down to the ground in a silky puddle around her feet. She wore nothing underneath it. Paul's slender hold dissolved with it as well.

The flames burning inside him exploded and he pulled her against his body as need overcame all other rational thought. The feel of her soft skin under his callused hands pulled at his conscience to handle her with care even as he wanted to do nothing more than bury himself balls deep inside her. She deserved better he kept repeating to himself in a mantra, hoping it would keep him from acting like some uncouth barbarian.

"Fuck!" He groaned as her distended nipples brushed along his chest. "I'm not going to last this first time. Forgive me," he choked out hoarsely. "Forgive me, Morian."

"Don't stop," Morian whispered desperately, running her hands through the coarse hair on his chest and over his smooth shoulders. She ached so bad with need it had become a physical pain. She gripped his shoulders, her short nails leaving crescent moons in his skin. "Don't stop, Paul, please," she wailed as the fire in her scorched her and her dragon howled with need.

Paul slid his hands around her, lowering her back down on the divan. He briefly dropped one hand down between her parted legs, searching and finding the heated channel. He moaned as his fingers sank into her liquid sheath.

She was more than ready for him. Her cry resonated in his head and heart when he withdrew his fingers so he could grip his cock to align it with her heated core. His own cry mingled with hers when her hips shifted. The movement was enough that the tip of his cock slid into the entrance of her slick channel. Both of them froze for a moment, staring deeply into each other's eyes as if on a precipice of discovering something explosive.

"You are fucking mine," Paul suddenly growled out before impaling his cock as far as it could go inside her molten vagina. "Forever!"

Morian's eyes widened in shock and awe as his steely length slid deep inside her. Every nerve was so in tune with him that it was like he was touching her very soul. Her dragon roared out in triumph, exploding into a frenzy of passion as the dragon's fire burst in all directions.

The combination was too much for her and she arched under him, screaming out as her body erupted in her first orgasm. Her body tried to hold him in, almost as if it was afraid if he withdrew she would wake to discover it had all been a dream. When she felt him pull back, she wound her arms around his neck and pulled him down until her lips touched his vulnerable neck.

"As you are mine," she snarled back before sinking her teeth into him and breathing the century's worth of pent up dragon's fire into him.

The little she had breathed before was nothing compared to what she released now. She held nothing back. She didn't think - didn't fear what could happen. Deep down she knew he was strong enough to handle anything that was thrown at him. She felt his body stiffen as the waves of heat mixed in with his bloodstream. She released a long moan as his cock swelled, stretching her already sensitive channel even more as she continued to breathe the dragon's fire. His arms tightened around her and he began moving, pressing harder and faster with each stroke. Only when the last of the dragon's fire had been released did she pull away to look up at his face.

Paul's face twisted, almost as if in pain, as the waves of fire danced through his body. His cock had never felt so full or so heavy before. He looked down with blazing eyes, gazing into Morian's gold ones as he pounded into her.

He felt his cock touching her womb as he drove deeper and deeper into the hot haven of her body. He had loved his first wife with a gentle and tender passion. With Morian, he took her with the driving need of a male for his female. He needed to lay his claim to her, seal her to him so she would never leave him. He took her with the thirst of a man denied a drink after crossing the desert.

"Yes," he moaned as his balls drew up tight. "Yes!" He shouted as he felt her clench him again as his orgasm ignited her own and her vagina fisted his cock, holding him inside her as he emptied his seed into her marking her as his.

The sound of their heavy pants echoed in the small room. Paul lowered his head, pressing a kiss into Morian's sweat dampened shoulder. His shaky arms were the only thing keeping his weight from crushing her even as his hips continued to move slowly, grinding against her. He pulled back enough to look down at her with worried eyes. He had not been tender with her.

"Are you alright?" He asked huskily.

Morian smiled up at him, her eyes softening until they glowed a dark gold. "Yes," she whispered before a low groan escaped her. "Can you feel it?" She gasped.

Paul's eyes narrowed as his body responded to her husky question. Flames licked at his nerve endings, causing his cock to swell and his heart to race. He gritted his teeth as a wave broke over him, causing sweat to bead on his forehead as he fought the urge to take her savagely again and again.

"What the hell is happening?" He asked harshly as a shudder ran through him.

"The dragon's fire," Morian gasped as she raised her legs to wrap around him. "It's starting again."

Paul swore as his body heated up again. "What the fuck is the dragon's fire?" He bit out.

Morian's eyes filled with tears as her fear of alienating him filled her. "I've claimed you, Paul. You are my life. I claim you as my true mate. No other may have you. I will live to protect you. I love you, my fierce warrior," she choked out before sealing her lips to his in a kiss that conveyed all her hopes, fears, and longing.

# Chapter 9

Paul didn't understand what the hell was happening. At the moment, he was beyond caring. All he could think about was the soft woman he held in his arms. His body felt like it was on fire from the inside out. A primitive need to claim, mark, and possess pulled at him. His cock, which should have been spent after the intense orgasm he had just had, was still rock hard and throbbing painfully.

He groaned as a particularly fierce wave burst through him. He ripped his lips from hers and ran them down along the sweet curve of her jaw. Running his tongue along the smooth skin of her neck, he nipped it before sucking to soothe the bite.

"Hold on to me," he demanded in a soft, rough voice.

Morian gasped as he suddenly rolled over so she was on top of him. She had never been in this position before. Jalo had always dominated her as was the way of the Valdier warrior. The thought of a female being on top would have equated to giving her control over him.

A shudder ran through her body as the huge male beneath her rose up. Her head fell backwards as his cock sank impossibly deeper into her body. She had never felt such fullness or power as a female.

"Paul," she moaned loudly as her fingers kneaded his shoulders.

"Ride me, Morian," he demanded.

Morian's head fell forward as she rose up on her knees before sinking down on him again. She leaned forward, keeping her golden eyes locked with his darker brown ones. A gasp left her lips as he reached up and cupped her breasts, running the rough pad of his thumbs over her ultra-sensitive nipples.

She started out slow, tentatively rising up and down as he fell into the pattern with her. Her fingers kneaded his shoulders as she increased the speed of her rhythm until a low wail built inside her as her orgasm rushed to wash over her.

The wail turned to a scream of ecstasy when Paul suddenly released her breasts. He gripped her hips as he thrust upwards, meeting her as she came down on him. His lips wrapped around the distended nipple of her right breast where he sucked hard on it. Her body shattered into a million pieces as she sobbed his name over and over.

Paul jerked back as she came, arching up into her even as he pulled her down, impaling her on his throbbing length. The pulsing channel of her vagina gripped his cock, pulling his own orgasm out. He groaned loudly as he felt his hot seed pouring into her. His arms wrapped around her, pulling her down on top of his chest as she melted into him. He pressed a kiss into the pulse beating frantically on her neck. Everything inside him demanded that he bite her, mark her as his. He pulled her closer, breathing deeply until the feeling lessened.

He reluctantly loosened his arms enough so he could look into her face. "Did I hurt you?" He asked quietly. "I don't understand what is going on," he said, briefly closing his eyes as he felt another hot wave of need building. He had never, ever had such an uncontrollable desire before.

Morian raised a shaky hand to run it along his temple. Her eyes widened when she saw the flakes of glowing gold mixed in with the dark brown of his eyes. Her eyes moved to his neck where the clear image of a golden dragon with its wings spread marked the spot where she had bitten him.

"It's the Dragon's Fire," Morian responded with a tender smile. "When a true mate is found, our dragons release a chemical known as the Dragon's Fire into each other. It is how we claim our mates. My dragon wants you," she added huskily.

Paul grimaced as the heat continued to build. He refused to let it overtake him until he had some idea of what the hell was happening. Hell, if this was what happened every time they made love he wasn't sure how long he would last before he died of ecstasy.

"I don't think that is going to work too well," Paul said with a puzzled frown. "I'm human, not Valdier. I can't change into a dragon."

Morian bit her lip and rolled off of Paul's chest, hissing as his still stiff cock brushed against her sensitive skin. She knew that her sons' mates were able to transform from the Dragon's Fire mating, but she was not sure how it would work for her and Paul. She could see the beginning of the transformation, but what if it didn't work the same way?

Uncertainty pulled at her because her claim on Paul was a first on their world. As far as she was aware there had never been an incidence where a female had claimed a male from a different species. In fact, the treaty between the Valdier and the Sarafin was to have been the first of its kind where a female Valdier was to be given to another species.

Jalo had signed the treaty with Vox's father in the hope that the first daughter of Zoran would be united with the first born son of Vox. It had even been discussed that Vox d'Rojah, the leader of the Sarafin, might be joined with one of the few unmated Valdier women of distant royal blood but he had taken another human female as his mate. Now, she wasn't sure what would happen.

"I am not sure if you will be able to transform as your daughter and the other females have," Morian admitted. "A Valdier female has never mated with another species." She reached out and touched his temple again. "I can see the beginning of the transformation," she added huskily. "Your eyes have a touch of gold and my mark on you is…." She drew in a deep breath as she let her fingers trace the dragon's mark on his neck. "It is beautiful."

The fire in Paul leapt as she touched the mark on his neck as if in answer. A low growl broke from him and he reached up and wrapped his hand in her hair, fisting it so he could draw her closer. His eyes blazed with hunger as he slowly rose up until he was a breath away from her swollen lips.

"If the fire burning inside me is any indication that this 'Dragon's Fire' is still working its magic on trying to transform me then I guess we should see what happens," he purred, twisting up and around until he was back on top of her. "One thing is for sure….." he said as he gazed down at her with a devilish grin.

"What is that?" Morian asked breathlessly.

"You are going to be well and truly fucked by the time we are done," Paul responded before crushing his lips to hers.

*Oh yeah,* Morian heard her dragon moan. *My mate is hot.*

*You can say that again,* Morian agreed as the fire exploded over them again.

\* \* \*

Paul stood next to his bed later the next morning watching as Morian turned over onto her side in her sleep. Her hand reached out, searching for him. He sat on the edge of the bed and wrapped his larger hand around her delicate fingers. Instinctively, her fingers closed around his and a soft, sweet sigh escaped her as she relaxed back into a deeper sleep.

A small smile pulled at the corner of his lips. It was amazing he could even function after the marathon love making session they'd had in the atrium. It had been the middle of the night before he finally roused enough to pull his pants on. Morian had been so exhausted she didn't even stir as he wrapped her tenderly in the light blanket that lay across the back of the divan. He had carried her through the silent corridors back to his living quarters where they would be more comfortable.

Once there, he had been unable to resist making love to her again. This time, slowly – tenderly. Afterwards, they had both fallen into a deep, sated sleep. He didn't know if the transformation had been successful. He didn't feel any different. Morian had quietly explained how Abby shyly told her about seeing scales forming on her arms and chest during her transformation. He knew Morian was disappointed as neither of them had seen any on him.

It appeared the only difference after their lovemaking, besides his ability to keep an erection that any man would love to brag about, was the mark on his neck and the gold she insisted was in his eyes now. He carefully raised the slender fingers to his lips and pressed them against his lips. His eyes closed briefly as he realized the gnawing emptiness that had filled him since Evelyn's death was no longer there. His eyes stared tenderly down at the flushed cheeks of the beautiful woman lying in his bed. He would do everything in his power to keep her safe.

His eyes grew cold and he carefully lowered her hand back down to the bed, covering it with the comforter. He needed to meet with Zoran, Kelan, Mandra, and Trelon. Creon hadn't returned yet, but he and Carmen were on their way back. It was time to find out everything he could about Raffvin. He refused to wait around for the bastard to strike against his family again. It was time to settle this once and for all. He wanted to know everything about the bastard down to what he ate and when he took a piss.

"Paul," Morian whispered sleepily.

"Shush," he responded, leaning over and brushing a kiss across her plump lips. "Sleep. I'll return later."

Morian forced her eyes open. "Where are you going?" She asked huskily.

Paul smiled reassuringly down at her as he brushed a strand of her dark hair back from her cheek. "The boys and I are going to have a little fun. I promised Trisha I would show them some moves that might help them. I'll return later this afternoon. Rest a little longer," he whispered in her ear. "You are going to need your strength for when I return."

Morian's eyes widened before a delighted chuckle escaped her. "You better make sure you don't tire yourself out," she giggled.

"If I do, you can always be the one on top," he retorted with a grin. "Hell, I may be exhausted just so you are."

Morian's cheeks turned a rosy pink, but her eyes twinkled with joy. "I would enjoy that very, very much," she admitted.

Paul groaned as he saw the flare of desire in her eyes. "Woman, you are going to be the death of me and I'm going to love every damn second of it," he said before he captured her lips in a hot, fierce kiss before he forced himself to pull away from her. "Rest," he demanded roughly before he stood up and strode from the room.

If her safety hadn't been his priority, he would never have had the strength to walk away from her lying naked in his bed. He shook his head and cursed. He was acting like a teenage boy who had just discovered the pleasure of being with a girl. His curse grew more colorful as he adjusted the front of his pants. His cock was definitely excited about the discovery, that was for damn sure.

*Yes, the woman was going to be the death of me,* he thought with a resigned sigh. *But, at least I'll die a happy man.*

## Chapter 10

"How in the Guall's balls does he do that?" Zoran snarled out as he wiped the sticky, red juice from his face. He grimaced as more slithered down under his vest and between his shoulder blades.

"I don't know, but I'm going to kill that bastard if he says 'tag' one more time," Trelon snapped out, tripping over a vine as he wiped gooey fruit off of his chest.

"You guys just don't like the fact that a human male is kicking your asses," Kelan chuckled humorously.

Mandra walked by him and flicked a chunk of the ripe fruit out of Kelan's hair. "Your ass is getting kicked right along with ours, dear brother," he said as he wiped his sticky fingers down Kelan's cheek.

"You boys are depending too much on your dragons and your symbiots to defend you," Paul said landing silently in the middle of the four huge Valdier warriors, pulling a curse from all of them as they jumped back startled. "You have to think like your enemy."

"How in the Gods did you learn so much about our fighting techniques in such a short time?" Zoran asked in irritation.

Paul looked steadily at the Valdier leader, waiting for Zoran to calm down a little. His lips twitched when he saw the huge male shift on his feet before his broad shoulders slumped just a hair. Morian's sons reminded him a lot of the Navy Seals and Marines he trained back home. They were cocky, full of confidence, and headstrong. All three traits were admirable, but they could also get them killed, as he had proven to them over and over. They needed to realize that there were other ways of defeating the enemy than brute strength. Stealth, cunning, and understanding not only your enemy's weakness, but your own were vitally important if you wanted to not only be successful, but remain alive.

"I studied you," Paul said bluntly. "I trained with the warriors on the *V'ager*. And, I did my research. Right now, all of you would be dead if this was a real battle. That is unacceptable to me."

Zoran snarled and took a menacing step closer to Paul. "If this had been a real battle, I would have gutted you already," he growled, his eyes narrowing dangerously.

Paul continued to study Zoran for a moment. His mind raced through one scenario after another. He knew that Zoran was feeling threatened by him. The other male's attitude changed the moment he noticed the mark on Paul's neck and he realized what it meant.

The other males appeared to take it in stride. Hell, Mandra had all but given his permission while Trelon had enough on his hands to worry about and Kelan just grinned and nodded to him. Zoran was different. As the leader and Morian's oldest son, he was much more territorial and protective.

Paul shook his head in disagreement. "You are an excellent warrior. I am not arguing that point," he said quietly in the same tone he used when he was teaching one of his men. "Trisha recognized that you have your areas of weakness and asked that I assess it." He looked over at Kelan who nodded to him.

"It's true, Zoran," Kelan admitted with a nod of his head. "Four of Valdier's best trackers and I hunted for Trisha through some of the wildest terrain and still missed her."

Zoran looked sharply at his younger brother. "That is not true," he said, glaring back at Kelan. "You found her."

Kelan shook his head again. "No, she found us. We found where she stayed, but she was always one step ahead of us. She came at us and could have easily killed all four of us if she had wanted," he explained before taking a step closer to Zoran. "She recognized our weakness just as Paul has, brother. He is very good. I vote we listen to him."

Zoran's mouth tightened and he shot an annoyed glance at Paul. "We have fought the Sarafin and Curizan in the Great Wars and survived. Why should we change our ways now?" He asked in a low voice.

Paul stepped up closer to Zoran until they were staring each other in the eye. He let his own cold determination shine through. It was time he let the big male know he was not going anywhere and he wasn't going to stand down as long as there was a threat to his family.

"If I can defeat you so can Raffvin," Paul said coldly. "The key to winning is not only knowing your enemy, but knowing yourself. You have to be prepared. That bastard has already tried to kill my daughter and grandson. He almost killed your brother, which would have also taken the life of someone I care about very much. I am offering my service and expertise to help protect those I care about, Zoran. That includes your mother."

Zoran studied Paul for several long seconds before he drew in a deep breath. "She has claimed you," he said, glancing briefly at the dragon's mark on Paul's neck before staring into the dark brown and gold eyes.

Paul nodded. "As I have claimed her," he responded quietly. "I will protect her with my life and do everything I can to make her happy. Now, are you ready to listen or do I have to kick your ass again?"

Trelon began to chuckle. A moment later, Kelan and Mandra joined in. Zoran felt the corner of his mouth quiver before a deep chuckle escaped. Paul looked at the four males with a perplexed expression.

Kelan came up and slapped Paul on the shoulder, knocking him forward a step. "Our father used to say that to us all the time," he laughed. "Now, show us how we can NOT get ourselves killed."

Paul looked over to where Zoran was standing and saw him nod. No words were needed to know that he had passed some test the Valdier leader had given him. He felt the mark on his neck burn briefly as Zoran's eyes passed over it again with a thoughtful expression on his face.

Rolling his shoulders, a shiver ran down his spine. It was as if something had moved deep inside him.

The feeling was so fleeting that he thought he must have imagined it. With a lift of his shoulder in answer to Zoran's questioning look, Paul began explaining what he had observed about each of their movements, what he discerned as a weakness that could leave them vulnerable, and methods to prevent their enemies from using it against them.

* * *

The next several weeks fell into a pattern. He made passionate love to Morian anywhere and everywhere he could, he trained with Zoran and the others, and he continued to research every shred of information he could about Raffvin. The picture he was developing was one of a very cunning, very jealous, extremely unstable man. A man who not only coveted the power of ruling the Valdier but of controlling Morian and the Hive.

"Tell me of Raffvin," Paul asked late one night as Morian lay pressed against his side.

Morian trembled, snuggling closer to her mate's heat. "He was a handsome but arrogant warrior even as a young boy. He had little care for others including his younger brother," she murmured, remembering the first time she met Jalo and Raffvin when she was still a child.

"Jalo?" Paul asked quietly.

Morian tilted her head so she could look into Paul's dark eyes. "Yes," she replied with a sigh. "Raffvin was very jealous of Jalo for some reason. Where Raffvin was harsh, rough – Jalo was the opposite. Raffvin resented that Jalo had been better at just about everything than he was. It wasn't because it was easy, it was because Jalo listened, watched, and learned. He was patient and did not like violence for the sake of violence. Raffvin would often start a fight among the other warriors just to see them pitted against each other."

"Raffvin was older yet he was not the leader of the Valdier. Why?" He asked, rubbing his hands up and down her back as she shivered.

Morian drew in a deep breath before replying. "To understand that you need to understand about me," she said, pulling away and sitting up.

She reached for her robe on the side of the bed and slipped it on before rising gracefully and walking over to the windows. She stared with unseeing eyes out over the walls of the palace and down over the city far below. She could no longer feel the pull of her dragon wanting her to release it so it could fly.

The restlessness of her other self had died away and now a haunting lethargy was slowly gripping her and ripping her apart on the inside. It didn't seem to matter how much Dragon's Fire she breathed into Paul, there was no sign of any further transformation than his eyes becoming more golden.

Her dragon was beside herself, wanting her mate, but unable to touch or feel him. The last few days had been especially difficult as they both came to the realization that her feelings for Paul might be one sided. If so, it would mean a half-life for her as her dragon would never be allowed to touch her mate.

She had felt her dragon's withdrawal. It had given up hope and, in doing so, meant that Morian was slowly dying. She had been able to survive with Jalo because she had not tasted her true mate. Now that she had, it was impossible to live without the three parts that made her up.

Morian jerked when Paul's warm arms slid around her, calling her back to the present. "Tell me," he encouraged, pulling her back against his hard body and resting his chin on the top of her head.

"I was very wild and carefree when I was young," she started with a small smile. "I didn't understand why I had a symbiot. None of the other females I knew had them except for my mother. I would later learn that only the Priestess to the Hive had a symbiot of her own. It was an enormous responsibility that I remember telling my mother I did not want. I wanted to be a warrior, just like my cousins," she explained.

Paul chuckled, the warmth of his breath stirring her hair. "Something tells me that didn't go over very well," he speculated.

Morian's own shoulders shook as she laughed. "No, it didn't. My mother was very much the Queen Mother of Valdier. She was very delicate and my father and his brothers made sure she was protected at all times. She relished having them cater to her."

"And you?" He asked.

Morian tilted her head back and grinned. "I was forever dressing up as a boy and sneaking out to fight the imaginary Sarafin cats or defeat the cursed Curizan warriors who were determined to battle the fiercest warrior of all – me! As a royal, I could transform into a dragon. Not many females can do that unless they are the true mate of a warrior. I did not have those restrictions. I had a dragon. I had a symbiot. I was a warrior, pure and simple as far as I was concerned."

Paul nodded. "But…."

Morian turned back around to stare out into the night. "But, I soon learned I was more when the Queen of the Hive called to me. No-one knew the location of the Hive back then. The secret of its location had been concealed by the Gods and Goddesses," she murmured.

"I thought the ruling King of Valdier knew where it was," Paul said.

Morian nodded. "Now, but not then. There was no King then. The symbiot would come to a newborn shortly after it is born. No-one knew where it came from, only that it did," she whispered, lost in her memories.

Paul waited while Morian gathered her thoughts. He didn't rush her, sensing it was important to her to tell him in her own good time. A shudder went through her body before she wrapped her arms around his. He leaned down and pressed a kiss into her shoulder in comfort.

She drew in a shaky breath before she spoke again. "There were more females back then," she said distractedly. "Before the war, there were almost as many females as there were males. Because the symbiots bonded with the males, infighting among clans began when one tribe had more males than females. Soon, one clan bonded with another until it was as strong as the clan my parents ruled. The difference between the clans was my mother was a Priestess to the Hive. She was the only female who had a symbiot. One day she was out looking for me. She was captured by the rival clan," her voice faded as she wiped a tear that trailed down her cheek.

"I thought she had a symbiot," Paul said.

Morian turned in his arms and looked up at him. "She did, but she sent it to me," Morian whispered. "My symbiot was too small to protect me. She ordered her symbiot to take me to safety. It did and that act cost my mother and father their lives."

Paul drew her against his bare chest, holding her close at the pain he heard in her voice. "What happened?"

Morian wrapped her arms tightly around Paul's waist and breathed his scent, finding comfort in it. "Her symbiot took me to the Queen of the Hive. As my mother died, her symbiot dissolved before my eyes and turned into the form of the *Juuli,* what you would call the Gods' Revenge. The Goddess' Arosa and Arilla, in the guise of a great flying serpent warned me that if the clans did not cease their fighting the blood of the Gods would be taken from them and all would perish. To prove that they meant what they said, every symbiot was absorbed into the soil of Valdier and returned to the Hive to wait and watch. If a way was not found before the next twin moons were full, then the death of our people would soon follow."

Paul looked over her head as anger swirled inside him that a young girl was burdened with so much responsibility. His arms tightened around her protectively. He couldn't imagine what it must have been like to be so young and have the weight of the world on his shoulders while grieving the senseless loss of his family.

"What did you do?" He asked huskily.

Morian pulled back and looked solemnly up at him. "I did want I was expected to do. I swore I would stop the wars between my people and I would protect the Hive with my life. I returned to my clan and explained to my uncles what the Gods had told me. It was decided I would mate with the son of the leader of the clan who had taken my mother. Raffvin was the eldest, but my uncles refused to give me to him. They saw the greed in his eyes. My symbiot and dragon tried to attack him. It was Jalo's gentle touch that calmed my symbiot and dragon. It was said to be a sign of the Gods that Jalo and I were to join and he would rule," she said with a serene smile. "I fell in love with the man," she added looking up at Paul with a sad smile. "He was not my true mate, but he was a very good mate. He gave me five beautiful sons and he was a good friend. I miss him still."

Paul felt his stomach knot for a moment as a taste of jealousy washed through him to be replaced with understanding. Jalo had been the love of her youth just as Evelyn had been for him. Her love for her mate had shaped her into the beautiful, strong woman she was today. He also reluctantly admitted if it hadn't been for her son, he might never have found her.

He tenderly brushed her hair back from her face before he leaned down to brush her lips with his own. The tender, comforting kiss turned to something entirely different once he had captured her lips though. A hot wave washed through him again and the mark on his neck burned fiercely. He groaned as he felt her answering response as her lips parted for him.

"I want you again," he murmured hungrily.

Morian wrapped her arms around his neck as he lifted her. "You are my true mate," she breathed out as she pressed her lips against his neck. "I love you, Paul Grove."

# Chapter 11

Paul held the wiggling body of Amber while Mandra made faces at her making her squeal in delight. Trelon was carrying Jade, who was doing her best to bite him on the ear again. From the drool hanging off of his earlobe, he suspected she had already been successful. Zoran carried Zohar, who was babbling away while Kelan held a sleeping Bálint. The guys decided to take the kids out for a walk while the women spent time with Carmen who had given birth earlier that morning.

"Creon couldn't have cut it any closer if he tried," Trelon said, wincing when Jade grabbed his hair with both of her tiny fists and jerked his head close enough to latch onto his ear. He sighed loudly when she growled and started shaking her head back and forth. "I feel for him if his girls are anything like these two," he said tiredly. "I don't think I've ever been so exhausted as I have since I met Cara," he admitted grudgingly.

Kelan laughed as he rocked his tiny son in his arms. "At least she can keep up with them so you can get a few hours of sleep. Bálint is already sleeping through most nights," he bragged.

"Rub it in," Zoran growled out. "Zohar still wakes at least twice a night. Abby has started making me get up so I can bring him to her. The only good thing is since she is awake I can take advantage of the time to spend it with her practicing to make more babies," he added with a wicked grin.

"TMI, Zoran," Paul said with a laugh as he hung Amber over his shoulder and tried to nibble on her toes. "That was way more information than we needed to know."

Mandra reached over and scooped the squealing baby off of Paul's shoulder and into his arms. He held her upside down and growled teasingly at her. Amber's delighted giggles were enough to distract her sister who wanted to know what was going on.

Jade released her father's ear that she had been chewing on to gaze eagerly at Mandra and her sister. Trelon breathed out a sigh of relief as he shifted her to his other arm. The sigh turned to a grimaced as he tried to dry his ear off on his shoulder.

"I heard Creon passed out when Carmen went into labor," Trelon said with a chuckle. "I'll have to tease him about that. He has always said he could handle any situation."

"Just remember he wasn't the only one to hit the floor," Mandra reminded him. "You couldn't even handle finding out Cara was expecting these two bundles of energy. I wonder if my daughter will be like them."

All the men stopped to stare at a grinning Mandra. "Congratulations, Mandra," Paul said with a huge smile. "But, I don't think you should be worrying about if your daughter has as much energy as Amber and Jade so much as if she has the love of animals like her mother. You might be in for an adventure if she does."

Mandra paled as he thought of all the creatures running around his home already. Hell, if he wasn't careful they often ended up in his bed as well. This morning he had woken up to see a *Slithering*, or snake, as Ariel called it, staring down at him from the canopy of their bed. Ariel had giggled when they started hissing at each other. She said it had escaped from its container a few days before and she had wondered where it had gotten to.

Paul listened as the brothers shared more horror stories with Mandra about diaper duty, baby puke, and how all the warriors were going to be wanting to date his beautiful daughter. He chuckled even as his eyes searched the shadowed edges of the forests.

They were not far from the palace having come to a large park area where they could let the little ones crawl and play. He enjoyed spending time with the four brothers and looked forward to meeting Creon. Any man, or alien, that could love and heal his surrogate daughter, Carmen, was alright in his book.

Ariel and Carmen had lived at his and Trisha's house almost as much as they had lived in their own. Hell, after their parents were killed in a car accident, Carmen had spent her senior year of high school with him. Less than a week after she graduated, he had walked her down the aisle.

His throat tightened as he remembered how beautiful she was and how her first husband, Scott, swore to Paul he would always love and protect her. When Scott was murdered it had almost killed Carmen. He knew the last few years she had been focused solely on seeking revenge against the man responsible for Scott's death. He was glad that Creon had found her and that she had finally found happiness again. She had suffered enough loss in her short life.

Paul's eyes moved to the symbiots that were playing together. He chuckled as they bounced and rolled around in the grassy meadow. The symbiots here were smaller as they had divided in half so that part could remain with the women while the other part followed the men and the children. Each child had their own symbiots, even Amber and Jade, though they were very small.

Paul turned when he heard Trelon telling Mandra about how one of the girls spewed what she had eaten all over the front of him the night before. He was about to tell them about Trisha doing the same thing when the hair on the back of his neck suddenly stood up in warning.

"Stop!" He barked out sharply.

All four men froze, recognizing the warning in his voice. "What is it?" Zoran asked, pulling Zohar protectively to his chest.

"I don't know," Paul said, shifting his feet into a defensive stance. "I feel something." He nodded toward the symbiots. "Look, they sense it too."

Kelan cursed as he looked around. Bálint woke with a whimper as his father's arms tightened around him. He called out for his symbiot to come to him. Within moments, a small golden skimmer formed. Kelan leaned forward and laid Bálint down in it.

"Put the children in Bio," Kelan said harshly even as he reached for his dragon.

"Paul, protect them," Zoran said as he placed Zohar next to his cousin.

"Amber, Jade," Trelon said sternly, looking at his daughters as he set Jade down next to Amber whom Mandra was gently lowering next to Zohar. "No biting. Be good," he whispered, running his fingers over both of their chubby little faces. A smile tugged at his lips as Jade growled menacingly while Amber looked at him with big, bright shining eyes filled with warmth and laughter.

Paul stood back as he watched Bio seal the babies within its protective shield. He nodded to the four men who were now in the shape of their dragons. A cold, calm settled over him as he scanned the darkened area. His gaze jerked up to the sky when it suddenly darkened. What looked like hundreds of skimmers filled the air even as dark-clad warriors shimmered and formed all around them.

"Son of a bitch," he swore under his breath as he pulled his long hunting knife out.

The roars of the four brothers shook the ground as they surrounded the golden capsule holding its precious cargo. Paul looked up again as enemy fire began raining down on them like hot spears of lightning. He knew the men would not be able to fight like they needed to as long as they were trying to protect their young. Forces from the palace would be here soon, but not soon enough to save his sons if he did not remove the obstacle holding them back.

"Let's even the odds a little," he growled before jumping on top of Bio. "Form grips," he commanded.

Bio immediately shifted, forming hand and foot holds for Paul. "Remember the cavern we were at last week?" He asked. A grin formed as he felt the answering shiver. "Let's go."

Bio shifted slightly, becoming longer and sleeker. In a burst of unexpected speed, the golden figure pushed forward through the empty space created by Kelan's dragon as it communicated its intent. Paul clung determinedly to the weaving golden form. It burst through into the dense woods surrounding the large park, leaving behind the roar of the dragons and the sounds of battle.

Four skimmers broke formation to follow him. Paul glanced over his shoulder as one fired on him. With a quietly muttered command, Bio dipped down under fallen trees before turning on its side to squeeze through the narrow opening between two huge trunks.

Paul felt the muscles in his arms and legs tighten as he held on. He tucked his head close to the body of the symbiot in an effort to keep it attached to the rest of him as they passed through the narrow opening. The skimmers were forced to go up and around the trees if they didn't want to crash.

He would head to the palace using the underground passageway he had discovered during his research. It would appear one of their ancestors enjoyed sneaking out for a midnight swim. He had shown the hidden passage to Zoran and the others after he determined it could be dangerous if the enemy ever discovered it.

Paul mentally ran through each scenario. He had to trust that the brothers would survive. His gut twisted at the thought of losing any of the 'boys' as he thought of them.

He recognized deep down that he thought of them as the sons he never had. His main focus needed to remain on protecting the precious cargo contained inside Bio. A warmth spread through him as gold bands wrapped around his arms and legs, securing him to the skimmer.

He glanced over his shoulder and saw the skimmers behind him reforming into formation. His eyes flickered back and forth until he saw a large grouping of trees up ahead. A plan began to form in his mind.

He sent a mental image to the symbiot of what he wanted it to do. A shudder of furious denial shook the symbiot, but Paul was determined that it would follow through with his plan. The children had to be protected no matter what. It was only when he sent his own assurance that he would be careful that Bio reluctantly agreed to release the bands around his arms and legs.

Paul waited until the last minute before he rolled off the top of the symbiot and landed on a large moss-covered branch. He watched for a brief second as the symbiot sped off. Turning and crouching, he gripped the long hunting knife in his hand and waited as the first three skimmers passed under him.

He counted under his breath the speed of the skimmers as they passed so he could time when to jump. By the time the fourth skimmer passed under him, he was ready. He dropped down, landing behind the pilot. His feet slid on the slick outer surface of the skimmer but his hands held tight to the back of the seat. The pilot of the skimmer turned, revealing a dark purple face.

Paul grinned nastily before he reached up with his right hand and pulled the surprised purple pilot out of his seat by the back of his jacket. The alien's hands and feet flew over the side as Paul tossed him out. Unfortunately, the skimmer tilted at the same time.

Paul glanced up with a curse as he saw it was heading straight for one of the mammoth tree trunks. He flung himself off it, hitting the soft fern and moss covered ground. He rolled several times before he came to a stop.

The loud crash of the skimmer resonated through the dark forest. Paul rolled over onto his belly and saw two of the other skimmers turning back around. He immediately pulled back deeper into the chest-high ferns and began weaving to the west.

He caught a glimpse of movement to his left and knew that the pilot from the skimmer was up and moving around as well. A dark smile curved Paul's lips. He needed a skimmer – fast. He would not take a chance of those bastards hurting his grandbabies.

Moving like a ghost through the undergrowth, Paul slipped further into the shadows as the two skimmers landed and the pilots disembarked. A moment later, the pilot from the third skimmer walked within inches of where he was standing inside a tangle of hanging vines.

"What happened?" A slender purple male asked.

"The male on the golden creature jumped me from behind," the pilot grumbled. "He is somewhere close."

"Let's find and kill him. Raffvin said he wanted all but the Leader of the Valdier killed," a feminine voice replied. "I do not like his plan, but I like his credits. Let us get done with this."

"Where did Pehr go? We could use his help," one of the men asked.

"He chased the golden symbiot. Raffvin wants one of those as well. How he expects us to capture one, I don't know. Pehr can try all he wants. He never was very smart," the female replied with a toss of her head.

Both men chuckled. "You do not sound like you want him as your lover any longer?" One of them joked. "I could kill him for you."

The female moved to stand closer to the tall, slender male who had spoken. "If he doesn't die here, then I accept your offer," she purred. "Now, let's find and kill the one that attacked, Keebe."

Paul decided certain alien females should not be considered off limits when it came time to attack or kill them. That had been the hardest thing for him to overcome when he was training the soldiers who came to him. The realization that some women were as deadly and dangerous as any male was a hard lesson to teach. Everything inside him was programmed to protect and care for a woman above all else. Trisha had demonstrated to those training under him just how lethal a lone female could be in a given situation.

Paul waited until they had walked by him before he moved again. Keeping low to the ground, he quickly cut some vines hanging down. He decided he needed to capture and bound at least one of them for interrogation. He decided since he didn't like the idea of killing a female, he would choose her as the one he would keep alive.

He listened as they moved off in different directions. Each carried what looked like some type of laser pistol similar to what Kelan had shown him. The tall, slender male also carried a long rifle pressed against his shoulder.

From the noise they were making, Paul had to guess they were not used to fighting in a wooded environment. A menacing grin curved his lips as he moved in behind the male he had thrown off the skimmer. Rising up behind him silently, Paul wrapped his right hand around the male's mouth while his left hand slid the blade silently across the thick, purple throat. He dropped the body down into the coverage of the ferns while keeping his hand firmly over the male's mouth until he knew he was dead. The other two never even heard him.

"Keebe, go to the left," the female yelled out about twenty yards ahead to the northwest. "Keebe?"

The slender male turned in a slow circle. "Keebe!" The male called out harshly. "Where did he go? You do not think he returned to the ship do you?"

The female snorted. "You are almost as stupid as Pehr!" She growled out raising her pistol up. "He wouldn't dare leave. He knows I'd slit his throat."

Paul waited until she turned back around before he rose up and threw his knife. He had disappeared again by the time the slender male's finger squeezed on the trigger of the laser rifle he was holding. Paul crawled quickly through the ferns making sure he didn't give his position away as he moved stealthily through the dark coverage.

The female was alone now. His hunting knife was buried to the hilt in the middle of the male's chest. He came up behind a thick tree and glanced around quickly. The female was holding the pistol up as she reached down for the laser rifle. He could hear her cursing under her breath.

"You are dead, Valdier," she yelled out viciously. "Why don't you and your dragon come play?"

Paul quickly wrapped a smooth rock around each end of one of the pieces of vine he had cut. Twirling it over his head, he stepped out from behind the tree just as the female stood up. Her eyes widened when she saw how close he was to her.

Before she could turn either weapon on him, Paul released the modified sling he had made. The female's curses were cut off as it wrapped around her neck. One of the rocks struck her in the chin with a loud pop. She teetered for a moment before collapsing backwards from the blow.

Paul moved swiftly toward her, pulling more pieces of vine from his pocket. He quickly bound her before removing the tight fiber from around her neck. He had already wasted precious minutes dealing with these three. He could only hope that Bio was able to shake the other male who had been pursuing it.

Rising up, he left the unconscious female lying on the moist ground. He quickly gathered the weapons from the fallen attackers before he pulled his hunting knife from the chest of the slender male. He jogged over to the skimmers. He didn't want to take a chance of leaving a skimmer just in case the female managed to escape.

Looking at the laser rifle, he set it to full charge before sliding it part ways into the engine compartment. Sliding onto the other skimmer, he silently thanked Mandra for showing him how one worked during the many hours of training. Since he couldn't shift like the other Valdier warriors, Mandra had shown him how to operate one of their skimmers so he could follow them to the different areas they had used over the last few weeks. Once he was far enough away, he aimed the laser pistol he had confiscated at the charged rifle and squeezed the trigger. The skimmer exploded, raining debris down around the waist high ferns.

Paul turned the skimmer around and headed toward the direction he had ordered Bio to head in. If the other mercenary was able to follow the golden symbiot he could only hope that it would be able to protect the little ones. He knew they were supposed to be powerful and had glimpsed a little of what they were capable of but he didn't want to take any chances.

Pressing his foot down on the accelerator, he shot forward easily navigating through the dark shadows of the forest. He traveled several miles when he felt a stirring deep down as if warning him that danger was near. He was close to the edge of the forest where the cliffs leading down to the turbulent waters of the ocean fell far below.

He slowed and gradually lowered the skimmer down until it rested on the outer edge of the dark woods. He slipped off the skimmer, gripping the laser pistol in his right hand. He could see the other skimmer doing a slow sweep back and forth along the edge of the cliff.

"Let's see if you can swim you son-of-a-bitch," Paul muttered under his breath as he aimed the laser pistol at one of the stabilizing elevators.

He fired five shots in rapid succession. The skimmer tilted at a sharp angle as the shots tore through the stabilizer. He watched as the slender purple figure of the male called Pehr fought to regain control as it lost elevation.

The nose of the skimmer tilted at an awkward angle before it began to spin. Paul watched as the male threw himself off the skimmer as the nose connected with the rocky surface of the cliff. He moved cautiously forward as it plummeted to the rocks jutting out of the waters along the base of the cliff.

He was almost to the edge when he saw a dark purple hand reach out to grip wildly for a hand hold. Paul walked over to the drop off and looked down into the cold, black eyes that glared back up at him. Kneeling down, he returned the glare with an icy look of his own. Paul grinned when he saw the male's eyes widen in bewilderment to be staring into the eyes of a human male instead of a Valdier warrior.

"Not what you expected?" Paul asked in a quiet, deadly voice. "Where is Raffvin?"

"What are you?" Pehr asked as he struggled to get a better grip as his feet slid on the narrow rock face. "You are not a Valdier."

Paul leaned forward just a little and grinned menacingly. "Answer my question first. Where is Raffvin and what does he want?"

Pehr grunted as his hands began to slip on the thin turf of grass he held. "Help me up and I will tell you," he snarled out as the rock under his feet began to crumble and he slipped down half an inch.

"Answer my questions and I might help you," Paul said with a shake of his head. "Where is Raffvin and what does he want?" He demanded again.

Pehr looked up at Paul with a furious expression. "I tell you and I'm dead. I don't tell you and I'm dead. Looks like I am dead either way," he growled as he slipped even further.

Paul reached out and grabbed Pehr's wrist as he started to slide. He stared down at him through narrow eyes. "You don't have to die," he responded tightly. "Tell me what I want to know and you might live," Paul said before adding with a grin. "But if you do, I wouldn't trust the female that was with you. I don't think she likes you anymore," he added.

\* \* \*

Pehr's eyes narrowed on the strange alien species holding his life in his hand. He had planned on using this mission to break free of his required assignment. He might be a Marastin Dow, but he had discovered that there was a life much different from the one he had been raised to believe.

He knew his life expectancy would be cut short the longer he was aboard the *Hoarder*. He was the second officer aboard it and officers did not last long if they were not careful. He knew Kasha, the female the strange alien was talking about, had her eye on replacing him. He had already caught her trying to poison him. He hoped he would be able to slip away during this assignment, but his commander, paranoid that he meant to take his position, had sent him down with the attacking force.

Pehr looked into the strange dark brown and gold eyes before making a decision. It was true what he had said, he was dead either way. Still, he had a better chance of escaping from this being than from either Raffvin or the rest of the members of the crew of the Marastin Dow.

"I will tell you what I know in exchange for a chance to disappear," Pehr said grimly.

Paul studied the black eyes of the creature he was holding. "Try anything and I'll blast a hole through your ass," Paul bit out harshly. "Don't fuck with me," he warned. "You were after my grandbabies."

Pehr released a weary sigh and shook his head. "Actually, I wasn't," Pehr reluctantly confided. "I was hoping if I followed the golden skimmer it would lead me away from everyone else," he admitted honestly. "But I promise, I had no desire to capture it. I was just trying to figure out a place to hide until everyone else was killed or gone."

Pehr knew it sounded crazy coming from a male of his species, but it was the truth. There was an uprising going on back on his home planet. Many of the younger generation were rebelling against the way they were being raised.

As the younger Marastin Dow interacted with other species, they were realizing there was more to life than raising their young to be killers, thieves, and the low-life of the star systems. Now, a large section of the Marastin Dow had decided that was not how they wanted to continue to live. Pehr and his brothers had started a rebellion that was building into a major revolution for change.

His older brother was the leader of the rebellion. Pehr knew he was under suspicion when he was transferred to his current assignment. It had become time for him to 'die' quietly somewhere. Raffvin's offer of credits to mount this suicide attack couldn't have come at a better time for him.

He waited as the unusual male decided his fate. The only regret he had if the male decided it was time for him to die was that he would not be a part of the changes coming to his own home world. He wanted to one day see it prosper like those of many of the other star systems, including the Valdier, Sarafin, and Curizan. A relieved sigh escaped him when he heard the male mutter a dark curse before he found he was being pulled upward instead of slipping further down.

"You better damn well not try anything," the male cursed as he gripped Pehr's arm and jerked him up with surprising strength.

"I have more to live for than to die for," Pehr admitted as he rolled over onto his back on the hard ground and held his hands out in surrender as Paul stepped back and aimed the laser pistol at his chest.

"And why is that?" Paul demanded as he stared at Pehr with narrow, suspicious eyes.

"I want freedom for my world," Pehr replied quietly, sitting up and lowering his hands to his side. "This is my chance to become a shadow so I can fight for the survival of my people from the tyranny that is currently governing it."

Paul looked at the seriousness in the male's eyes. He could not only see, but hear the truth behind his words. With a look of disgust, Paul lowered his weapon, but remained alert.

"Where is Raffvin?" Paul asked harshly.

Pehr shook his head. "I don't know," he said calmly before he raised his hands again when Paul pointed the laser pistol at him again. "I speak the truth. He used an encrypted code to block his signal so we couldn't pinpoint his location. He transferred credits to one of our holders as a retainer to attack the Valdier royals when the signal was given. I do know there is a traitor in the palace who is relaying information to him. No name was given but it is the only way your location could have been pinpointed and we knew you were away from the palace. He had a Curizan freighter fitted for members of my crew to use so we could beam down. In addition, there is a small, hidden base to the northeast. It is buried under the sands. That is where we came from. He had skimmers ready for our use."

"What were your exact orders?" Paul asked, trying to understand what Raffvin was after.

Pehr shrugged his shoulders. "To kill all but the leader of the Valdier if possible. Capture a symbiot and return with it," he said not taking his eyes off the huge man standing in front of him.

"And," Paul prompted.

Pehr frowned for a moment, a puzzled look on his face. "To draw as many warriors away from the palace as possible."

Paul paled. "Did he say why?"

Pehr shook his head. "No. Though I did hear him say something rather strange right before the transmission ended. I don't think he was even aware he had spoken aloud," Pehr admitted as he thought of Raffvin's last muttered words before the transmission was cut.

Paul could feel his gut clench in fear. He felt the movement of something deep inside him as if it was suddenly pushing, trying to get out as the fear grew. He swore loudly as he turned toward the skimmer. He paused a moment, turning back around to face the male who remained unmoving.

"What did he say?" Paul growled out harshly.

Pehr studied Paul's suddenly frozen expression and for the first time realized just how lucky he had been to have received mercy from the predator standing in front of him. He made a mental note that if the two of them ever crossed paths again, he wanted to make sure they were on the same side.

"She is mine at last," Pehr said, not understanding what the words meant.

It didn't matter whether he understood the words or not, the other male did. The words were no sooner out of Pehr's mouth before the strange alien was running for the woods. A moment later, a skimmer burst out of the trees curving back in the direction of the palace. Pehr stood up and wiped the dirt off the back of his pants. He flicked open his communicator and sent the emergency signal to his younger brother. He had his own war to wage.

*I am now officially dead*, he thought as he felt the familiar rush of adrenaline wash over him as he thought of the changes to come.

## Chapter 12

Morian smiled down softly at the infant she held in her arms. She had returned to Carmen and Creon's living quarters an hour before to check on them. Carmen was resting with Spring, her oldest daughter, while Abby, Cara, Trisha, and Ariel had left to go get some lunch. Morian couldn't help but chuckle as she watched their symbiots trotting beside them in a wide variety of shapes.

Her symbiot was her constant companion since she returned from the atrium where she had gone to shed tears of joy after the birth of her latest great-children. She knew it could feel the weakness sweeping through her as her dragon became more and more withdrawn and was concerned.

"*Dola*, are you well?" Creon asked from behind her.

Morian turned and smiled at her youngest son. "Of course. Phoenix is beautiful, just like her mother," she responded lightly as she caressed the soft, pink cheek of the little girl she held tenderly against her.

Creon looked suspiciously at her. A hint of worry darkened his golden eyes as he noticed that she seemed unusually pale. Even her eyes seemed duller than ever before, including after the death of their father.

"Tell me what is wrong," he demanded. "Has the human male harmed you? Mandra told me he is your true mate. Has he done something to upset you?"

Morian laughed at the fierce expression on Creon's face. He looked like he was ready to defend her honor against some great foe. She walked over to gently lay his tiny, dark haired daughter in his outstretched arms. Only when the sleeping babe was securely in his arms did she lay her hand tenderly against his cheek.

"No, he has not harmed me," she assured him quietly, rubbing her thumb back and forth on his rough cheek. "He is my true mate and he has been wonderful. I am happy to have known the joys of what having a true mate can bring. I am just tired. Perhaps I will go rest for a little while. I am not as young as I used to be," she admitted with a tired sigh.

Creon's face softened as he saw the shadows under her eyes. "Thank you for your help this morning. I don't think I have ever been more afraid or more thankful to have you here. I love you, *Dola*," he said with a warm smile.

"I love you as well, my son," Morian replied softly. "I am so proud of you. Take good care of your mate and your younglings. You will be a good father to your daughters," she said turning to leave.

Creon watched his mother walk gracefully toward the door. He called out as she opened the door, gazing at her with a worried frown on his face.

"You are sure you are just tired?" He asked again, studying her carefully.

Morian nodded and smiled before she stepped out of the room and gently shut the door behind her. The lump in her throat prevented her from responding to his searching question. She drew in a deep breath before heading back to the atrium where she could seek the peace of her plants. Her symbiot brushed against her in support.

Morian moved more out of habit than of awareness. She reached for her dragon and tenderly stroked its white scales. She felt it shudder as she gave the mental caress.

*I am so sorry, my friend,* she murmured in sorrow. *I love him so much.*

*Love my mate,* her dragon responded weakly. *Need his touch. Why I not good enough for my mate?* Her dragon asked in mourning.

*Do not think that!* Morian responded sternly. *You are more than good enough. It was just not meant to be. We should be thankful to have at least known the love of our true mate. It is not your fault he is unable to transform. It was not the will of the Gods to grant us this gift. We should be thankful for what we have and cherish it as long as we can.*

Her dragon did not respond. It just rolled over and curled up. Its despair pulled at Morian. She could feel its pain and loneliness tearing at her fragile control. She brushed the tear that coursed down her cheek away with an impatient hand. She would not feel sorry for herself or dwell on things she could not change. She would hold every second she had with Paul to her as if it was a precious gift.

*It is a precious gift,* she told herself fiercely. *Not many women are given the chance to love not once, but twice in their lifetime. I will not tarnish our love with useless dreams or hopeless wishes.*

Morian was so focused on the argument she was having with herself that she didn't recognize the warning that brushed across her mind until it was too late. The hand that wrapped around her throat, pulled a startled gasp from her even as her symbiot moved to attack.

"I'll kill her," the raspy, harsh voice warned. "Not even you will be able to heal her from the wound I would inflict."

"Raffvin!" Morian choked out.

The dark, menacing chuckle in her ear sent ripples of fear through her. "Yes, my beautiful mate. I finally have you," Raffvin murmured as he wrapped his other arm around her and breathed in her scent. Morian's cry was cut off as his hand tightened around her neck, cutting off her ability to breathe. "I smell another male on you!"

Morian's hands clawed at the grip he had around her neck until he loosened it just enough for her to draw in a desperate breath. Her symbiot snarled in rage and frustration as it paced just inside the top step of the atrium. It shivered in fear and revulsion when a very small symbiot of pure black snaked in between its body and the body of its mistress.

Morian's eyes widened in fear as she saw the abomination Raffvin had created out of what remained of his symbiot. Her horror that he could take something so pure and turn it into something so horrid froze her. She knew what had happened to the symbiots of the guards who were protecting Trisha. She would not allow hers to be destroyed that way.

"Stay back," she whispered. "Do not let it touch you."

Raffvin chuckled as he pulled her closer. "Very smart, but you always were," he purred as he rubbed his nose along her neck. "Now, tell me whose scent covers you," he demanded again, squeezing her until she was sure her ribs would crack.

"My mate," she cried out painfully. "My true mate."

Raffvin pulled her backwards with a hiss to his symbiot to keep the other one away from them. Turning Morian roughly around, he struck her across the face. Morian cried out again, but was unable to pull away from him due to the steely grasp he had on her wrist.

"I am your true mate!" He growled out. "You are mine! You have always been mine. I was born to control you, the Hive, and the Valdier."

"No," Morian responded in a trembling voice. "The elders saw what was in your heart and rejected you."

"It was your mother and father who rejected my claim," Raffvin snarled pulling her by her hair until she was standing in front of him again.

"What are you talking about?" Morian asked in shock.

"I watched you for years until you were old enough to claim. You were different from any other woman I had ever seen," Raffvin said with a cruel smile curving his lips. "You were always slipping away with the help of your symbiot. You would run through the forests playing and fighting imaginary creatures while your symbiot played with you. I knew you must have been special. It was said your mother could talk to the Gods. You must have been able to as well. With the power of the Gods behind me, I could defeat any who challenged me," he murmured as he slid his hand down over the heated flesh of the cheek he had struck. "With you by my side, I would rule our world."

Morian stared up into the insane eyes of Jalo's brother and thanked the Gods that the elders had seen back then what she and Jalo missed for so long. Raffvin was truly insane. His greed had turned his blood black with the sickness of it. She jerked when she heard her symbiot cry out in pain. Struggling against the hold on her, she tried to get to it.

"No!" She cried out in horror as Raffvin's black symbiot whipped out a long, black tentacle and ran it along the smooth, golden side leaving a blistering trail along it. "Please, I'll do anything. You know if you harm my symbiot, I cannot survive," she said desperately.

"Just like your son and his mate intended to leave me," Raffvin responded harshly. "I was too smart for them. I kept a part of my symbiot hidden so no other could find it."

"Your symbiot is hurting," she whispered, feeling the agony running through it. "This is not its normal state. You are destroying it."

"Then it is good that I am about to get more, isn't it?" Raffvin said softly against her throat. "So soft, so silky. Once the stench of the other male is replaced with mine you will belong to me at last."

Morian whimpered and closed her eyes as she felt his teeth lengthen and scrape against her neck. She could not let him mark her. It was more than she could bear.

* * *

Paul cursed as he pressed the accelerator as far as it would go on the skimmer. He could see the palace in the distance. His heart had frozen as the purple alien related what he had overheard.

Paul could see the sky filled with dragons battling the invading force. He would let the boys handle it. He knew the children were safe. All he wanted to do was make sure the women, namely Morian, was safe inside the palace.

He flew over the walls of the palace swerving around Abby, Cara and Trisha who were blowing streams of heated blue flames at the few skimmers that had broken formation and were attacking the palace walls. He jumped off the skimmer before it had even shut down and was running through the courtyard.

One of the guards pulled the door open and he rolled through it just as laser fire cut a dark path where he had been. The guard had shifted and his roar echoed as he and his symbiot were hit. Paul turned his head in time to see the skimmer that had fired on him explode as Creon burst out of the clouds and ripped it apart with his claws. The sight was magnificent as the solid black dragon turned and disappeared into the smoke of the destroyed vehicle.

"Morian?" Paul said, rising as he saw Ariel and Carmen hurrying toward him. Each held a newborn protectively against their body.

"I saw her heading for the atrium earlier, but I haven't seen her since the fighting began," Ariel gasped out as the doors shook from another explosion. "How did they get through the palace defenses?"

"There is a traitor inside the palace," Paul grunted as he pulled both women and babes toward a staircase. "Take cover under the stairwell," he ordered them. He raised his hand to stop their protest. "There is a passageway at the bottom of it. Tap the fifth, eighth, and fifteenth stone in that order and a door will open. I need you to be with the other babies. Bio has them in a cave hidden beneath the palace."

Carmen drew in a deep breath and nodded. "We'll protect the little ones. Go find Morian. I have a feeling there is more to this attack than what meets the eye," she replied before she turned. "Come on, Ariel."

"Paul," Ariel said quietly. Balancing Spring against her breast, she laid her hand on his arm as he turned. "Be careful."

Paul's eyes softened as he saw the worry in her eyes. "I will. Take care of the little ones," he said again before he looked at Carmen's retreating back. "And your sister."

"Always," Ariel said with a smile before she hurried down the steps after her sister.

Paul watched for a fraction of a second before he took off at a loping run through the long corridors. He slid around the corners, took the stairs three at a time, and kept his eyes sharp as he finally reached the level leading to the narrow staircase leading up to the secluded atrium. It was because of his awareness that he was able to dive into a roll when he reached the last step to the long corridor leading to the entrance to the atrium.

The laser fire tore through his sleeve and sliced along his arm, but he refused to acknowledge the pain. He continued rolling until he came up behind one of the huge planters lining the walls. Another blast shattered the huge curved container. Paul used the distraction of flowing dirt and plants to run for the shallow alcove near the window. He fired as he went and was rewarded with a low grunt.

"Give up," Paul called out. "You'll never get out of here alive."

Paul wasn't too surprised when he didn't receive a response. It wasn't like the guy trying to kill him wanted to sit down and enjoy a cup of tea while discussing techniques. Still, he hoped to get an idea if he was facing one or more threats.

He laid his head back as he pictured the corridor in his mind. There were planters every ten feet. His target was twenty feet away. His eyes narrowed as he looked down at the shiny floor. A grin curved his lips as he remembered the polished floors of his home growing up.

*You could slide on them forever,* he remembered. *Never under-estimate the power of surprise,* he thought. *Let's see if I still have it in me.*

Paul rocked back and forth on his heels before he jumped out and began running along the long narrow corridor. As he suspected, his target moved out to aim for him. The moment he did, Paul went into a slide reminiscent of his high school baseball days. He slid ten feet, firing rapidly as he went. The look of surprise showed on the face of the male as a large hole opened in the old man's chest.

Paul curled his leg under him and hopped up as the male collapsed. Keeping his pistol aimed at the dying man, he moved closer to him, his eyes scanning to make sure there were no other threats. Using his foot, he kicked the other man's weapon away from where it lay by his side where he had slid down the wall.

"Where is Lady Morian?" Paul demanded of the man whose eyes were already beginning to cloud with death.

The male opened his mouth, but nothing came out as his eyes grew dim. Paul cursed as he knelt beside the man and felt for a pulse knowing it was hopeless. His frown grew darker as he wondered why the male did not have his symbiot with him. It should have been able to help not only defend him but heal the wound. His eyes fell on the dark band of black that appeared to wither and dissolve before his eyes. A harsh black blister marked the man's wrist.

Paul's mind worked through the evidence, even as he rose to cautiously climb the stairwell leading to the atrium. The man must have been the traitor in the palace. Whether he was the only one or not, Paul would leave to Zoran and the others to discover. His immediate concern was for his mate.

He shivered as he felt the feeling of something moving inside him again. The feeling had been building inside him until at times he swore he was about to burst. He pushed it aside. He couldn't afford any distractions right now.

He carefully scanned the entrance of the atrium before he rose up and began searching for the woman who held his heart in her delicate hands. He wanted to shout for her. He wanted to demand that she let him know that she was alright, but the hairs standing up on the back of his neck were warning him that everything was not as it appeared.

"Well, well, well," a dark chuckled echoed from the shadows to his left. "Is this weak alien the one you insist is your mate? How disappointing," Raffvin murmured sarcastically as he pulled Morian in front of him.

Paul turned calmly and stared at the man he had been studying intensively since he first heard his name. Long, greasy strands of dark hair hung in limp clumps around a face carved with madness. Eyes as black as oil focused on him.

The figure was no longer filled out, but was a hollow shell of the man he must have been at one time. The only indication that he would be a ruthless opponent was the cruel hold he held on Morian. Dark bruising marred her cheek, chin, and neck.

"Paul," Morian began fearfully before she whimpered as Raffvin tightened his hold on her. Dark bands similar to those on the old man he had killed wove around her wrists.

"What are you?" Raffvin looked Paul over with disdain. "I at least expected an opponent worthy of my attention."

Paul's lip pulled back into a sneer. "By all means, let her go and you can see just how worthy I am. I would hate to disappoint you," he mocked.

Raffvin's eyes narrowed suspiciously. "I don't think so. I will have to satisfy myself with knowing you will not be able to stop my claim of such a beautiful female," Raffvin said, turning his head just enough to run his tongue along Morian's bent neck. "She will taste all the sweeter when she is screaming my name."

Paul knew better than to give away his rage. He calmly took a step closer to where Raffvin stood partially in the shadows of the plants hanging down. His eyes took in the thick blackness holding the plants at bay.

Every time a vine tried to thread through toward Raffvin, the blackness would touch it and the plant would wither and withdraw. Whatever in the hell that thing was, he needed to get Morian away from it and Raffvin.

"It will never happen," Paul said quietly. "I'll kill you before you get a chance to claim her."

Raffvin lifted his head and sniffed before he shook his head. "I don't think so. You are no match for my dragon," he said before he shifted.

Paul burst forward as the hard claws wrapped around Morian. Her symbiot moved at the same time, but was thrown backwards by the dark ribbons snaking out around Raffvin. Paul heard the symbiot hiss in pain and rage, but his focus was on preventing Raffvin from taking Morian away. He pulled his hunting knife, ducking when Raffvin blew a stream of blistering heat at him. He swiveled, slicing a clean cut along one thick, scaled thigh. Raffvin's roar shook the glass enclosure.

Paul jumped to the side as Raffvin swung his tail at him before rolling onto his haunches. "Let her go," Paul snarled in a deadly voice. "If you want to fight, fight like a man."

Raffvin's harsh laugh sent shivers down Paul's spine. The edge of insanity clearly visible in the sound. There was no reasoning with the other male. His only hope was working on his pride.

"What's the matter, Raffvin? I thought you were tough. Hiding behind a woman is weak, even for you," Paul taunted. "Next you'll be crying like a baby and sucking your fucking thumb."

Raffvin roared and blew a stream of dragon fire at Paul. His rage expanded when he missed the male.

He swung around, shaking Morian as if she was a rag doll. He shifted back into his two-legged form.

"Surrender to me or she dies," Raffvin hissed out loud.

Paul looked coldly at Raffvin from where he was shielded from the dragon fire by Morian's symbiot. "You won't kill her," he stated confidently. "You need her. She is your only link to the Hive. Your symbiot is dying. Even I can feel it weakening and without it, you and your dragon are dead. It's only a matter time. If we wait you'll be dead without us having to lift a hand."

Raffvin's furious snarl of rage was enough to let Paul know he had hit the nail on the head. Raffvin's appearance, the weakened size of the symbiot, and the slowness in his dragon form proved that the other male was fast losing his battle for supremacy.

"You are right. I do need her," Raffvin replied in a low voice. "But, I only need her alive…. a little. She doesn't have to be whole either," he said with an evil smile.

Morian's agonizing screams suddenly filled the atrium as the black bands wrapped around her wrists began smoking and sizzling. Paul's eyes widened in horror as he saw cuts open and blood began pouring from under the black bands. His stomach twisted as Morian collapsed against Raffvin, hoarse screams and horrendous sobs escaping her as the bands twisted, cutting deeper.

"Stop!" Paul said, stepping around the golden symbiot which was shaking uncontrollably. He threw the hunting knife away from him and raised his hands. "Stop torturing her," he begged hoarsely.

Raffvin hissed out a command and the bands loosened. Morian collapsed, unconscious as the pressure was released. Dark ribbons of red blood flowed down from her wrists to pool on the floor. Paul choked back helpless rage as Raffvin raised one of Morian's tattered wrists to his lips and dragged his tongue over the ravaged flesh.

"Delicious," Raffvin whispered.

"What are you going to do now? There is no escape for you," Paul asked harshly, his body humming with pinned up rage.

"Yes, Uncle, what are you going to do now?" Creon asked coldly as he stepped off the staircase. "We have captured not only the traitors you had planted in the palace, but your ships in orbit have been destroyed and the hidden base in the sands has been taken. You were not as careful as you believed."

Raffvin looked with hatred at Creon. "You are just as arrogant as your father. I should have ordered Aria to kill you, though the information you gave her proved very rewarding."

Creon no longer felt the weight of guilt the name of his ex-lover would have brought. His love for Carmen had healed that time in his life when his love for another had caused the death of many of his men. He shrugged his broad shoulders and pulled his laser sword.

"That is a mistake you will not have to worry about for much longer. Release my *Dola* and fight as a warrior, Uncle. It will be the last opportunity you will have to pretend you were ever one," Creon said with a nasty smile.

Raffvin's eyes narrowed. "I think not," he retorted shifting Morian as she regained consciousness.

"Creon, Paul," she whispered softly. "Kill him. Do not let his threat to me stop you. He cannot be allowed to learn the location of the Hive. Kill him," she begged.

"Morian, my beautiful, sweet queen," Raffvin laughed. "So melodramatic. They are Valdier warriors. They cannot kill their queen, their priestess... or a mother and a true mate. That is their weakness. But I can remedy at least one of those obstacles for them, my dear."

Before anyone realized what he meant, Raffvin hissed out a command and a long rope of black energy shot out, piercing Paul through the stomach and exiting out his back. Morian screamed in agony as she watched her true mate's body jerk as the spear of black energy passed through him. Creon's loud curse echoed as he caught Paul's body.

Everything seemed to happen in slow motion. Raffvin shifted back into his dragon form, the black symbiot covering him in thin armor and lifted upward on long, leathery wings. Morian's eyes never left the sight of her youngest son holding her mate in his arms. Even the tears blurring her eyes could not wash away the heartbreaking sight. Glass shattered as Raffvin broke through the ceiling of the atrium. Creon leaned over Paul as it rained down around them, trying to protect his body as best he could.

"Paul," Morian whispered in agony before she closed her eyes and let the blackness take her once again.

# Chapter 13

"Zoran!" Creon yelled out as he rushed down the stairwell with Paul in his arms. "Zoran!"

Zoran looked up from where he was checking over Zohar and Abby to make sure neither one of them had been hurt. His eyes widened in shock when he saw the human male who had become as much of a friend to him and his brothers as a father figure. Over the last several weeks of training, Zoran not only came to appreciate the male's intelligence in tactical maneuvers, but also his compassion, easy humor, and his calm guidance on them all.

"What happened?" Zoran asked just as an anguished cry sounded behind him.

"Daddy!" Trisha cried out horrified, handing Bálint to Kelan so she could rush to his side. "No.... No! Daddy!" She sobbed.

Creon gently lowered Paul down onto the smooth marble flooring. Trisha dropped down next to her father's left side. Her hands went to circle the seeping hole through his stomach. His breathing was erratic and his blood pressure was dropping due to the amount of blood he had lost. Morian's symbiot tried to move over him, but the traces of black energy still lined the wound, making it unable to heal the injury.

"Kelan, help him," Trisha begged, turning to gaze up at her mate. "Please, you have to save him," she pleaded desperately as tears coursed down her cheeks.

Zoran knelt next to Trisha and pulled Paul's hand back so he could see the damage. "Forget about me,"

Paul gasped out, gritting his teeth against the pain. "You have to go after that bastard. He has Morian," he rasped out as his vision began to blur.

"It is too late," Zoran said sadly, shaking his head as he looked at the mortal wound. "She is lost when you die," he said, his voice thick with sorrow, even as Paul's head fell limply back as he lost consciousness again.

Zoran's eyes moved to the mark on Paul's neck as it began to glow. The gold of the dragon burned brighter. When the mark started to move, Zoran's symbiot sent him an image. His head jerked around to stare in wonder as each of the symbiots, including those of the guards who had come to surround them, moved closer and began bowing in respect.

His eyes shifted back to the mark and he hissed, falling back away from Paul as the mark expanded until Paul's body began to glow as well. Zoran grabbed Trisha who was sobbing quietly, her head on her father's chest and her hands wrapped around him. He pulled her roughly away from Paul's body.

Trisha's cry of protest died on her lips as a golden mist began swirling around her father. Each symbiot came forward, moving until they surrounded the body of the human male. Rising up from the mist two figures began to form, merging until the forms of twin dragons appeared only to shimmer once again and become the translucent bodies of two women.

"What.... What is that?" Trisha asked, slowly rising as she looked at the golden bodies hovering over her father's lifeless form.

Kelan drew Trisha back protectively under his arm. Bálint gazed at the glowing figures and he cooed loudly, blowing bubbles. Kelan and Trisha looked down at their son and saw his eyes shining a dark, dark gold. Seconds later, the sound of the other children could be heard.

Amber and Jade's giggles, Zohar's loud sigh, even Spring and Phoenix reacted by squealing and waving their tiny arms. The figures floated inches above Paul's silent body. Ribbons of gold began streaming from all the symbiots surrounding them, flowing from their bodies in thin, weaving bands before raining down over Paul until he glowed a dark gold. The black threads that prevented Morian's symbiot from healing him before began to bubble, hiss, and dissolve in brilliant bursts of color as the stream of gold poured into the wound in Paul's stomach.

"Zoran," Abby whispered as she held a mesmerized Zohar against her. "What is happening?"

"The Gods and Goddesses have heard our mother's plea for her mate," he replied in awe.

One of the figures turned and looked at Zoran with a warm look. Even though he could see right through the shimmering gold that made up her form, he had never seen anything so awe inspiring, not even the Hive. The figure tilted her head and looked down at his son before letting her eyes move to each infant, pausing on Phoenix for several long seconds. Carmen pulled her daughter closer to her and tilted her chin in defiance drawing a smile from the figure.

Slowly, the ribbons of gold began to grow thinner and thinner until the gold looked more like dust motes dancing in the sunlight. Both figures turned back to Zoran and nodded before they dissolved. The symbiots circling Paul's body stood up and began moving back, forcing those standing on the outer rim to step away.

"Daddy?" Trisha called out, stepping forward only to be stopped by Kelan when he wrapped his arm around her.

"Wait, Trisha," he murmured in a hushed voice.

The symbiots parted, each taking the opposite side of the other until they formed a path that lined either side leading to where Paul's body had been moments before. Trisha's surprised gasp was followed by those of all who turned their eyes to the figure that had been hidden by the huge bodies of the symbiots. The figure of an injured human male was no longer lying on the hard marble floor. Instead, a different figure stood – tall, proud, majestic.

\* \* \*

Images flashed through Paul's mind. He knew the wound he had received was mortal, but all he cared about was his beautiful, fragile mate. He was sure the look in her eyes would haunt him even in death.

He refused to believe she was lost to him. He cursed his distraction. When the band of black had begun cutting through Morian's wrists and her screams of agony rose, all he could think about was doing whatever was necessary to stop Raffvin from hurting her anymore. The pain and terror in her eyes filled him with rage and the desire for revenge.

Creon's sudden appearance gave Paul a glimmer of hope that between the two of them, they would be able to defeat Raffvin before he could escape. He had not expected Morian to plead for them to kill Raffvin, regardless of her safety. He had also not expected Raffvin to use the black symbiot on him in the way he had. He barely felt it as it sliced through his body.

*No,* he thought as he felt his life blood draining away, *the pain I felt from my mate's ravaged screams caused me more pain than anything physical could have,* he acknowledged with despair.

He vaguely remembered Creon lifting him as if he weighed no more than one of the babies. He rolled in and out of consciousness as light and shadows from the windows and corridors flashed by in a kaleidoscope of colors. Regret pulled at him when he heard the anguished cry of his baby girl.

A part of him felt the cold, hard stone of the floor as Creon laid him down while another part became numb with hopelessness and grief. He knew from the look in Zoran's eyes that there was nothing that could be done to save him. His last thought was of Morian's beautiful face just that morning as her eyes sparkled with delight when the news came that Carmen had gone into labor. He had kissed her passionately, wanting to wrap himself in her warmth and love. If it wasn't for the fact that one of the healers was frantically begging for her assistance he would have taken her back to their bed and made love to her all morning.

A frown creased his brow as gold light suddenly filled his vision. He thought everything would turn dark.... black even as death came to claim him. His frown deepened as he realized that his body was actually feeling very warm at the moment. In fact, it was getting pretty damn hot. He knew he hadn't been an angel during his life, but hell, surely, he hadn't done anything so bad as to send him to hell.

Soft laughter drew his attention. He turned his head, moving as if in a dream world. The gold light was getting brighter until he wondered if he could conjure up a pair of sunglasses to help him see the figures approaching him better.

*I like your humor, human,* one of the figures said in a warm, lyrical tone.

Paul raised an eyebrow. *Is that a good thing or a bad thing?* He asked in a husky voice.

*Good thing,* the second figure replied with a light chuckle. *You are right, sister. He is the chosen one.*

*Chosen one?* Paul asked with a puzzled frown. *Am I supposed to understand what that means?* He asked curiously as he watched them come closer. He might be going to hell, but at least he wasn't hurting anymore.

Both figures chuckled as they glided around him, assessing him. *He will be good for her. He will free her so she can run free once again,* one said to the other as if he wasn't standing between them.

*Yes, it has been too long since she has been free. I miss that. We should have brought her true mate to her sooner,* the first figure responded.

*He was not ready. Neither was she,* the second one snorted. *Everything in its time, sister.*

*I know, but it took so long,* the first sister said with a sigh. *It has been hard standing aside and watching.*

*We could not interfere until we were sure,* the second sister insisted.

*Ladies, as charming as your company is, can either one of you tell me what the hell is going on?* Paul asked impatiently. *In case you didn't know, my mate is in danger.*

*Of course we know,* the second one said with a roll of her eyes. *I am Arosa.*

*And I am Arilla,* the first figure said with a smile.

Paul studied both of them for several seconds before he shook his head in frustration. *Is this supposed to mean something to me?* Paul asked with a raised eyebrow wondering if he had ended up in the Valdier version of heaven or hell.

*Neither,* both figures stated at the same time as if they could read his mind. *We needed to know that you were the one for our daughter. You will save her, protect her, love her and let her be who she needs to be. You see who she is beneath the mask she wears. You dare her to be true to herself and you will do the same for her dragon.*

*Isn't that what a true mate is?* Paul asked drily. *You accept them for who they are, for better or for worse. I'm not exactly a saint, you know.*

*No, you are not,* Arosa purred. *I like that.*

*Arosa, he is not for you to seduce,* Arilla snapped.

Paul shook his head. *Sorry ladies, you couldn't seduce me if you wanted to. My heart is already taken,* he responded lightly. *No offense intended,* he added quickly.

Both Arilla and Arosa laughed in delight. *He is quick witted as well,* Arilla said.

Arosa's eyes turned serious as she looked deeply into Paul's eyes. *You have been chosen to protect the daughter of the Hive. You must defeat Raffvin and prevent him from gaining access to the blood of the Gods. If he is successful, the lives of all Valdier and their dragons will fall,* Arosa stated in a voice that resonated through Paul.

Arilla opened her hand to reveal a bright red stone set in silver. Paul recognized it immediately as the necklace that Mandra and Ariel had shown him. It had been a gift to Ariel by the strange creatures who needed her help with returning some critters to their world.

Ariel had explained that when the black symbiot that had attacked and wounded Mandra tried to kill his symbiot, she had stepped in front of it. The stone had absorbed the negative energy, pulling it away from the symbiot trapped within.

*Wear this and no harm can come to you,* Arilla said.

*How can I find my mate?* Paul asked. *Raffvin flew off with her.*

*Your dragon will know,* they both whispered as they began to fade.

*I don't have a dragon….,* Paul started to say before his words faded as the world suddenly tilted.

*You do now,* the golden goddesses giggled at the same time knowing the golden blood that ran through him was just what he needed to wake his dragon up.

Fire burst inside him, burning like lava as the pressure that had been building inside him suddenly exploded outward. His body shook for a moment as he rose. His vision was clearer, sharper. He turned his head to gaze down at the wound in his stomach only to realize that not only was the wound gone, so was his stomach as he knew it.

His eyes narrowed as he quickly processed the changes. He raised his head as he felt the pull of his mate. Rage burned as hot as the heat pulsing through him. Paul let out a roar that shook the walls of the palace, shattering the windows around him. He looked down as the symbiots formed a passage for him. The gold from his body swirled with the colors in the corridor before solidifying in the same gold of the symbiots.

"Daddy?" Trisha breathed out in awe, pulling away from Kelan's grasp.

Paul watched through narrowed eyes as his baby girl came closer to him and raised her hand. He lowered his head and brushed it gently against her hand before he pulled back and nodded to Zoran. It was time to go get his mate back. He would pursue her to hell and back if he had to, but he would bring her back. He made sure Zoran knew his intent.

"Go!" Zoran said in a rough voice. "Bring her back to us."

Paul snarled out to Morian's symbiot which transformed into a huge Were Cat. Two guards rushed to open the large double doors leading out of the palace. Paul could feel Morian's pain and sorrow, even from a distance. She believed he was dead. It was time to let his mate know that not only was he very much alive but so was his dragon.

Morian's symbiot charged through the double doors, transforming once it was clear into a huge golden eagle. Paul was right behind it. As soon as he was outside, he used his dragon's ability to reflect his surroundings and vanished.

"Kelan!" Trisha cried out terrified as she watched her father disappear before her eyes. "Where is he?"

"He is fine, *mi elila*," Kelan assured her coming up to stand next to her.

"That is totally wicked!" Cara whispered. "He's just like the symbiots! He's a big dragon symbiot!" She said with a touch of envy. "I could totally drive you nuts if I could do that, Trelon." Amber's loud squeal and bouncing showed she approved of the idea.

"Like you don't do that already," Trelon muttered as he tried to get Jade to release his hair that she was shaking back and forth in her mouth like it was a bone. He was going to have to wash the drool out of it again, he thought with a sigh.

"Heck, he's even bigger than Mandra!" Ariel giggled, looking up at her huge mate. "He can totally kick your butt now."

Mandra growled and scooped Ariel up into his arms. "You think that is funny, do you?"

"Oh yes," Ariel breathed out with sparkling eyes.

"Do you think he will bring Morian back safely?" Abby asked, shifting Zohar in her arms as he began rooting around the front of her top.

Zoran wrapped his arm around his mate. "Yes," he replied confidently. "Yes, he will bring her home safely."

"We need to repair the damage," Creon said, rocking Spring in his arms where she had fallen asleep. "There are a few prisoners. We will get what information we can out of them," he said before turning to look at Carmen who was beginning to wilt next to him. "You must rest. There has been too much excitement for you. You gave birth just this morning."

Carmen smiled wearily up at her mate, deciding she wasn't going to argue with him this time. "Ariel, would you mind helping me?" Carmen asked, turning to her sister who was still in her mate's arms. "Sorry Mandra but I think I need her more than you do right now," she added with a waning smile.

"Of course, Carmen," Mandra said, brushing a kiss over Ariel's lips. "It would be better for her to rest as well."

Ariel rolled her eyes, but grinned at her sister. "He's turning into a worry wort," she teased as he set her on her feet.

Carmen laughed when Mandra grunted under his breath about unappreciative, stubborn human women. "We're appreciative, Mandra. We just don't want you to know it," Carmen teased.

Abby watched as the sisters walked away. She looked up at her mate who was staring out the opened doors. She knew from the dark frown on his face that he was more worried than he was letting on. She rubbed her head against his arm and smiled up at him.

Zoran smiled down at her before he looked at Trisha who stopped in front of him. "My dad is the best there is," she said softly. "He'll get her back. No one can defeat him when he is hunting them. No one."

Zoran nodded. "I know," he said, letting his gaze move once more to the bright sky outside. "I know," he repeated.

## Chapter 14

Paul soared through the air, letting the pull of his mate guide him. The symbiot beside him was using its ability to reflect the environment around it to vanish as well. Paul's eyes picked up the slight distortion. He let his gaze travel over the ground below him, marking places that would be good for setting traps, escape routes, and places to hide.

He thought of everything he had learned about Raffvin from the files he had read and from his brief encounter with him. The male was a coward, but a smart and ruthless one. He would hide behind Morian, perhaps even kill her if he had to in order to escape. Still, he was also becoming dangerously weak. Raffvin's gaunt look and the ease with which he had been able to injure Raffvin's dragon told him that Raffvin was not up for a lengthy battle.

In addition, Raffvin might have his symbiot but it was not capable of healing him. He had turned it into a weapon. Paul sent a command for the symbiot to focus on Morian when they reached her. Once Paul had separated her from Raffvin, she would need the healing powers and added strength of it.

*Us too,* his dragon growled back silently. *Our mates need us. Mine not know I live now. I want her.*

*You will be with her soon, my friend,* Paul assured his dragon, amused that it was acting like a stubborn, horny teenager. *It is important that we get her to safety so that we can see what her injuries are and heal them.*

*I kill Raffvin,* his dragon snapped, rage making him shimmer.

*Calm, my friend*, Paul said with an icy calm. *He will die, but our first concern must be our mate. We cannot take the chance of her dying on us.*

*I feel her*, his dragon admitted. *I feel my mate's pain. She is very weak.*

*I feel it too, which is why we must care for her first*, Paul said soothingly. *Besides, I think she might like to help us roast Raffvin's ass.*

Paul's dragon snorted. *She sure not going to bite it! I not allow my mate to eat rot.*

Paul chuckled. *I agree! The only place she is putting that delectable mouth is on us.*

*Agree*, his dragon hummed in delight. *We are close! He too weak to take her far.*

*It didn't hurt that you were flying like a bat out of hell, either*, Paul responded drily even as he slowed. *There!*

Ahead of him was a patch of heavy forest. The pull to get to his mate was stronger than ever. Paul fought to remain calm as he felt the fragile strand that connect him and Morian growing weaker.

There was no time to waste. He had to get her away from Raffvin fast. He glided down on silent wings, weaving in and out between the dense clusters of trees, the symbiot following closely behind him. The shadows were no problem for his sharpened eyesight.

He glided between the heavy foliage before sweeping his wings up to land on a thick branch on the outer edge of a small clearing. A makeshift camp had been set up. There were approximately fifty warriors moving down below. In the center, Paul watched as Raffvin exited a tent.

*There is our target,* he thought with a menacing curl of his lip. *How light are you on your feet?* He asked his dragon.

*Lighter than you!* It replied with a snort.

*Let's hope so,* Paul thought with a grin. *Let's go.*

\* \* \*

Morian rolled over onto her back on the hard surface of the ground. She gritted her teeth against the pain in her face and wrists before blinking several times trying to clear her vision so she could see where she had been taken. Her eyes welled with tears as she remembered Paul. Pain unlike anything she had ever felt before exploded through her at the loss of her true mate. She pulled in a shaky breath. A part of her was amazed she was still alive. The only reason she could think of was so she could kill Raffvin. She had nothing else to live for but revenge.

*Please, let my mate not have hurt for too long,* she prayed silently as she sat up.

*He come!* Her dragon rose up inside her so fast Morian groaned with disorientation as her head spun. *He come!* Her dragon said urgently… excitedly.

*Stop!* Morian groaned again as she swallowed back the nausea from the blood suddenly leaving her head. She breathed deeply and looked down at her battered wrists that were still bound together by the thin black bands of symbiot. *Why should you be excited that Raffvin is coming?* She moaned out to her dragon.

*Not Raffvin,* her dragon snorted in disgust. *Our mates come!*

*Our... my mate is dead,* Morian choked out as tears overflowed down her cheeks. *Raffvin killed him,* she whispered as overwhelming grief flooded her and she lay back down to bury her face in her arms.

She didn't care if Raffvin killed her or her heartache did. She just wanted the pain to go away. Only, her dragon wasn't acting like its heart had just been torn from its chest. No, her dragon was bouncing around like she was a dragonling once again. Morian rolled over and wiped angrily at her damp, dirty cheeks.

*What is wrong with you!* She cried out in fury. *Didn't you hear me? I said my mate is dead!*

*No he not,* her dragon chortled in delight. *I feel my mate. If I feel my mate, your mate has to be alive.*

*Fine! Live what little life we have being delusional. See if I care,* Morian retorted with a growl.

*Okay, you not care, but I not delusional,* her dragon giggled. *I have mate!*

Morian felt a sliver of hope slip through her guard. She sat up and looked around. What if her dragon was right? She bit her lip and shook her head.

*NO! It is impossible,* she argued with herself. *He couldn't shift and there was no way he could have survived the wound he received.*

Her hands clenched into tight fists. She knew she was going to die, but she was going to take Raffvin's miserable ass with her. Her eyes flew around the large tent looking for a weapon. Her eyes gleamed with determination when she saw a small knife resting on a table near some fruit.

*His carelessness would be his downfall,* she thought savagely. *I'll rip his blackened heart out. He'll never touch another one of my loved ones again. I'll bury it so deep in his chest it will go all the way through the miserable bastard,* she swore passionately.

She rose on shaky legs and stumbled over to the table. Her fingers wrapped around the knife. She gritted her teeth as she felt the black bands around her wrists tighten, cutting into the tender flesh. She ignored the fresh wave of pain and rested against the table for a moment before she forced herself to straighten up with determination.

*It was time that crazy son-of-a-bitch met the devil, as Carmen would say…. hell, what all the girls would say… well, except for maybe Abby, who would say something a little less crude,* Morian thought with a bittersweet smile. *Yes, it was time to take him out permanently.*

Morian stumbled toward the entrance of the tent just as the flaps blew open before closing again. She swayed as her heart settled back down only to squeak in surprise as she found herself pulled forward by invisible hands… or claws. Her mouth dropped open as first the head, then the body of a huge golden dragon slowly appeared.

"Paul?" Morian whispered in wonder.

The huge golden head lowered and a soft purr escaped from its chest. Morian gaped as one eyelid slowly lowered in a wink even as the golden lip curled back in the semblance of a smile. She would recognize that smirk anywhere.

"Oh shit!" She muttered before her eyes rolled back in her head as she fainted.

* * *

Paul smiled down at the sweet, delicate face of his mate. It was bruised, dirty, and tear-stained and he had never, ever seen anything more beautiful. It had been easier than he expected to sneak through the camp. His dragon had been true to his word about being light on his feet – for the most part. Paul had brought only a small amount of Morian's symbiot with him, not wanting to take a chance of it being injured if Raffvin had more of his twisted essence hanging around.

He had landed just inside the outer rim of the camp and wove his way through the maze of tents that were set up. He noticed a variety of species within the mix. Most were of the purple species that had attacked them earlier.

There were a few Sarafin, and of course, a Valdier or two. He recognized most of the species from being on Kelan's warship only none of these looked like they were of the same caliber of warrior. All of these warriors looked like they were born and bred mercenaries. These were hired killers who would betray Raffvin if they got a better offer.

He had to pull his dragon back a couple of times when he wanted to cause a touch of mischief. Paul had sternly warned him tripping the warriors, gobbling them up, or torching a tent or two would

NOT be conducive to a stealth rescue mission. Havoc and destruction could come once their mate was safely tucked away somewhere. Until then, they would stick with their plan.

*Your plan*, his dragon had grumbled. *It not much fun.*

Paul chuckled even as he felt edgy. He was riding an adrenaline high right now. He would love nothing better than to slit every one of the bastards' throats but that would have to wait. He grinned as he thought of Raffvin's surprise and rage when he discovered that Morian had been whisked away right from under his nose. He was really looking forward to showing that bastard he wasn't as easy to kill as Raffvin thought. The playing fields were even now.

*Not even*, his dragon snorted. *I kill with my eyes closed.*

Paul shook his head at his dragon. *Well, it would not hurt my feelings if you wanted to do it with them open. Remember, the asshole doesn't fight fair.*

*And you think I do?* His dragon snorted as it flicked its tail just enough to knock the leg out from under a table of food causing it to crash to the ground amid a chorus of loud curses. *Oops*, he grinned.

*You are going to get us caught*, Paul growled out.

*No one see me*, his dragon replied indignantly as he slid around the corner of another tent and straight into the path of a large purple warrior. *Well, except for this one*, he muttered right before he wrapped his front claws around the male's head and twisted it quickly.

Paul cursed as he wondered what in the hell to do with the body. His dragon shrugged his huge golden shoulders, pulled back a flap on the closest tent, peeked in, and then tossed the body behind a pile of crates piled up in it. No one heard the loud thump over all the yelling and arguing over the spilt food.

*They not know until he smell,* his dragon said, backing out of the tent and continuing to move toward the center tent. *We be gone by then.*

*For Pete's sake, you are worse than any of the Seals or Marines I trained,* Paul retorted in a gruff voice. *We need to have a serious talk when we get the hell out of here about tactical attacks.*

*I not know this Pete or Seal or Marine,* his dragon said as he sucked in his stomach as another warrior walked a little too close only to stick his tail out at the last minute. Paul rolled his eyes as the warrior passed by and promptly fell on his face in the dirt. The warrior jumped up and looked around suspiciously before stomping off in the opposite direction.

*Later,* Paul said with a sigh of resignation. *Just get us to the damn tent.*

*We here,* his dragon huffed and blew the flaps open enough so he could squeeze through unseen.

*Morian,* Paul whispered as he saw his mate swaying by a small table. His lips curled into a broad grin when he saw the small knife in her hand. *That's my girl,* he thought proudly even as his dragon reached greedily for her.

He felt her jerk of surprise before her eyes widened in confusion. "Paul?" She whispered.

Paul and his dragon were both unable to resist her anguished cry. He thought afterwards that there might have been a less dramatic way of appearing before her, but truthfully, all rational thought disappeared from his mind when he saw her. He swept her up into his arms as he shifted back into his two-legged form. His dragon hissed a warning to not take too long.

He quickly lowered her down to the ground. Still cradling her with one arm, he pulled the ruby red crystal hanging around his neck out from under his shirt and brushed it over the black bands around her wrists. Almost immediately, the strands of black were pulled into the glowing crystal leaving the dull gold of Raffvin's symbiot.

The thin ropes of Morian's symbiot dissolved from around his wrists and flowed over both Raffvin's remnants and over the open wounds on her wrists. Paul watched as the deep cuts slowly sealed. She would need more than the little bit of healing he could provide now, but it would help relieve some of her pain.

"Paul?" Morian moaned softly.

Paul ran his hand tenderly over her battered face. "I'm here, baby," he whispered. "I need to get you out of here."

Morian's eyelashes fluttered for a moment before the blazing gold of her eyes struck him. She stared at him for several long seconds before reaching up to wrap her arms around his neck and pulling him closer. She sniffed and pressed her face against his neck, her body trembling with the overwhelming emotions threatening to paralyze her.

"Don't you ever do that to me again!" She whispered brokenly. "Don't you ever die on me again!"

Paul buried his face in her shoulder and bit back the chuckle threatening to escape. "It's not like I planned it or anything," he assured her. "Come on. I need to get you out of here and heal you properly." He pulled back and looked down at her with a dark scowl. "You scared the hell out of me. Don't you ever put yourself in danger again. You are mine, damn it. I need you," he said gruffly before pressing a quick, hot kiss to her lips.

He didn't wait for her to respond. He rose up with her in his arms. With a quick thought, he shifted back into the huge golden dragon as if he had been doing it for centuries. Morian released an awed sigh as she ran her hand over his broad chest. Shivers of need and rage shook the large figure holding her as if she was made of the finest spun glass that Abby could create.

"You are beautiful," she breathed out, looking up at him again.

Paul turned his head down to gaze at the woman he held protectively in his claws. He puffed out a hot breath in answer before he wrapped his wings around her until she was completely enclosed within them. A second later, another hot breeze blew the flaps of the tent open again. Not one warrior, including Raffvin, saw a thing.

# Chapter 15

Paul's dragon moved silently through the camp. He was not about to take any chances with his injured mate securely enclosed against his body. Once he reached the outer rim, he glanced over his shoulder. A dark look glittered in his eyes as he saw Raffvin conversing with several warriors. It took every bit of his self-control not to roar out a challenge.

*Soon,* Paul promised. *Soon, we will kill him.*

Paul decided it was more the small, soft hand that caressed his chest, reminding him of his priorities instead of his promise that motivated his dragon to turn and vanish into the dark forest. As soon as he felt he was far enough away, he unwound his wings from around Morian and lifted off. He sent a silent call to her symbiot to catch up with them. He would take her to one of the areas he spied during his time here. He thought it would be better to camp for the night and heal her.

Morian sighed in his arms, relaxing back as she turned her face to the waning sunlight. She wrapped one slender hand over his thick forearm and gently stroked his scales. Another deep sigh escaped her as she turned her head to rub her uninjured cheek against his chest before closing her eyes.

Paul couldn't contain the deep purr that vibrated through him at her touch. Hell, he was going to be showing the world how horny he was if he didn't stop thinking about how good her tender touch felt. He needed to focus on something else but between her scent, her touch, and the adrenaline coursing through his body it was damn near impossible.

*Focus on her needs,* Paul repeated over and over. *Focus on her needs.*

*What do you think I doing?* His dragon snarled out. *Her dragon need me. She want me as much as your mate want you.*

*Yes, but MY mate needs to be healed first, damn it!* Paul snapped back impatiently before he bit back a chuckle at his dragon's response.

His dragon was muttering darkly under its breath about he needed to hurry the hell up then because he was getting tired of waiting. They traveled north before turning east. His first thought was to return immediately to the palace, but he was not sure how badly Morian was hurt and didn't want to take a chance of leaving any injury unattended for long.

He glided low along a narrow canyon that cut through a series of mountains. He had been through this way once before with Mandra when they were out exploring one day several weeks before. He vaguely remembered that there had been what he suspected was a cave not far from a series of lower falls.

He descended until he was only a few dozen feet or so above the rapidly moving water. He used his ability to reflect the surrounding environment on his back and wings while the front of him was visible. Anyone coming from above him would not see anything but water. The tips of his wings touched the water at times, creating dewy drops on the ends that glittered like diamonds. As he approached the second set of falls, he saw what he was looking for, a low overhanging ledge and the darkened interior of a cave. A group of large boulders lay in the rushing water at the entrance to it.

Paul swung upward, flapping his wings strongly as he navigated between the strong wind blowing through the canyon and the pull of the water. He landed lightly on the largest of the three boulders. Gingerly, he hopped from one to the other until he was in front of the cave. He would have to jump and shift at the same time to be able to fit. It would be tricky, but not impossible.

"Show off," Morian whispered huskily as she found herself held by a pair of strong, deeply tanned arms.

"So you were impressed, huh?" Paul asked teasingly as he moved further into the darkened area.

"I have been from the first moment I heard about you," she admitted shyly.

Paul glanced down and saw the tears glistening on her eyelashes. "You aren't the only one, sweetheart," he murmured.

Paul didn't have to ask his dragon for assistance. Almost immediately, his dragon surfaced far enough that his vision sharpened. He glanced around the cave. It wasn't real large, more of a bowl-shaped carved over centuries by the rise and flow of the river. Tree branches were swept up along one wall from previous floods. He was about to bemoan the fact there was nothing soft to lay Morian on when the golden symbiot that had landed behind him and shifted into a Were Cat shifted again into a bed.

"Shit, I could get used to that," he murmured as he gently laid her down on it.

Morian giggled even as her symbiot sent waves of healing warmth and long, narrow bands running up and over her body. She closed her eyes as it healed the bruising and small cuts on her face, chin and lips. She released a relieved sigh as it moved over her still aching wrists. Her eyes opened when she felt a different warmth touching her. This one had rough calluses on it, but was tender as it caressed her, soothing the ache in her heart.

"Did he hurt you anywhere else?" Paul asked in a low, husky voice. His eyes scanned hers carefully as he waited for her reply. "I need to know," he added gently.

Morian raised her hand and placed it over his in comfort. "No, just what you saw. I have to admit I was a bit of what Cara would call a 'wuss'. I remember very little after he took me," she said, her voice breaking as her eyes filled again. "Damn it! I'm still being one."

Paul leaned over her and brushed a kiss against her soft lips. "You can be as big a wuss as you want," he assured her. "I won't think any less of you."

Morian's lips trembled as a single tear escaped to run down the side of her face. "I bet you have never been a wuss in your life," she responded with a sniff.

"Are you kidding?" Paul asked with a surprised tone. "Hell, I can tell you a dozen times when I have been the world's biggest wuss! I bet I even have a certificate or two to prove it."

"Oh, right," Morian sniffed again in disbelief. "Give me an example," she retorted.

"Okay," Paul thought for a moment before he grinned. "One time was the night that Trisha was born. Hell no, that was the second time. The first time was when Evelyn told me she was pregnant. I was shaking like a leaf. I was thinking I didn't know a damn thing about babies. What was I supposed to do with one?"

Morian tilted her head as her symbiot ran down along her neck to heal the bruises from where Raffvin had grabbed her. "What did you do?" She asked, needing to hear the sound of his voice as much as being curious about what he was saying.

Paul grinned as his eyes followed and documented each mark on her delicate skin. He was taking notes because he fully intended to exact retribution for each one. His eyes darkened as her symbiot slipped down under the bodice of her torn blouse.

His head jerked up when Morian squeezed his hand that he still held against her cheek. "Oh, I found out she wasn't as breakable as I thought. Trisha was a beautiful baby. She had a head full of curly hair and the most beautiful brown eyes that followed me everywhere," he said softly as he remembered the first time he held his baby girl.

"Tell me another time," Morian said as she drew his hand down to rest on her stomach.

Paul bit back a silent curse as his hand brushed over her breast. His jeans were suddenly feeling very tight. He tried to think of another time he had been a wuss. He figured it was probably Trisha's first real birthday party-slash-slumber party after Evelyn had died.

He told Morian about what it was like to have a half-dozen little four and five year old girls running squealing through the house. Everything had been fine until about one in the morning when the tears started because they all wanted their mommies and daddies. It had taken several huge bowls of popcorn and three consecutive showings of the *Little Mermaid* before they fell asleep.

He couldn't stomach listening to that damn crab sing ever again. He could barely stomach eating crab after that night because all he could think about was that it might suddenly jump up and start into a version of *Under the Sea*.

They both chuckled over his 'wuss' moments until he felt the warmth coming from the symbiot that Morian was completely healed. "Let me get a fire going. I'll also see if I can catch us something to eat. How do you feel about fresh fish?" Paul asked, watching Morian's eyes droop in exhaustion.

"Wonderful," she murmured sleepily. "Would you mind if I rested for a little bit?"

"No," he replied, knowing that she didn't hear his quietly spoken words as she had already drifted off.

* * *

Paul spent the next hour and a half making their temporary shelter more secure and habitable. He was able to catch several large fish similar to river trout back home. He quickly filetted them out and had them roasting over the small fire he had built from the dried driftwood. He had to admit, being able to shift into a dragon made life a lot easier. He didn't need to make a spear or work at building a fire.

*Great,* his dragon snorted with a dry humor. *You use me as fishing pole and match.*

*Hell,* Paul chuckled. *You have to admit you do a great job as both.*

*Anything for my mate,* his dragon replied as Paul's eyes shifted back to where Morian was still sleeping. *She be alright?* His dragon asked in a hesitant voice.

*Yeah,* Paul said with a small smile, looking back to adjust their dinner in the coals of the fire. *It's been a long day. She was with Carmen first thing this morning, then the attack, then what that asshole did to her. She just needs some extra rest.* "I haven't exactly let her get much sleep either," he added in a rueful whisper as guilt washed over him.

He started when he felt a light hand on his shoulder. "I haven't complained," Morian said quietly before sitting next to him on the log he had pulled up near the fire.

Paul looked at his mate carefully. She looked…. Breathtaking. Her hair hung down around her waist, tousled from her sleep. Her eyes still held a hint of drowsiness, but the dark shadows were gone. Her

cheeks and lips were rosy and clear of the bruising
and cuts from earlier.

He leaned over and wrapped his hand in her hair,
pulling her forward. He paused to look deeply into
her eyes for a moment before he tenderly captured
her lips. He drank long and deep from her. He
needed her. He needed to touch her, taste her, hold
her and never let her go. He had come so close to
losing her today and it had scared the shit out of him.

"I love you, Morian," he said fiercely, pulling back
to look back down at her in the soft glow of the
firelight. "I don't ever want to come close to losing
you again," he murmured. "I can't live without you. I
don't want to."

Morian smiled and touched his lips tenderly with
the tips of her fingers before looking back up into his
eyes. "I love you too," she breathed. "What
happened? I saw you. I saw what Raffvin...." Her
voice faded as the dark memory came back. "There
was no way you could have survived such a wound."

Paul reluctantly pulled away and stood up. "Let
me dish up dinner and I'll tell you about the weirdest
damn dream I've ever had and maybe you can help
me understand everything that happened."

Morian nodded and watched as Paul pulled out
two thin sheets of slate that he had found. He had
lined each with large leaves. He carefully used a long
stick to pull the two leaf-wrapped bundles out from
the coals of the fire. She watched in fascination as he
unwrapped first one, then the other and placed a
large section of fish on each leaf-lined slate. He

opened up another leaf filled with different fruits that he had harvested from the forest above the river. He added it as a side.

"Bon appétit," Paul said with a grin as he handed one of the thin slates to Morian before sitting on the ground next to her with his own.

Morian settled the thin stone on her lap and pulled a piece of the hot meat off with her fingers. She was amazed at how tender and delicate it tasted. She was also surprised to find she was starving. She eagerly pulled more off, moaning as it practically melted on her tongue.

"This is good," she said with a surprised grin.

Paul chuckled as he popped a piece of fruit into his mouth. "I'm a much better open fire cook than I am a kitchen cook. Trisha used to beg me to take her camping just so she could have some 'real' home cooked food," he laughed as he leaned back against the log.

"Tell me what happened?" Morian asked softly as she picked up a piece of her fruit and nibbled on it.

Paul looked toward the entrance of the cave. He didn't want to sink into the comfort of staring into the fire. That was a mistake that many rookie soldiers did. Not only did it lure them into becoming comfortable, it took away their night vision. He knew the symbiot was positioned near the entrance of the cave right now, but he still didn't want to take a chance with the enemy still out there and them being outnumbered.

"I could still kick myself for not expecting Raffvin's attack but that would be useless," Paul said quietly as he reflected on the afternoon. "Instead, I'll learn from it. I didn't feel any pain at first," he admitted looking over at her for a moment before turning to gaze back out into the darkness. "My only focus was on you – getting you away from him."

Morian listened as Paul described what happened after the attack on him. A shiver of awe swept through her as she listened to him describe how the goddesses, Arosa and Arilla, came to him. He laughed quietly when he told her how he thought he was either in some Valdier version of heaven or hell.

"When I woke, I was in the form of a golden dragon," he added as he finished his tale. "I had been feeling like something was moving inside me for weeks. Now, I know what it was. I have to tell you, it is a pretty awesome feeling," Paul said, looking at Morian with a twinkle in his eye. "He is one horny son-of-a-bitch. All I've heard since he woke up inside me was he wanted you."

Morian set her empty slate on the ground next to the fire and stood up. "Really?" She asked with a curious tilt to her head. "Show him to me," she demanded.

Paul set his slate aside as well and stood up. "Are you sure?" He asked in a gruff voice. "I'm not sure if I'll be able to hold him back," he admitted in a rough voice.

"Who said anything about wanting you to?" Morian whispered as she slowly undid the ties holding her torn shirt on.

With a shrug of her shoulders, the soft cloth floated to the floor. Paul's swift intake of breath sounded loud in the cave. His eyes drifted down over her shoulders to her breasts that were lit by the dancing light from the fire.

The rosy tips were hard and swollen. They seemed to harden further as he stared at them with unashamed desire. Her hands moved down to the fastening on her pants. A dark rumble echoed through the cave as they joined her discarded shirt. She proudly stood nude in front of him.

"You see me," she whispered. "Now, show me you."

Paul moved away from the fire and closed his eyes briefly, calling for his dragon. Within seconds, a huge golden dragon stared at Morian with undisguised desire. His rich dark gold eyes followed every move she made from the flow of her hair swinging around her buttocks to the movement of her hands as she reached out to touch him.

His eyelids drooped as she ran a delicate hand over one of his nostrils. He reached around with his tail. Very gently, he ran the tip of it over her shoulder and down her back. At the last minute he flicked it, slapping her sharply on her ass.

"Oh!" She gasped at the sting before she felt the soothing touch of his tail rubbing it. "You are a very bad dragon," she moaned out as she felt the tip caress the dark line between her buttocks. "Very bad," she said hoarsely as the tail continued to move along the inside of her thigh. "I want to explore you as well," she admitted even as she leaned closer to the sharp teeth revealed by the dark smile.

Paul blew a light wave of heated breath over Morian's body. He wanted to taste her so bad it was almost like an unbearable craving for something sweet - forbidden. He flicked his tongue out and let the tip of it touch the side of her neck as she wrapped her arms around his head. The slightly salty-sweet taste just made the craving worse. His chest rumbled with heavy purrs as she traced the ridges above his eyes down the length of his jaw and back again.

"Grrr," he growled as her breast came up against his lips as she stood on the tips of her toes to reach the top of his ear. He ran his tongue up and over the swollen mound, letting the rough texture of his tongue lap her distended nipple.

"Paul," she shuddered. "My dragon needs you."

The answering rumble was the only warning, she got before her dragon pushed forward in answer to her mate's demand. Paul's tail and front claws wrapped around the white dragon suddenly standing in front of him. Her long neck was bent backwards exposing the tender flesh. The huge male struck quickly with only one thing on his mind... claiming his mate.

The hoarse cry echoed as the smaller female was held immobile as the larger male breathed his dragon's fire into her. Waves of fiery heat scorched her as he flooded her with a need… a desire… a love so fierce that the threads binding them together melded them as one being. The smaller female struggled as the heat built to a point that she wasn't sure she could survive it, but the male refused to release his hold on her, pulling her closer to his body instead.

*I can't,* Morian groaned as an intense hot wave broke over her leaving her trembling.

*You can,* Paul murmured in response as he continued to alternate between drinking the sweet, tangy taste of her blood and exchanging it with his essence.

After several long minutes, he released her neck. Brushing his tongue along the thick puncture wounds out of instinct, he lovingly traced the mark he had left. It was the first, but wouldn't be the last. He pulled back as she raised her head. Her long tongue came out and brushed against the curve of his lips. A deep growl escaped him as he released her with his front claws and used his tail to suddenly twist her around.

Her snarl faded to a startled squeal as he pushed her down until she was bent over. His tail slid down from her waist and wrapped around her tail as he jerked her up and mounted her swiftly. His only focus at this point was filling the smaller dragon under him with his essence.

He would mark her again so there was no mistaking who she belonged to. Pushing down with his broad chest against her back, he pulled her up by her tail and began moving – driving deeper and deeper into her.

*Mine!* His dragon snarled as he heard the whimper of his mate. *So good, my mate,* he groaned.

*Yes,* Morian's dragon whimpered as she tilted her hips so he could go even deeper. *Waited too long,* she cried out as she felt the first wave of heat washing through her pulling her closer to her orgasm. *More!* She begged as she tried to rock back into the driving shaft buried deep inside her.

The huge dragon grunted as he gripped her tail tighter and he leaned a little further forward, his front claws on each side of the smaller dragon's shoulders. His hips moved like a piston, moving with a speed and ferocity that pulled along the sensitive lining of the female's slick channel. His muffled roar shattered the heavy echo of pants in the dark cavern.

He pulsed deep as the female clutched him, pulling him deeper and locking him to her as she came with him. He turned his head clamping down on her shoulder at the curve above her wings. Her shudder pulled another orgasm out of them as her body reacted to the pleasure/pain of his bite.

The huge dragon reluctantly released his hold on the female, shuddering as the last of his seed pulsed into her. He would be locked to her for several long minutes before he could pull out of her. When he was able, he would take her again and again. His golden eyes turned toward the symbiot who was staring out at the night.

The image of a clear starry sky was returned to his silent question. *Our mates,* the symbiot sent. *We protect our mates,* it sighed.

Paul's dragon nodded his head once in agreement. *We protect our mates,* he responded.

# Chapter 16

"Where is she!" Raffvin roared as he flipped the table, scattering left over food everywhere in the center tent. "She was bound! She was in the middle of a camp filled with warriors! There is no way she can just have vanished," he snarled as he turned to look at the three men who were in charge of the warriors.

"Tracks were found leading from the outer rim of the forest into the camp," the large Sarafin male said staring with shuttered eyes at Raffvin.

Raffvin turned to look coldly at the warrior. A scar ran down the left side of his face from the corner of his eye to the corner of his mouth. "What kind of tracks?" Raffvin asked in a frigid tone.

"Dragon tracks," the male responded with a shrug. "No one saw a thing. It was as if the dragon was invisible. The tracks lead to where a table of food was knocked over and one of the warriors swore something tripped him but he didn't see a thing."

"The body of a Marastin Dow was found in one of the supply tents. His neck broken. Puncture wounds from a dragon's claws in his throat," the Valdier warrior added dispassionately. "It was only feet from where a large group of warriors were."

Raffvin's eyes narrowed as he listened to the information. He cursed as he tried to think how a full grown dragon could sneak through their defenses. How did Morian escape the symbiot bindings? He had ordered it to slice her hands from her body if she tried to escape. He had absolute control over his symbiot. He reached up and grabbed his head with one hand as it began to pound. His dragon snarled at the loss of the female. It was fighting him more and more. He fought to hold onto the little bit of sanity he had but it was becoming harder and harder. He needed to find the Hive. He needed more of the God's blood. It would heal him. He and his dragon could not survive much longer without it. An evil grin curved his lips as a new plan began to form in his fractured mind.

"Fine," he growled out in a dark voice. Turning, he looked at the men standing in front of him. "There is another way to get what I want," he said as a malevolent smile curled his lips. "If the Priestess won't guide me to the Hive then her oldest son will."

The huge Marastin Dow warrior looked skeptical. "How do you propose that? By asking him?" He asked with a cynical look.

Raffvin's grin turned so ugly that all three men took a step back and looked at him warily. "Once I have his infant son, he will do whatever I tell him to do. It will give me great joy to crush his son's head between my hands," Raffvin laughed out insanely. "It will give me even more pleasure watching Zoran's face as I do it."

The Valdier warrior and Marastin Dow chuckled darkly while the Sarafin Warrior stared at the dark face before him coldly. He had no problem fighting a warrior who could defend himself, but even he had to draw a line when it came to using children. He wisely kept that thought to himself.

* * *

Paul stared out the entrance of the cavern. His body felt totally sated. He no longer had the aching feeling of emptiness he had when he was back on Earth. He felt – complete, whole. It was the first time in his life that he could remember feeling that way.

He had been happy – even content with Evelyn but there had still been a restlessness in him. He thought it was because he had been young and ambitious to provide for his family, but he realized now it was more than that. Even after her death, and as he grew older, the restlessness and emptiness continued to plague him.

He rubbed his chin against the dark hair of his mate. She lay tucked safely in his arms. He had loved her hard and fast and slowly and tenderly throughout the night. It was as if he couldn't get enough of her. His hand moved lovingly over her side, his fingers brushing over one of the many marks he had left on her.

This one was on her right hip. They had made love in both forms so many times he had lost count. It often depended on which form was more demanding at the time.

"I think I have a matching mark on my other hip," Morian murmured as she rolled over to lay on his chest. "I think I have about a dozen or so of them, in fact," she added with a twitch of her lips.

Paul rose up far enough to give her a quick peck on the lips. "I wouldn't complain if I were you," he whispered with a fierce look. "I bet I could count that many on my own body."

Morian blushed as a husky laugh escaped her. "I bet you could," she retorted with a quick kiss of her own. "I need a bath," she said as she rolled off him and sat up on the golden bed.

Paul's eyes darkened as he thought about how he had used the symbiot to hold Morian down last night. He was going to have to remember that for future use. Right now, the thin cover it had created over them dissolved back into the bed, leaving her body bare to his gaze.

"My body isn't the only one bare," she whispered before she quickly rose off the golden bed with a chuckle when he reached for her again. "Bath and food," she teased before her smile dissolved like the cover. "Then, we need to return to the palace. I want to let my sons know I am safe and I need to make sure they are as well."

Paul released a disgruntled sigh as he rose off the bed. As soon as he did, the symbiot shifted into a Were Cat again and shook. Waves of gold shimmered and rolled before it trotted over to the entrance of the cavern. Paul stretched his arms above his head and rolled his shoulders, laughing as Morian's eyes remained glued to his body as he did.

"Bath, then food," he reminded her as he reached over and pulled her against his body. "When this is over, I want to bring you back here," he said as he ran his hands under her hair and along her back.

Morian rested her head against his chest as he hugged her. "I want to take you to my hidden home," she murmured. "Not even Raffvin has been there. It belonged to my family long before I knew Jalo and Raffvin. Only my sons know about it."

Paul let her go, threading his fingers with hers as he pulled her toward the back of the cave. "I look forward to going there with you," Paul said as he guided her toward the shallow pool of water. "There is a small area back here where the water flows through a crack. We can bathe there. I'll warm it for us," he said before he released her hand and shifted into his dragon.

The huge golden dragon bent over the small pool of water and breathed a steady flow of blue flame at the water until it bubbled and steam rose from it. Once he was confident it was warm, he turned and raised his eyebrows up and down at Morian before sticking his tail in the water and swirling it around to mix the hot and cold water. He turned and blew a little more blue flame before he was satisfied. With a wink, he shifted back and swept a giggling Morian up into his arms.

"Madam," Paul said formerly, stepping down into the shallow pool. "Your bath awaits you."

Morian fluttered her eyelashes up at him, trying to hide the smile pulling at the corner of her mouth. "Are you always so chivalrous?" She asked as the warm water swirled around her.

"Only with you," he said quietly. "You fill me up, Morian. I feel whole when I touch you. I've felt so empty for so long," he told her in a low voice. "I don't ever want to be empty again."

Morian gazed at him with love shining through her dark golden eyes. "Neither do I."

\* \* \*

After their bath, they ate a quick meal of fresh fruit before they departed. Paul shifted as soon as he was outside of the cave and scanned the area thoroughly before he sent a message to Morian's symbiot. Morian had balked at first about riding in the skimmer her symbiot formed, but finally gave in when she realized it was too dangerous for both of them if they were caught. Inside the skimmer, her symbiot could vanish the same way as Paul did. He would fly alongside them so he could survey the area more closely as they went.

The trip proved to be surprisingly uneventful. Paul had taken a brief detour to fly over the encampment in the meadow only to find it empty. Raffvin had smartly moved his base camp. Paul wasn't stupid enough to believe they had heard the last of him.

The feeling in his gut made sure that he didn't let his guard down. Paul made a brief search of the area. He frowned as he noticed an unusual mark on the ground. It was almost like someone had left a marker.

He circled around the area several times, his sharp eyes looking for any signs of a trap. Once he felt confident that the area was indeed abandoned, he glided down to land near the suspicious marker he had noticed from the air. As he walked over the area, he paused several times to glance around.

*I no like this,* his dragon growled. *You should no shift. It too dangerous.*

*I need to see what is under the marker. Someone went to a lot of trouble to leave something behind. Something they wanted found,* he said calmly. *Just be ready in case I need to shift back and get the hell out of here in a hurry.*

*Let me sniff first,* his dragon insisted. *I see if anything dangerous left. You not look good in pieces if it go boom.*

Paul shook his head at the image his dragon formed of his body scattered in little, bloody pieces all over the field. *I hate to tell you this, mate, you and I are one. If I get blown to smithereens then so do you.*

*Great! Just great!* His dragon growled out. *Get mate and get balls blown off. Not what I want.*

*Me either, dude,* Paul laughed as he let his dragon take a sniff to make sure it couldn't smell any explosives.

*Nothing,* his dragon said, looking around once more before he let Paul take over and shift into his two-legged form.

Paul knelt down and carefully observed the rock with the strange mark on it. It was as if a cat had raked his claws across it, but in both directions, making an X that could be seen clearly from the air.

This told him that whoever was here expected someone to return. Paul looked around for a long stick. He found one a short distance away and walked over to grab it. He returned back to the rock and reached out, turning it over with a wince when it thudded as it toppled over. Under the rock was a small piece of fabric with one name written on it. He bent over and gingerly picked it up.

Paul's eyes narrowed dangerously. Even though it was written in a language he didn't understand yet, he did recognize what the symbols of the Valdier language meant. He had seen it many times. It was the name of a future king – Zohar.

Paul cursed as he realized that the palace wasn't the only one with a traitor in it. Raffvin had one in his camp as well. With a curse, he shifted back into his dragon form and lifted up. Moving on powerful wings, he soon caught up with the symbiot that had slowed while it waited for his return. He sent a swift mental image showing the need to return to the palace as quickly as possible.

"Paul, what is it?" Morian asked as they flew. "I know something is wrong, I can sense it."

Paul sent an image to the symbiot of his discovery that was quickly related to Morian. He felt both of their shock and her fear. He also conveyed that they had someone working on their side to warn them.

"Thank you," Morian said as she sent a wave of warmth to Paul.

She wanted him to know how much it meant to her that he let her know what was happening. Jalo had always protected and shielded her from what was going on. She had loved that he was so protective of her but she had also felt frustrated. She wanted to be his partner in every sense of the word. Yes, she knew she could never have been his true mate but she could be his partner. He never shared with her the political side of the royal house that was formed. Even during the Great War between the Sarafin, Curizan and Valdier. He never consulted with her how she would feel about forcing Zoran's child into an alliance with the Sarafin. The forced marriage between Zoran's future daughter and the future son of Vox had been repulsive to her for the simple fact she knew what it was like to be forced into a match not of her choice. True, it had worked out, but she had also seen times when it had not.

Paul was showing he would not hold information back from her. She was his partner in every sense of the word. He would not try to hide things from her simply because he thought it might be too much for her.

A wave of warmth flooded her as his dragon communicated with her symbiot. The images showed her having to deal with the grown kids when he snuck off with the little ones to teach them how to survive in the woods, especially Trelon. Morian's laughter filled the symbiot skimmer as he sent all kinds of other things he could do so she could help him deal with the consequences.

"It will be hard to deal with it if I am your accomplice in all these crimes," she responded happily. "Get us home, Paul. We need to warn Zoran and the others."

The increase in speed showed that Paul was pouring everything he had into getting them back in time. Paul reluctantly realized that the golden skimmer could travel much faster than he could. With a swift command, he swerved toward the skimmer shifting at the last minute as it opened for him. He felt the golden bands wrap around him as they steadied him from colliding with the other side of it.

"Go!" He ordered even as a seat formed under him next to Morian.

Morian reached for his hand as they were pressed back against the back of the seat as the golden symbiot put on a burst of speed that was just shy of being deadly. It knew better than to use its full ability within the confines of the atmosphere as it could disrupt it with deadly consequences. No symbiot would ever endanger the Valdier or the Hive in that way, not even Raffvin's black bands would as it would destroy itself as well as its other halves.

"Do you think the message really means Raffvin is going after Zohar?" Morian asked fearfully.

Paul squeezed Morian's hand in reassurance. "Yes," he said heavily. "I've seen men back on Earth do the same. In some countries, the children are used for ransom. If the parents are hesitant or refuse to pay, the men send the children back – one piece at a time," he added grimly.

Morian shook her head and looked out at the rapidly passing terrain. "Then we must make sure that does not happen," she responded with a hard edge to her voice.

"That's my girl," Paul grinned at her. "Do you know how sexy you sound when you are pissed off?" He asked with a teasing smile.

She rolled her eyes. "How can you not be upset about this?" She asked curiously looking at him even as the palace came into view in the distance.

Paul grinned even larger showing his suddenly longer canines. "Because I've never lost when I am hunting," he said with a confident and deadly glint in his eye. "I'm going to kill Raffvin. It isn't so much if as when. If he even tries to harm one hair on any of my boys' children, I'll gut him where he stands."

Morian's eyes lit up with love at the reference to her children being referred to as 'his boys'. "I'll be right next to you, helping you," she promised.

Paul nodded as they came in for a landing in the middle of the courtyard that had been cleaned of the fight from the day before. It was hard to believe that so much had occurred in such a short period of time. Guards came out in force as the symbiot reappeared. Paul stepped out first, turning to hold his hand out for Morian as she stepped out into the opening.

"*Dola!*" Mandra yelled with a laugh, running down the steps of the palace. He pulled her away from Paul giving her a bear hug. "Ariel said he would find you and bring you home! I knew he would as well. I have fought against him."

"You big ox," Ariel said, smacking Mandra on the ass. "Put her down before you squish her."

Mandra gently put his mother down before swinging around and picking his mate up with a low growl. "I warned you what would happen if you smacked me there again," he muttered.

Ariel threaded her fingers through his long hair and pulled his face to within a few inches of hers. "You know you love it," she whispered with a wink. "Now, let's get into the house – palace – whatever in the hell you call that thing," she said with a sigh. "I miss our little place in the mountains," she added.

Mandra turned with an apologetic glance at his mother. "Welcome home, *Dola*. I'm happy you are safe," he said before he headed toward the entrance. "I told you," he responded in a low voice to Ariel's sigh, "we will return once the threat has been taken care of. I will not risk your life or our unborn youngling's life while Raffvin is alive," he growled out.

Morian looked at Paul who was nodding. "Where is Zoran?" Paul asked as they entered the huge open foyer. "I need to speak with all of you," he said grimly.

Mandra glanced over his shoulder at the hard edge in Paul's voice. "I will call a meeting. He went to check on Abby, who was visiting with those who were injured. It was not just warriors that were injured during the attack. Many of those in the city were also hurt. Abby insisted on visiting with them."

"How many were killed?" Morian asked in a worried voice.

Mandra held Ariel closer to his body as he thought of those lost yesterday. "Seventy," he said gruffly. "Most by falling debris from buildings."

Morian nodded and lowered her head as tears filled her eyes at such a waste of life caused by a man who should have been protecting them. She looked up when Paul slid his arm around her. She nodded to his unspoken question if she was alright. She pulled her shoulders back and walked with her head held high. She was the Priestess for the Hive and the Queen Mother to the ruler of Valdier. She would not show weakness in front of her people.

"I'm so proud of you," Paul murmured for her ears only. "We'll kill the bastard."

"As Carmen would say, you're damn right we will," Morian responded as they swept into the conference room.

Mandra lowered Ariel down near the table. Leaning over, he pressed the viewscreen. Almost immediately, images of each brother appeared. Paul shook his head at the technology available on this world. He couldn't help but think that if he ever returned to Earth it would seem even stranger to him now than this world had at first.

"Zoran," Paul said as the leader of Valdier appeared. "We need to meet at once."

Zoran gazed over Paul's shoulder. His lips curved in a satisfied smile when he saw his mother standing slightly behind him. His eyes turned back to stare at Paul with a look of respect and gratitude.

"Five minutes," he responded with a curt nod.

# Chapter 17

Paul was surprised when several men he had never seen before arrived with Zoran and the others. His eyes narrow suspiciously as he watched them. At this point, he didn't trust anyone but the brothers. He waited with a grim stare until introductions were made.

Zoran nodded for everyone to sit. Paul watched as Morian murmured to her oldest son before she left the room with Ariel. The two women decided it was better to leave the men to discuss what was going on. Paul knew what Morian was really going to do. She was going to tell the women what they had found. She wanted to make sure the little ones were safe and surrounded by their mothers and their symbiots while the men worked on a plan to capture Raffvin.

"Paul," Zoran called out. "I would like to introduce you to some of the most experienced and deadly warriors in the known galaxies," he said with a grin.

"Don't forget the best looking," Ha'ven drawled out with a roll of his eyes.

"Everyone knows the Curizans all look alike," Calo chuckled, earning him a handful of fingers.

"Shit! You guys have been hanging around human females, haven't you?" Cree said with a disgruntled look at his twin and a tired sigh.

"Your mate hasn't used it on you, has she?" Kor asked Cree in surprise. "She seems like such a polite little thing. Not that either one of you would never deserve it," he added with a snicker.

Calo snorted as Cree scowled back at the huge Valdier tracker. "Go fuck yourself," Cree grunted out.

"Oh yeah," Adalard laughed. "I just bet both of them have heard that more than once from her. I heard tell from your cousins that she is giving you both a bit of difficulty. Are you two having a hard time keeping up with her?" He asked with a grin.

Calo threw the small knife he had in his hand at Adalard who caught it with a flick of his wrists. "You're getting slow old man," Adalard chuckled. "I think the little human female has tired you out."

"Enough!" Creon growled as he leaned forward. "Adalard, if you aren't careful you are going to end up with another scar to match the one on your face. Let's get back to business," he growled out looking at Zoran who raised his eyebrow at his younger brother. "The babies didn't sleep well last night," Creon muttered before sitting back in his seat.

Trelon grunted out in empathy. "Mine never do," he muttered. "They escaped again last night. They are up to something new."

Ha'ven rolled his eyes. "This is why I never want to find a mate. It turns a man…."

"…. Into a man," Paul said, standing up. "Especially when their young are in danger," he stated looking intently at each man sitting at the table. "I found a message hidden at Raffvin's deserted camp. It was left on purpose. There is someone in the camp helping us," he said, looking at Zoran now.

"What did the message say and do you know who might be helping us?" Zoran asked reaching for the piece of cloth that Paul held out. Zoran's eyes darkened to a thunderous gold color as his eyes snapped back up to Paul's grim ones.

"He is one of my men," Vox said as he strode into the room.

Half the table of men rose as another warrior walked into the room. Loud curses filled the room before Ha'ven began to laugh. Soon, all the men were stepping up and slapping the huge man on the back with bone breaking thumps. Paul watched with wry amusement.

*Yes, this is worse than having the Seals and Marines doing a survival competition,* he thought with a weary sigh as he sat back in his seat.

Paul cleared his throat nosily to get everyone back on track. "Gentlemen, we have a situation that needs to be dealt with," he said calmly. "Vox, is it?" Paul waited until the male turned to look at him coldly. "Can you tell us if we can trust the man you say is yours?"

"Who are you?" Vox asked, sniffing loudly before he frowned in confusion. "You look and smell human, but there is another smell on you."

A chorus of smothered chortles met his statement. Zoran sighed and sat down with a wave of his hand. "He is – was – human. He is *Dola's* true mate," Zoran informed the spotted male who sat down across from Paul.

"Hey Vox," Palto called out, teasingly. "Have you killed any more jackets lately?"

Paul could feel the room about to explode into another wave of comradely laughter. He looked at Zoran with a shake of his head, unable to hide the smile curving his lips. His eyes danced with mirth as he listened as the group started asking how mated life was for him. There was one warrior sitting off to the side who did not join in. His eyes looked sad, withdrawn as he watched his friends.

"Paul?" Zoran called out again.

Paul pulled his eyes away from the warrior and looked back at the other men who were suddenly completely serious. They had finished picking on each other and were ready to get back to business. The expressions on their faces told they were more than capable of dealing with the fight that was to come. Each man had scars. Some wore them on the outside like Adalard and others on the inside like the warrior sitting off to the side.

Paul cleared his throat. "Gentlemen, the women and children are in danger. Raffvin needs to be stopped. Here is what I propose doing to kill the bastard once and for all....."

Over the next several hours, Paul outlined his plan with input from all the warriors at the table. His confidence that the reign of terror was about to come to an end grew as the warriors around him offered suggestions, defined where they would be stationed, and how best to ensure the women and children would be kept safe at all cost.

\* \* \*

Morian's heart swelled with love as the women she thought of as her daughters surrounded her. She laughed with them as they asked her if she had kicked any ass and shed a tear when she told them about discovering that her true mate was not dead after all.

"So, Raffvin is still alive," Carmen said in a calm voice. "What is the plan?"

Morian looked at the daughter she had worried the most about. She looked tired this morning, but that was to be expected after just having twins. She was currently nursing her oldest daughter, Spring. The girls might have been twins, but they were as opposite as night and day. Morian looked at the dark haired infant Ariel held protectively against her. The babe turned her head and looked at Morian with eyes far older than what they should have been. Morian drew in a shuddering breath before she looked away in confusion.

"Morian," Abby said softly. "Are you alright? Do you need to lay down for a little while?"

Morian smiled up at Abby. She was indeed a true queen for the Valdier. Her soft, caring manner, her compassion, and her strength were what their people needed. She shook her head and glanced back at Phoenix who was now sleeping peacefully. That little one had some surprise hidden deep inside her, Morian could feel it.

"We need to plan," she said, looking at the group of young women. "Raffvin plans to use Zohar to force Zoran to take him to the Hive," she explained.

"I say we let him try to get his hands on our kids," Cara said with a low growl. "I'll show him was it really means to have a stick up his ass."

"I think we should go after him, use the element of surprise," Carmen suggested. "Do we have any idea where he might be hiding?"

"What do Zoran and the others say?" Abby asked, pouring a cup of tea and handing it to Morian before scooping Zohar up protectively in her arms.

Morian looked at Abby's pale complexion and knew she had been right to inform the women of what was going on. Despite the obvious fear, there was a look of determination that nothing would harm her child. Morian sipped her tea and contemplated what could be done.

"What if we give him what he wants?" Trisha suggested, discreetly shifting Bálint to her other breast.

"Are you crazy?" Cara asked, grabbing Amber up as she tried to crawl up Abby's leg to get to Zohar who was grinning down at her. "Jade, don't eat Tigger, sweetheart," she admonished as Jade laid on her back with her gold symbiot in her mouth.

Morian looked at Trisha for several moments before she slowly nodded. "Why don't we?" She murmured. "Trisha, you and Carmen have the most experience with situations like this. Tell us what you are thinking."

Trisha grinned. "Probably the same thing as my dad. Raffvin is insane, but that doesn't mean he isn't smart. So, do the unexpected. Draw him out away from here and take him exactly where he wants to go. Only when he gets there, we capture him," she explains.

Carmen nodded in agreement. "That would work. It would also draw him away from any larger population that he might use against us like he did yesterday to steal Morian away," she said looking at Morian. "Is it possible to do it?"

Morian looked at her symbiot who was curled up near the windows. It rose and came to her. She gently laid her hand along its head, closed her eyes and opened her mind. The answer she sought was quick. She opened her eyes in surprise as the Hive Queen gave her one last instruction.

"The answer is yes," Morian replied, looking at all the women who were waiting for her to respond. "But, it must be only Paul and myself that lead him. I will not risk any of you or the children."

Carmen shrugged her shoulders. "Well, I guess that leaves the rest of his miserable followers for us to beat the crap out of," she said with a devilish grin. "I was needing to work some of this baby fat off."

Ariel looked at the body of her slender sister and rolled her eyes. "Whatever!" She grumbled.

* * *

Morian ignored the glaring looks and deep snarls later that night. Trisha was right about her idea, Paul had already presented one almost identical to the men. They were not happy about using their *Dola, as* bait, but they conceded that it was better than using one of the babies.

Morian would sneak out of the palace and pretend that she wanted to make a deal with Raffvin. She would take him to the location of the Hive if he promised to let her family live. Paul would be by her side the entire time in the shape of his dragon. Her symbiot would be waiting for them at the entrance to the Hive. None of the men liked the idea of allowing Morian to be in danger but Paul was confident she could handle herself after he spent the rest of the afternoon showing her defensive moves. The exercises she did when she was younger, and still practiced when she was alone, took him by surprise. She admitted to having studied the younger warriors as they trained when she was a child and often watched Zoran and her other sons, even now.

"I liked being able to do the same moves that they did," she admitted as they moved to sit down at the long table. "I wanted to be a warrior, remember?"

"You are a warrior, darling," Paul said as he rubbed the bruise on his forearm. "You knocked the crap out of me more than once today."

Morian giggled and blushed at the compliment. Paul had not been easy on her. He had pushed her beyond anything she had ever expected. He told her it didn't matter if she was a woman or a man, if her life was in danger she was the one who needed to know how to not only defend herself but defeat her opponent.

"Always study his weakness," Paul had told her as he knocked her off her feet for the tenth time. "You always lead in with your right foot. Change it up.

Don't let your opponent know which side is your weakest one. Make both of them just as strong," he growled out over and over.

Morian climbed to her feet and moved swiftly at him, striking with one arm then switching to the other. Rotating on her heel and approaching from a different side over and over again until she was finally able to knock Paul on his ass. He had jumped up and attacked her again and again. Each time he would give her instructions on how to improve a blow or to escape one. Her muscles had been sore and she had been bruised but her symbiot quickly healed her so she could continue.

Paul looked along the table. He had to admit he had come to feel at home among the large warriors. Next to most of them were the smaller forms of their mates.

He took his time observing each of the human women who had been brought back to Valdier. He had a feeling that his "they must say yes first" rule had been stretched more than a few times looking at some of the defiant faces that were scowling back at the huge males who were doing everything they could to make the women happy.

There were three women in particular that he was concerned about. One was a small, dark haired girl sitting between the twin brothers he had met earlier. What concerned him was the wrist cuffs and gold chains attached to each of her wrists. Identical chains were attached to each brothers' wrist.

The only thing holding him back was the fact that the woman seemed to be holding her own. Every time one of the brothers went to take a drink or eat with the hand chained to her, she would jerk it making them drop or spill what they had in their hand, then shrug as if she didn't realize she was doing it.

His gaze moved to the other two women. They sat side by side. One of the women had long blonde hair that reached almost to her waist while the other had shorter blonde hair that reached past her shoulder blades.

The one sitting next to the warrior called Jaguin was looking down at her plate with a tense expression on her face. She shook her head when he tried to place food on it. The other one sat with a blank expression on her face. Her complexion was pale, almost translucent. He could tell she had beautiful blue eyes, but there was nothing in them to show she was aware of her location. She ignored everything going on around her.

"What is wrong with those two women?" Paul asked Morian in a low, husky voice.

Morian glanced down the table where the two women were sitting. Her eyes softened with concern as she observed them. Both women had been rescued from the man responsible for killing Carmen's husband and unborn child.

The man had been taking his revenge out on them since he could not find Carmen. Each had sustained serious physical and mental torture before they were rescued. Morian knew the one sitting next to Jaguin was his true mate. He refused to leave her for long. Her heart broke for the young warrior because she knew he would do whatever it took to help the young woman if she would let him.

Morian explained this to Paul knowing he was deeply upset about what happened. "No one knows much about the other female. She has not spoken to anyone since she woke up. She eats, she sleeps, and except for Sara, she won't let anyone else near her. Even Abby hasn't been able to break through her silence," Morian said, looking back at the small female. "Oh my," she whispered.

Paul looked back down the table and noticed that Ha'ven had taken a seat next to the woman. His jaw was tense as he placed food on her plate for her before filling his own. He held up a piece of meat to her lips, but the woman turned her head away in rejection of it.

Paul watched as Ha'ven tried several different items to entice the female to eat before he picked up a piece of fruit and held it in front of her lips. He leaned over and whispered something in her ear. For the first time, Paul saw a glimpse of fire in her eyes before it disappeared.

She pushed back her chair and rose. The female sitting next to her started to rise as well, but the smaller one laid her hand on her shoulder and shook her head before walking out of the room. A moment later, Ha'ven excused himself and left the room.

Paul could tell the female identified as Jaguin's mate had been surprised at the response. She watched the other girl leave before turning to look back at her plate, a small smile forming on her lips. Jaguin's hand disappeared under the table and he saw the blond start in surprise before she relaxed and used her free hand to pick up a piece of bread, slowly chewing on it.

# Chapter 18

"You will protect her with your life," Trelon bit out harshly to Paul. "Do not let her out of your sight."

"Do you have the knives I gave you?" Kelan asked anxiously to his mother. "Abby sewed special sleeves for them so they should be easy to access, but impossible to see."

"Do you remember the moves that Paul showed you in case you get in trouble?" Mandra asked, biting his lower lip like he did when he was a boy and worried about something.

"Just get the hell out of there as soon as you can if there is trouble," Zoran stated bluntly looking with worried eyes at both Paul and his mother. "Are you sure you can do this?" He asked Paul under his breath.

Paul gave Zoran a grin that made him swallow back a muttered oath. *Yes, Paul could handle it*, Zoran thought as he saw the man who had 'tagged' him and his brothers on more than one occasion during their trainings. Zoran didn't insult the man who was as deadly an opponent as he had ever encountered by asking again. Instead, he turned to look at Vox who was leaning against the wall near the door.

"Your man is sure that Raffvin will be coming?" Zoran asked the Sarafin leader and one of Creon's closest friends.

"He says he'll be there, then he'll be there," Vox said confidently. "I know the man personally. He is trustworthy."

"How can you be sure?" Zoran asked skeptically. "Raffvin has bought a lot of loyalty."

"He can't buy Blaze," Creon said as he watched his mother check the weapons she had hidden on her one last time.

"How do you know?" Zoran insisted. "I don't like trusting *Dola's* safety to an unknown warrior that has been in the service of Raffvin for the last ten years."

Creon looked at his older brother before he looked at Vox who gave a brief nod. "Blaze is Vox's brother. He has been working on finding the traitors involved on the Sarafin side. He and Vox decided he needed to join with Raffvin to locate who tried to kill his adoptive parents," Creon said reluctantly.

"Won't he be recognized?" Mandra asked, looking at Vox who had moved to stand next to Creon.

"No," Vox said bluntly.

"Why?" Kelan and Trelon asked at the same time.

Vox turned to look at the men in the room with a dark look. "Because everyone believes he died when he was a youngling. Including my parents," Vox replied. "I can tell you no more than that and the information should not leave this room."

Zoran stared at the Sarafin King before he bowed his head in acknowledgement. "Very well," he responded quietly. "I will trust your judgement."

Vox grinned. "Hell, I wish I could get Riley to trust me as easily. She is still cursing my ass for getting her pregnant. She swears she is having a litter of wild cats. I keep telling her there is just the one in her belly," he said.

"You will have to bring her to visit after the babe is born," Morian said with a smile. "He might enjoy playing with the others and I would love to meet your mate."

Vox sighed and rubbed the back of his neck. "She wanted to come, but I feared placing her in danger with her being so far along. Her sister and Grandma Pearl...." Vox shuddered as he said the last name. "That female can be scary..... Anyway, both are with her as well."

"It's time to go," Paul said, sliding his hand along Morian's back. "Are you ready?"

Morian turned and looked at her mate. "Let's go kick some ass," she responded with a determined grin.

"Aw shit," Kelan muttered with a groan. "She's been hanging around the girls way too much."

All the men chuckled, knowing they were just trying to cover up their own reservations about letting Morian participate in a fight that could end tragically for any one of them. The men had to threaten to tie up all the other women and place them in the dungeon if they so much as left the hidden cavern under the palace. They were to stay there with the children until the men returned.

"Let's go," Zoran said with a nod to Vox. "Your ships are ready for those in orbit?"

"Of course," Vox responded as he turned to Kelan. "The *V'ager* is ready?"

"As is the *D'stroyer*," Mandra said, moving to stand next to his brother. "We will give you the coverage you need to destroy the Marastin Dow ships that the radars picked up entering our Star System. They will think we are just completing maintenance at the Space docks and an easy target."

"Viper has the *Shifter* in position with several other of our warships," Vox assured him. "Creon, where is Ha'ven?"

"I'm here," Ha'ven scowled coming in. "I have the shields in place. Nothing can get into the palace without us knowing. I designed the damn thing myself. Just do me a favor?" He asked, looking specifically at Trelon.

"What's that?" Trelon asked even as his lips twitched as he knew the answer.

"Keep your damn mate away from it!" Ha'ven said with a sigh. "She has already been driving me nuts trying to get to it."

Trelon grinned as he thought of Cara's endless questions. "I'll do the best I can but you know what she is like," he replied as he imagined coming back to see the shield turned into a big disco ball or some other such device.

"Zoran, we'll meet you inside the Hive," Paul said quietly. "Good luck, men."

Each man bowed their head and placed their fist over their heart. "Fight well, live for another day," Ha'ven said quietly.

"Live for our mates," Kelan added.

* * *

Paul watched as Morian moved with her elegant grace toward the edge of the terrace where a small wall separated it from the cliff. Vox's brother, Blaze, had contacted Vox to let him know that Raffvin was about to make his move. It was a bold and daring one.

Raffvin was going to use his knowledge of the palace to use seldom used passages to sneak in and take Zohar. He knew the areas of weakness of the palace. What he would not expect was that Paul had also reviewed the layout and marked them.

Paul was able to view the palace from a fresh viewpoint. There were thick woods along one edge of the huge terrace area with plants providing coverage along the other side. The original blueprint of the palace showed there was a hidden door along the wall leading down to the ocean far below. A narrow path on the other side of the door led down to a cave entrance just above the breaking waves of the ocean far below.

It was too narrow for a skimmer or other spacecraft to land, but it was large enough for a dragon to get close to and a man in his two-legged form to jump to, much like he did on the boulders on the river. It would be tricky and far more dangerous, but it was possible. Paul had practiced it several times to see if it could be done.

It was decided that Morian would be in his way, presenting him with the perfect opportunity to take her instead. She would offer a small resistance before offering him a plea deal. To make her appear less threatening, she had insisted on wearing one of the gowns she normally reserved for her Prietess ceremonies. She not only looked beautiful, but fragile and ethereal. It would be hard for Raffvin to see her as a threat, at least that was what Paul was hoping as he felt his stomach tighten at the thought of all that could go wrong.

*Be safe, my love,* Paul thought silently as he shifted into his dragon and flew to the top of one of the trees overlooking the terrace.

Morian stopped at the small wall and stared out at the brilliant ocean laid out before her. Her thoughts turning to everything that had happened since Paul came into her life. He had given her the strength to believe in herself as an individual again. She felt young, strong, and brave.

She smiled as she thought of how she felt when she was a young girl. She closed her eyes and turned her face to the waning sun as it started to settle on the horizon. She felt like she could fly up and touch the stars. Maybe she would ask Kelan to take her to them. She had never left Valdier before. She would like to see what the other worlds were like.

*I will take you,* a soft male voice echoed in her mind.

Morian had to force herself to remain still as she felt Paul's voice in her mind. She was wearing teardrop earrings of gold and the traditional gold necklace and headband. While he was in his dragon form, her symbiot had refused to leave him defenseless.

It had created the normal body armor around his head, chest, and legs. The brilliant ruby necklace was blended into the chest plate. A shiver went through her as she remembered seeing what he looked like earlier.

"So beautiful," a harsh voice rasped out from behind her drawing a startled gasp from her.

Morian turned so quickly that she lost her balance and fell against the wall. Raffvin reached out and snared her arm in a hard grasp. He shook his head. His lank, dirty hair swinging back and forth.

"I would hate to see such beauty wasted on the rocks below," he murmured, letting his hand move up her arm to her throat. "But then, you could always shift into your dragon," he muttered.

"I haven't shifted in so long I can no longer feel my dragon," Morian lied in a trembling voice as his fingers tightened around her throat. "I sometimes believe I dreamed I could shift."

"But you have a true mate," Raffvin spit out. "You have felt the Dragon's Fire. You have been given the power to transform."

"No… o, I told you, I cannot shift," she whispered as his fingers began to squeeze. "My mate is human. He does not have the Dragon's Fire to give me."

"But he lives," Raffvin said more than asked. "He should have died. How did he live?"

"Ple… plea… please," she whispered as her vision began to grow dark as he began to cut off her oxygen. "I can't breathe," she stuttered as she swayed.

Raffvin loosened his hold enough for her to draw in a swift breath. "Don't try to scream. I'll slice your throat before you get a sound out," he said, letting one of his fingers shift until a sharp, dark claw pressed against her skin. "Your mate lives?"

"Yes," she whispered. "Barely. He is very weak. The wound does not close all the way. We are waiting to see if a new device the Curizans have developed will heal him. If he dies, so do I."

Raffvin paused as he heard the trembling in her voice. He tilted his head. A cruel smile curved his lips as he thought for several moments. He leaned forward, rubbing his nose against her jaw.

"I could give you what you need to save him – for a price," he hissed in her ear.

Morian would have pulled back if not for the tight hold on her neck. "How?" She begged in a strangled whispered. "How can you save him? What would you want in return?"

Raffvin pulled back and wrapped his other arm around her waist. "I can remove the blackness that keeps the wound open. Although, I suspect you already know how to remove it. You removed it from your wrists when I had you before. How did you escape from the camp, Morian?" He demanded pulling her against his body. "Tell me how you escaped the bands and the camp."

Morian started to struggle, her eyes moving to the tall tree where Paul stood perched. She knew he would come to her in a heartbeat, but she also knew he wouldn't be able to reach her before Raffvin killed her. She could feel the sharp claws through the thin material of her gown. He could sever her spine, pierce her heart, or slit her throat. These were all wounds that would be impossible to repair in time to save her life.

She licked her suddenly dry lips. "I am the Priestess of the Hive," she replied. "Even the black symbiot cannot deny a request if presented correctly. It was hurting. I was able to draw the essence hurting it into myself," she lied.

"How did you escape?" He asked harshly as he cursed his lack of planning for her power over the symbiot.

"I…. I used my symbiot," she said, thinking quickly. "I called it to me. I had it shift into the form of a dragon. It carried me through your camp. You know a symbiot has the ability to reflect its environment. I had it do that. I was too weak to make it on my own."

Morian hoped she had not given too much information. She tried to stick as close to the truth so Raffvin wouldn't smell the lies. She knew he was confused about her remarks about being able to draw the dark essence from his symbiot.

"Please," she said in a quaking voice. "You promised you would help me save my mate. What price do you demand?"

Raffvin pulled her back into the shadows as Creon came out onto the top of the terrace. "Wave to him as if nothing is wrong?" He hissed letting his claws cut through the back of her gown.

Morian smiled and raised her hand to Creon who nodded and disappeared back inside the palace. "He's gone," she whispered.

"Take me to the Hive," Raffvin demanded.

Morian drew in a sharp breath. "You know…." She stopped with a small cry as his claws pierced the skin of her back. "Will you promise to leave my family alone if I take you?"

Raffvin chuckled. "Of course," he said.

"Swear!" She demanded, turning to look at him. "Swear you will not harm any of my family and I will take you. I cannot stand living knowing they are in danger any longer. Even if I die, I need to know you will spare my sons and their mates or I will not help you."

Raffvin grinned. "You always did have fire in your blood," he replied through narrowed eyes. "I will spare your bastards, even that male you think is your true mate, but you will be mine. That is the price."

Morian drew in an unsteady breath before she reluctantly nodded. "Very well. For your promise that my family will be safe, I will take you to the Hive and…." Her voice faded as she stared into his black eyes. "…. And become yours."

"Then let us not wait," Raffvin said, grabbing Morian around her waist and throwing both of them over the side of the small wall. Morian's scream was cut off as Raffvin shifted into his dragon as they fell.

Raffvin made his second mistake of the evening. His first was believing that Morian would ever belong to him. His second was not looking behind him. If he had, he would have seen Creon and Trelon step out onto the terrace just feet from where he and Morian had been standing. Raffvin would never have seen the golden dragon that was flying right above him. No one saw it, not even his mate.

## Chapter 19

Paul followed closely behind and slightly above Raffvin. He had fought a major battle with his dragon back on the terrace. It had taken everything in him not to attack Raffvin when he had grabbed Morian.

Her cry of pain was what held him back. He would not take a chance of her being mortally wounded. He needed to be patient, let Raffvin drop his guard when he thought he had won. The man's ego would be his downfall.

Paul watched as Raffvin's dragon swerved to the east. Raffvin was heading away from the cliffs out over the ocean. Paul hadn't flown out this far before. After almost an hour of flying, a series of rocky columns rose up out of the ocean from a small island that stood like a lighthouse against the vast waters surrounding it. A misty haze rose up around the lower part of the island, obscuring it from view.

As they drew closer, the winds picked up. Paul's breath drew in as Raffvin fought against the fierce jet stream cutting through the towers. Raffvin suddenly plummeted down closer to the waves breaking against the rocks before disappearing into the heavy mists.

Paul dropped down to follow him. He swerved as a large wave rose up barely missing it as it crashed against the smaller rocks rising out of the sea floor as a natural barrier. He turned and slid between two of the boulders with only inches to spare. Once on the other side of the barrier, the waters and wind calmed as it opened into a small cove.

Paul pulled up and circled around as Raffvin dropped Morian onto a narrow sandy section of the beach. He looked for a safe place to land so as to not give away the fact he was there. He settled for a spot further along the rocky shore.

The beach area had only spotty sections of sandy areas. He couldn't use those as his footprints would show. He needed to chose a rocky section, but he would have to be careful to not make any noise. He cursed as he realized that he wouldn't be able to remain in his dragon form once he was down.

His eyes skimmed the area as he circled one more time. His eyes narrowed as the symbiot on him pointed him to a narrow open shaft in the rocks. It showed him a way to the Hive but it would mean he would have to go up and then down the narrow opening. The warmth of the symbiot assured him it would do what it could to help him.

*Thank you, my friend,* Paul responded. *You know, now would be a good time to name you. What do you think? What name would you like?*

The symbiot shook with joy at the thought of having a name like the other symbiots it played with. Different images flashed through it before it settled on one. It sent the picture to Paul, a shiver of excitement coursing through it.

Paul chuckled silently even as he shifted into his two-legged form at the last minute just inches from the rocky terrain and the hard surface of one of the towers. His hands reached out to stop his forward momentum before he turned to fold his larger frame into the shadows of an indentation in the rock. He leaned back as the symbiot shifted into a long golden rope leading upward to the opening it had pointed out just minutes earlier.

*Crash it is,* Paul thought with approval. *I think that is a wonderful name. Let's go save the Hive, rescue the not-so-damsel in distress and kill the bastard who thinks his shit doesn't stink.*

Crash's shiver of delight ran through him as it responded. Paul wondered how Morian was going to feel about him naming her symbiot and then rolled his eyes. She would probably think he was as crazy as the girls. He would have to remember to explain it was a human custom. He grabbed the golden length of rope and began climbing.

The rock was smooth for the first twenty feet before it became pitted from wind and erosion. He was able to use hand and foot holds when he reached that section to work his way upward. He looked up and estimated he had another ten feet or so before he reached the darkened shaft.

The muscles in his forearms bulged as he pulled himself up the last few feet. He gripped the edge, lifting his upper body onto the small ledge before swinging his leg over. His dragon came forward enough so he could see down into the darkened interior. The walls on the inside were smooth as glass.

*I'm going to need your help with this one, pal,* Paul asked, brushing his fingers across the gold that was still attached to his wrists.

Crash immediately formed a long, thick rope of gold. Paul swung his other leg over the side and grabbed the rope. He slid down it, jumping the last few feet to the hard smooth surface. Crash flowed down shifting into a small dog. The symbiot would meet up with the other half of itself in the Hive chamber. Crash looked up at Paul as he knelt down next to it and ran his hand over its golden head in appreciation.

"Let's end this," he whispered.

Crash sneezed and shook its body before taking off through the winding tunnel at a fast clip. Paul shifted enough so he could follow without having to worry about knocking himself out on any of the low hanging rocks. The cut of the tunnel reminded Paul of some of the lava tubes back home.

It was wide and rounded, with smooth walls and flooring. The ceiling was pitted and jagged at times as though the heat had broken down parts of it. He could also see bits and pieces of seaweed and shells that gave the impression the tube had flooded in the past. He hoped the flooding wasn't dependent on the tides.

He was about to ask Crash when they rounded a narrow corner. Paul slowed as he saw a golden glow coming from the end of the narrow tube. He walked to the end and just stood in stunned awe at the huge cavern below him. His eyes moved slowly as he tried to take in the magnificent view of the Hive.

He swallowed as the figures inside turned to look at him. He hesitated for just a brief moment as golden steps formed from the entrance of the tunnel he was standing in and lead down to the main cavern twenty feet below. A shiver passed through him as he took the first step. He wondered how in the hell you were supposed to address a deity because one thing was for sure… he was in the presence of the Gods.

* * *

Morian stumbled and fell to her hands and knees in the soft sand as Raffvin's dragon released her to land next to her. Her hair fell forward around her face. It had been pulled free from the chignon she wore by the fierce winds that had buffeted them as they approached the island.

She cried out in pain as Raffvin reached down and grabbed her by the arm, jerking her roughly up to stand next to him. She wiped her free hand on her gown, brushing off the sand stuck to her palm, before she pushed the heavy strands of black hair back from her face. The winds were calmer here, but there was still enough to blow her hair back into her eyes.

"Where is it?" He asked impatiently, shaking her.

Morian jerked her arm out of his grasp and took a step back, almost falling again in the soft sand as she stumbled. "Remember your promise," she hissed back, glaring at him angrily. "I am holding you to it."

Raffvin laughed at her defiant expression. "So much fire wasted on my brother. Jalo never knew what he had," he said cruelly. "I asked him to share you but he refused - the fool. I could have stoked that fire to a blaze that would have scorched the three of us."

"Go to hell. That is not a good place, by the way," Morian spit out, her dark gold eyes flashing with rage. "Jalo was twice the warrior you could ever be. He knew how to lead our people and he knew how to love. That is three things you will never be able to do."

Raffvin grabbed Morian by the back of her neck and tugged her forward. His eyes burning with rage as he glared down at her. His eyes dropped to her lips before he crushed his mouth down on them, savagely kissing her. Morian struggled against the hold on her, trying to twist her head away from the horrid taste of him. He ground his lips against hers, trying to force her to open her mouth to his possession. Instead, she opened just far enough to clamp down on his lower lip with her small sharp teeth, drawing blood.

Raffvin jerked back. He raised his hand to strike her, but instead laughed darkly when she flinched. He touched his bleeding lip before drawing his fingers away to study it for a moment. A heated smile curved his lips as he ran his bloody fingers down along her cheek as she turned her head away from him.

"Yes, so much fire," he murmured thoughtfully. "I look forward to keeping it burning. When I spread you out beneath me and bury my shaft all the way to your womb, it will be my name you scream."

Morian turned to look at him in disgust. "Never," she vowed.

Raffvin looked at her with disdain. "Oh, I promise you'll scream my name," he said mockingly. "I didn't say you would be screaming it in pleasure. Just that you would be screaming it," he added with a harsh laugh before turning her toward the narrow opening cut in one of the tall columns. "Now, lead me to the Hive," he demanded, pushing her in front of him.

Morian ran her hands over the long skirt of her gown. She could feel the small knives that Kelan had given her. The tiny bit of symbiot on her let her know that Paul had reached the Hive and was waiting for them. She trembled as she made her way up to the entrance of the tunnels that would lead to the home of the Hive. She had only been to the main cavern a couple of times before, once she was little more than a child and the other shortly after Jalo's death.

Normally, Zoran took the infants who would be matched to the small chamber under the palace. Only a small river of the golden symbiot ran through that chamber. No one else had ever been in this chamber that she was aware of, including her mother. She would not have brought Raffvin if the Queen of the Hive had not requested it.

She stood for a moment in the darkened entrance long enough to allow her eyes to adjust. She stumbled forward when Raffvin pushed her roughly from behind. As she moved forward small ropes of gold began to glow, leading the way deeper into the rock tunnel.

After thirty feet, the tunnel began to slope downward. The golden glow wrapped in swirling designs, almost like it was playing as it ran along the walls. Morian glanced behind her and saw nothing but a blackness, deeper than that of space.

"Move," Raffvin said almost drooling. His dark eyes burned with increasing greed and madness the further they traveled. "Faster," he said impatiently pushing her roughly.

The moment he pushed her the swirling lights flickered and went out, leaving them in darkness. Raffvin's breathing sounded heavy in the confining space. He pulled his dragon forward, but even with its ability to see in the dark he couldn't see a thing.

He reached out blindly, his fingers shifting into claws. He wrapped it tightly around her arm, the tips piercing deeply into the skin of her forearm. She cried out in pain and collapsed onto her knees when the grip tightened to the point she thought he was about to crush the bone in her arm.

"Stop," she whimpered. "Please, you are hurting me."

"Why did they go out?" He asked harshly, trying to drag her back to her feet. "Why can't I see?" He snarled out shaking her like a rag doll.

"If you use violence they react," she choked out as nausea threatened her when his grip continued to tighten. "Let me go and see what happens."

Raffvin immediately let Morian's arm go. At once, the swirling beams of golden light lit along the wall. He turned to look at Morian who had stumbled over to lean against one smooth wall.

She was trembling and pale as she cradled her bloody arm against her chest. A single tear coursed down her face even as she tried to turn her head to hide it from him. For just a moment, sanity and regret touched his shattered mind.

He reached out and touched the tear, catching the dewy crystal on the tip of his finger. He pulled it closer to him to study for a moment before he touched it to the tip of his tongue. When he looked back at her, the madness had returned to his eyes. Morian couldn't help but wonder if she had imagined Raffvin feeling any emotion beyond his own greed.

"Go," he said, his voice echoing in the narrow passage.

Morian didn't say anything. She just nodded and pushed away from the wall, still holding her injured arm. They did not have much further to go. She was glad. She didn't know if she could handle much more without burying one of the small knives she carried into Raffvin's black, cold heart. She was through with being his punching bag.

*The only marks I want on my body are the ones that Paul put there,* she thought savagely.

*Hallelujah!* Her dragon muttered. *I ready to fry his ass.*

*What does that mean?* Morian asked curiously as she ducked around a low hanging ledge.

*Don't know,* her dragon said. *Heard Cara say it when she figured out what Ha'ven was doing. She happy and I like word. It funny sounding.*

Morian's lips twitched at her dragon's response. *Thank you for helping me find something good about all of this,* she said hesitantly.

*No problem,* her dragon said with a grin. *That another saying I like. Ariel say it a lot. I like Earth sayings. They fun. Make no sense, but fun. Our mates will take care of Raffvin. We help when time come.*

*Yes, it will be over soon,* she whispered silently as she rounded the last curve and saw the glow coming from the chamber ahead. *Very soon,* she thought as she felt Raffvin's breathing increase as he realized they were in the chamber to the Hive.

## Chapter 20

Paul walked slowly down the steps that had formed for him. His eyes slid from one golden figure to another as they changed and shifted, fading in and out of sight as they moved. Sometimes they appeared solid while at other times they were so translucent, mist from a shower would have been thicker.

His eyes lit up with humor when he saw Arosa and Arilla. Arosa waved to him from where she was lying back on a golden chair while Arilla was scooping up bits of symbiot from a flowing river and tossing it into the air.

Paul's breath caught as the bits of gold shifted into different shapes as it fell back toward the ground. Some of it shifted into the form of a bird. He watched as the bits flew up toward the ceiling of the cavern where they landed on small ledges. He turned his gaze back to the others that turned into huge flying insects the size of dinner plates, their wings shimmering with color before they floated off toward large mushroom shaped trees.

As he stepped off the last step, the golden staircase behind him dissolved. He turned his head and watched as it disappeared back into the river of gold. He chuckled and shook his head before turning his attention back to the figures.

There were eleven different ones standing, sitting or lying around the large cavern. It was hard at first to count them as they kept appearing and disappearing. Arosa and Arilla giggled as they winked at him. He bowed his head to them in return, drawing more giggles.

*Come forward,* an ethereal voice requested in a husky tone that echoed in his head.

Paul's lips parted in amazement as he spun to look as a twelfth figure suddenly appeared on a platform that rose above the cavern. The figure was tall and slender, wraith-like in appearance. It stood in a shimmering doorway of gold, encompassing what appeared to be deep space behind it.

He walked slowly toward the platform, following the stepping stones that appeared before him with each step he took. Small bits of gold symbiot danced around him. Some reached out to touch him while others flitted in front of him, as if curious about who he was.

Crash walked next to his side looking around with obvious joy from the warmth radiating from it. Paul didn't know how he could tell the difference, but when a larger shape of symbiot in the form of a Werecat stepped out in front of him, he knew deep down it was Crash's other half. Sure enough, the smaller bit of symbiot rushed forward flowing into the larger section. He could feel the peace as it became whole again. He raised his hand and let it slide over the body of the huge Werecat as he passed by it, loving the silky texture. It shivered in delight and emitted a low hum of contentment.

Paul paused at the bottom of the platform. He looked up, unsure of what the being expected of him. He started when he heard a giggle close to his ear.

*Go up,* Arosa said. *Go, human.*

*Arosa,* the voice said with a slight exasperation in its tone. *Come forward, Paul Grove.*

Paul looked at Arosa, who used her hands to shoo him forward. He shook his head in amusement before turning to slowly ascend the steps. He stared into the dark gold eyes.

A part of him thought they reminded him of Morian's beautiful eyes. When he reached the top, he took a step forward before sinking down onto one knee and bowing his head in respect. Since he had never been in this position before, he figured he would take a page out of some of the old movies he liked to watch with Trisha and use a touch of old-fashion gentility.

*Rise, Paul,* the figure requested gliding forward until it stood just a few feet in front of him.

Paul rose and stood in the military formation of being at-ease. His hands interlocked behind his back as the figure looked down at him. Even with him being almost six and a half feet tall he had to tilt his head back to look into the creature's eyes. Paul stared back at the form in front of him with a steady, calm look.

The creature's lips curved and it, he wasn't sure if it was a male or female, bowed its head. With a wave of its hand, the figure became more defined. The flowing hair, shimmering gown, and – Paul swallowed as breasts appeared, the creature was definitely feminine now. Humor glistened in her dark eyes.

* * *

Aikaterina studied the male standing in front of her. She had foretold of his arrival long before his planet had even formed. She had sent a touch of her own blood to the planet that would give life to his species on the rocks that she had cast into the heavens. It had taken billions of years, but time was of no consequence to her kind.

Aikaterina smiled as she looked around at others of her kind. These were her children. They were enjoying a respite on the world they had come to think of as their own. Most of her kind traveled through the different star systems, looking for planets that have the potential for life. When the world was ready, they would leave a part of themselves in the hopes it would grow and nurture life. On this planet, she had found a species that gave her life in return.

Aikaterina had discovered this planet by accident. She had been on the verge of dying when she first came across the dragon-shifting race. Her energy levels drained dangerous low from her travels, she had been seeking a newly formed world where she could rejuvenate.

Instead, she had discovered this planet. She had immediately fallen in love with it and its unique inhabitants. While the Valdier had already existed, they had been a dying species as well. Their dragons and two-legged form susceptible to many different kinds of diseases.

She had discovered her blood created a unique symbiotic relationship with the unusual species. She had never before found a life form that was compatible with the Hive's 'blood', the liquid essence that made up who they were. The fire within the dragons had merged with her energy. In return, she discovered the essence from both the two-legged and four-legged forms fed her, giving her the energy she needed to not only live, but multiply.

*It is perfect for my young,* she thought as she gazed at the flowing river of gold that made up her kind.

But no world is without its problems. Greed, fear, suspicion, and the desire for ultimate power lived in this world as it did on all worlds she had visited. The difference with this one was that she had bound their very existence to each other so one could not live without the other. Paul Grove's world was another that could sustain their blood with their essence. The problem was, it was still too immature to handle it.

*At least, most were immature,* she thought with satisfaction as she saw the hints of gold blazing in Paul's eyes. *Some are more ready than others.*

Paul cleared his throat. "I mean no disrespect, but my mate is in danger. You are also in danger," he said quietly.

"Yes, I know," Aikaterina replied, waving her hand to the other figures.

Paul looked over his shoulder and saw Arilla, Arosa and the other figures rising up and moving to a set of columns that circled the cavern. Each figure floated until they stood on one of the pillars. He frowned as he saw the small bits of symbiot rushing to plunge into the flowing river to hide. As they did, the chamber grew darker until only the glow from the twelve figures, the river, and Crash illuminated it.

He looked back at the figure in front of him. "What is happening?"

Aikaterina reached out her hand and brushed the side of Paul's face with a sad smile. "We cannot interfere with the battle between good and evil on any planet," she said, closing her eyes for a moment before opening them to look at him with a relieved look. "The battle above is going well. The evil cannot succeed with the combined forces of those who set aside their differences to seek peace instead of war," she said. "But the evil coming has the power to destroy the Valdier. If Raffvin should win, he would try to turn the good energy that gives life," she explained with a wave of her hand to the flowing river of gold, "to energy that would take it."

"Can't you stop it?" Paul asked, knowing he was in the presence of a force unlike anything man had ever imagined.

Aikaterina shook her head. "As I said, we cannot interfere. Raffvin has already learned how to not only change the good energy, but how to destroy it as well. He holds the power to destroy us," she said sadly.

"But, if the symbiot is destroyed…." Paul's voice faded as he looked back at the figures standing like silent sentinels over the birthing place of the symbiots. He looked back at the figure waiting for him to piece together the facts. "The Valdier will die," he said grimly.

"Yes," was all that Aikaterina said before she dissolved into a mist in front of him and reformed on the top pillar.

Paul looked up at her before spinning in a slow circle, looking at each figure with calm steady eyes. His family, his mate, his world rested on his shoulders. He was all that stood between Raffvin and the death of a world he had come to love.

Paul looked back up at Aikaterina with a dangerous glint in his eyes. "A brilliant man once said that 'the only thing necessary for the triumph of evil is for good men to do nothing.' I'll be damn if I do nothing," he growled out feeling a cold calm settle over him.

"Edmund Burke," Aikaterina murmured. "He was an interesting human," she said before her eyes moved to a different entrance to the cavern.

*Raffvin is here,* she whispered before she and the others standing on the pillars turned to solid golden statues.

* * *

Morian paused in the entrance as she looked down at the solitary figure standing in the center of the cavern on a stone platform. She started to step down the rough stone stairway, but Raffvin grabbed her by her shoulder, halting her. She looked over her shoulder in fury. Her dragon realized that she was tired of playing the helpless female.

With a low growl, she pushed back against him with enough force that he stumbled backwards. The moment his hand left her shoulder, she threw herself forward off the steps. She called forth her dragon as she fell.

A burst of joy swept through her as huge white wings unfolded and opened before sweeping up and down to allow her to circle around the huge cavern. The gold on the tips of her scales gleamed brilliantly against the white. She soared over the pillars before dipping down to drag her extended claws in the river of gold, painting them.

She drew up next to Paul, flapping her wings up and down as she settled next to him before folding them against her body. She turned to snarl at Raffvin who was standing at the entrance to the Hive with a sneer on his face.

"So, the Priestess shows her true colors," he laughed as he snapped his fingers. Dark shadows formed around him, forming into the body of his symbiot. Only the dark shadows continued to grow and grow, dividing into more than a dozen darkened, hissing masses of energy. "You are not the only one who has learned to harness the symbiots of others," he explained in a dark voice as he continued to stare coldly at them. His eyes flickered to where Paul stood motionless beside the huge white dragon. "I thought I killed you, human," he said with a look of disdain.

Paul's lips curved into a cold, deadly smile before he replied. "That's what you get for thinking, Raffvin," Paul drawled. "I think you will find I'm not that easy to kill," he added pulling a laser sword out and rotating it in his hand. "I'm letting you know now I'm going to kill your ass," he said before he jerked his head toward Morian, "and she is going to help me."

Raffvin's snarl turned into a growl as he thrust his hand out and pointed at the large white dragon that was crouching and hissing. "Kill her!" He ordered all but one of the dark masses to attack her.

"Go," Paul ordered to Morian who nodded and called for her symbiot to show her the quickest way out as she rose up with a powerful burst of speed.

Paul didn't take his eyes off of Raffvin. He had to trust that Morian would be able to handle this part of their plan. His focus was solely on destroying Raffvin once and for all. He would use the male's arrogance, greed, and madness against him. Raffvin roared out as the dark masses of symbiots followed Morian out through one of the larger tunnels leaving him and what was left alone with Paul.

"Do you think it matters that she is escaping?" Raffvin roared out in fury. "Once you are dead, she is as well! Nothing can save either one of you. You are doomed."

Paul laughed, knowing the sound would drive Raffvin to the breaking point, making him reckless. "Dude, it is going to take more than the grumblings of a bag of hot air to kill me. That's all I'm seeing," Paul taunted. "In the words of my daughter, it's time to tag your ass for good."

\* \* \*

Raffvin saw red at the human male's taunting. His mind splintering into uncontrollable rage. As he lost the last bit of his control, he lost control of his dragon.

It had been tortured for too long. The darkness eating away at its soul.

Raffvin had turned on the female who would have been his true mate, leaving her to die a brutal death instead of fighting for her or sharing her with the other Valdier warrior named Trevon, who had also been her true mate. The female had been Vox's aunt.

Raffvin had met her when she was very young, still too young to mate. His dragon and symbiot had known the moment they had seen her that she belonged to them. But, Raffvin had wanted Morian. He wanted power, not love.

When he had discovered that Rissa had mated with another Valdier he had sent word to the traitors working with him on Sarafin to have her and her mate destroyed, no matter what. He had not expected her death to have such a devastating effect on the other parts of who he was. His symbiot wanted to return to the Hive in its grief. His dragon refused to accept Morian or any other, slowly becoming mad with grief.

Raffvin knew without the three parts of himself, he would perish. He had worked tirelessly to find a way to force his essence to remain. He had eventually discovered that as his own blood grew darker so did the energy of his symbiot. As his dark power grew over it, he was able to force the symbiots of those weaker than him to become trapped within his making it larger, stronger until he was invincible.

Raffvin's insane roar shook the walls of the cavern, sending loose pieces of rock crashing down.

Thick molted gray wings unfolded from a body that was gaunt from its imprisonment as long, black claws dug into the stone floor. The dark mist swirled around him as the last of his symbiot formed around his body. His sharp yellow teeth snapped together as his tail flicked back and forth.

Raffvin's elongated head turned menacingly toward the small form of the human male staring at him. He blew out a stream of dark red fire. The male jumped to the side, rolling. Raffvin was forced to turn to follow him. The last straw came when the male stood up and shook his head in disgust at him.

"Damn, you are not only one ugly son-of-a-bitch, but your breath sinks almost as bad as you do," Paul said sarcastically as he waved his hand in front of his face. "Someone has really let their hygiene go to hell."

Raffvin, furious at being mocked, charged Paul.

* * *

*It's about time you stupid bastard*, Paul thought balancing on his heels.

He normally didn't badger his opponents, but then, his opponents didn't normally turn into fire breathing dragons. In the reports he read, he came across a medical one that had proved very interesting. It would appear Raffvin had received a significant injury when he was young while in his dragon form.

While his symbiot was able to heal his two-legged form, it had not been able to completely heal the wound to the back of his upper thigh. Several scales were missing. It was near a main artery. Perhaps it was time to start draining some of the black blood out of him.

Paul charged straight at Raffvin when the dragon came at him. He knew it would be the last thing that Raffvin would expect. Moving with the grace born of decades of training, Paul ducked the breath of fire aimed at him, twisting at the last moment to jump up on a large boulder as Raffvin moved past him and flipped over the huge gray dragon's back slicing with his laser sword as he went. He landed with one hand and one knee on the ground and rolled backwards up under the dragon's tail as it swung around at him coming up on the same side as he had begun.

He ducked again as the dragon twisted, trying to find him. Paul's smaller size was an advantage as he was able to move quickly. He sliced, opening foot long cuts as he went. Raffvin, bleeding heavily from the wounds he was receiving, launched himself up off the ground, breathing a ring of fire as he went. Paul rolled under a section of rock as a burst of superheated fire scorched the ground where he had been.

*I think I have his attention now,* Paul thought, hoping the battle wouldn't take too long.

He was worried about Morian. If the black symbiot caught up with her before she was able to get outside, she would never be able to survive. Paul pushed out of the shelter he had and turned as another blast hit him.

He had knelt down and pulled up the shield that Ha'ven had given him. The flames pulsed around him, but never broke through it. He waited until Raffvin broke off before he took off at a run for the far cliff.

"Halt human!" Raffvin's dark voice growled out. "Perhaps you need to see my true power!" He snarled before he pointed his finger at one of the golden statues standing on a pillar. "Destroy it!" His shrilled order echoed through the room.

Paul turned in horror as the black symbiot shot out at one of the pillars. The golden form withered, screaming in agony as the black bands wrapped around it. The river of gold rose up as a low hum of distress filled the room.

Grief filled Paul as the golden statue suddenly exploded. An unholy wail built until he knelt and covered his ears as the sound rose before fading to an eerie silence. The huge room dimmed as each of the golden statues and the river of gold reacted to the loss of one of their own.

Paul rose in anger. "Raffvin, you will kill us all if you continue," he shouted, stepping out from behind the boulder he had hidden behind. "You will die as well."

Raffvin's insane laugh bounced off the walls and ceiling. "If this world dies then I will find another. I have the power to conquer any world. Would you like to see, human?" He asked before he order the black symbiot to attack the statue of Aikaterina.

Paul had to lead the bastard away from the Hive. He took off running across the uneven ground, calling to his dragon. Jumping up on a small rock, he launched himself into the air, shifting. He blew a wave of dark blue flame in front of the black bands as they wound toward the pillar with the beautiful goddess. The bands split, shooting in different directions towards the other statues. Wails of pain rose again as they wrapped around the golden figures. Paul watched as Arilla and Arosa withered and cried out to him.

He wanted to go to them, but a larger band was trying to get to Aikaterina again. He knew he could not save them all. He could only hope the smaller bands would give him time to save those he could. He felt the thump against his chest as the ruby crystal moved. Reaching down with his left claw, he jerked the chain from around his slender neck, clutching it tightly in his palm. He needed to wrap it around Aikaterina.

He curved around the ceiling of the cavern as he flew toward the front of it again. His back legs pushed off the ceiling as Raffvin, back in his dragon form breathed a stream of hot red flames at him. He twirled as it flashed by him.

He was almost to the front platform where Aikaterina stood perched when he felt a piercing pain as Raffvin tackled him from behind, digging his claws into his back flank. Paul rolled as he grabbed at Raffvin's neck, angling it away from him with his free claw as the dragon tried to breathe fire at him again. They fought furiously, falling in a spiral before crashing into the hard surface of the floor. Raffvin was on top of Paul as they slid across the uneven surface coming to land against the bottom steps of the platform.

Paul jerked as Raffvin's claws ripped across his belly, leaving deep gouges. He tucked his back feet up under the gray dragon and tossed him over his head and rolled over onto his belly as Aikaterina's screams filled the cave. Pushing up, he snapped at Raffvin as he tried to grab him again. The gray dragon locked his claws onto the golden dragon's forearms and swung his tail. Paul fell heavily on his side, grunting when the large gray dragon landed on his ribs.

*Son of a bitch,* Paul snarled, royally pissed as he wrestled to break free of the other dragon. He hoped Morian was doing better than he was.

Paul reached around with his tail. He wrapped it around the gray dragon's back leg and pulled at the same time as he dragged his back claws down the front of the male's thighs cutting deep gashes. He had to get to the Hive Queen before she was destroyed.

The gray dragon had to let him go or risk getting his damn guts ripped open. Paul threw the gray dragon to the side and stumbled to his feet. He was covered in both their blood. His from the wounds Raffvin had inflicted and Raffvin's for the dozens of cuts Paul had given him.

Turning, he charged up the steps trying to get to Aikaterina whose screams had died down to whimpers as she slowly began to collapse. Paul could see the blisters forming all around her body as the black bands began to cut through her. He was almost to her when a band of the black symbiot shot out, piercing his left forearm. The force of the blow forced his claw open and the ruby crystal fell, rolling across the platform.

Paul's dragon roared out harshly as the band wound back around his front leg and started slicing through the scales into the flesh. He was barely aware of raising his tail to slash it across the gray dragon's face as he tried to attack from behind again. Instead, he pulled from the calm center deep inside him and pushed the pain away. He would not let evil win.

Strength flooded him as he felt Morian touch his mind. *We are almost there! Don't make me have to whip your ass! You get up and do what you have to until we get there.*

*This bastard is pissing me off!* He responded with a grunt as he caught a tail to his already tender side. *Where is he fucking getting his strength?*

*It is the symbiot,* she responded. *That is why his eyes are black. It took me a little while to figure it out. He must have it inside him.*

*Well, I'm about to do an autopsy to take it out,* Paul growled as he caught the offending tail as it swung at him again in his right claw and twisted it brutally before snapping the end.

Raffvin roared out in pain. *Breaking a tail bone hurts like hell, doesn't it?* Paul couldn't help but think with glee even as he snapped at the dark symbiot determined to slice his claw from his front leg.

Paul reached the ruby crystal and slammed his tortured forearm down on it. The black band hissed and screeched as it was pulled into the center of the stone. Turning onto his back, he caught the huge gray dragon as it charged him.

His eyes flickered up as he saw a golden eagle swoop down, talons out. With a flick of his wrist, he sent the necklace up into the air. The eagle caught the jewel in its talon and curved upward to the top of the golden statue. Dropping the stone around her neck, the crystal glowed a brilliant red as it absorbed the dark energy slowly draining Aikaterina of life.

Raffvin's dragon jerked back as the statue began to glow a dark gold again. His dragon stumbled backwards down the steps, turning in disbelief as the cavern began to glow brightly. His eyes turned to the forms of the other dragons appearing at each entrance to the Hive. Symbiots in a wide variety of shapes were dropping red stones over the other golden statues, absorbing the smaller bands of negative energy.

"No!" Raffvin screamed as he shifted back into his two-legged form. "No!" He screamed again, grabbing his head before turning to look with murder in his eyes at the huge golden dragon standing protectively in front of the Hive Queen. "You! You are to blame for this!"

Paul shifted and stood proudly in front of Aikaterina, Morian in the form of her white dragon stood behind him with her wings spread. He looked down dispassionately at the man who had brought so much pain to his new world. Who let greed and power corrupt him, his dragon, and even his symbiot to the point that there was nothing left but a gaunt shell of a Valdier warrior.

He let his gaze move to the entrances leading into the Hive. Zoran's red, gold and green dragon stood at one entrance while each of his brothers.... *my sons*, Paul thought, stood proudly at each of the others blocking any escape. Their symbiots had taken up position in front of each of the eleven remaining statues. He finally turned his gaze back to Raffvin who seemed to shrink further into his madness as he realized that he had failed.

Paul turned as he felt a hand slide along his lower back. "As the Priestess to the Hive, it is my responsibility to sentence him for the attack on it and to the damage that was done," she said with a quiet strength that spoke of her royal status.

He nodded his head in understanding but kept his eyes trained on Raffvin. The hair on the back of his neck was standing straight up and his gut was telling him that the bastard had a card up his sleeve. He would not give in gracefully.

He loosened his stance as Morian stepped slightly in front of him. His eyes narrowing on Raffvin's face as a multitude of emotions swept across it. They ranged from rage to hatred to madness.

## Chapter 21

Following her symbiot as it led her through the twisting maze of tunnels and air shafts, Morian folded her wings against her sides so she could fit through a narrower section of rock. She could feel the black symbiots gaining on her.

She swerved upward into a vertical shaft before twisting at the last minute into another horizontal one, bouncing off the smooth walls as she did and almost losing control. She rolled and picked up speed, ignoring the burning in her lungs and wings. She hadn't flown this hard or fast in centuries.

She burst into a large open area and swung around, beating her wings frantically as she waited for the black creatures to catch up with her. When the first one appeared, she used her tail as a club. Swinging it as hard as she could, she knocked the creature back into the others, snarling in pain as blisters formed where she touched it. Loud hisses of rage filled the narrow shaft and echoed up into the larger one sending a shiver through her petite white and gold body.

She didn't wait around to find out how angry she had just made them. Looking up, she saw the narrow opening at the top of one of the towers. It was too small for her to fit through. Putting on a burst of speed, she called to her symbiot to break through the narrow opening.

*Hurry, they are coming*, she breathed out with a mixture of excitement and fear.

*Crash protect you,* her symbiot responded. *The others wait just outside.*

*Crash?* Morian asked in confusion as she dodged the sharp spears of rock suddenly raining down as her symbiot burst through. From the sounds behind her, she was more successful at dodging them than the symbiots following her.

*Paul asked me for a name. I like Crash!* It responded as it shot through the ceiling in a perfect reflection of its name.

Morian twisted as she went through the opening and up into the nighttime sky. She flew straight up before turning and looking down as the black shapes emerged. She waited until she counted the last one. It would be close as they began to swarm around her. Her dragon shuddered as a long black band wrapped around her tail, leaving a long blister near the one she had just received.

Crash moved to attack it, but Morian hissed for it to stay back. *Now, Zoran,* she called out in dragon speak.

*With pleasure,* Zoran responded. *Trelon, let's hope your and Cara's crystals work.*

*They will,* Trelon said with a confident growl.

Trelon, Zoran, and Creon circled around Morian with their symbiots. Each of the dragons and their symbiots wore or carried hundreds of the ruby crystals that Trelon and Cara had been growing since Ariel and Mandra had returned. None of the crystals were as large as the one Ariel had brought back, but they were all just as powerful. Loud hissing and screeching filled the air as the black symbiots were being pulled away from the white dragon they had been seeking to destroy.

Long tethers of negative energy roped through the air and into the center of the crystals which began to glow brighter and brighter as it absorbed the energy and converted it. Thin bands of gold began appearing as the darkness was pulled away. The remains of the symbiots from Valdier warriors who had died under Raffvin's hand began raining back down into the open shaft.

Morian's heart burned with grief. Unable to ignore the pain radiating from the tiny remains, she folded her wings and dropped down below where the remaining black bands fought against the pull. Once clear, she rotated until she was able to glide back down through the narrow opening her symbiot had created so she could land on the smooth floor far below, shifting back into her two-legged form.

"Have hope, little ones," she murmured as she looked out over the tiny, shivering teardrops that lay in small pools on the hard, cold floor. "I will return you to your Queen."

Crash landed next to Morian and shifted into a Were Cat. It sent its own warmth out to the injured remains. When one symbiot is hurt or destroyed it resonated through the Hive to the others. Raffvin had committed a crime against the very fundamental beliefs of their people and the symbiotic relationship with the Hive. He could not be allowed to live.

"Crash," Morian said softly, turning to look at the symbiot with sorrow in her eyes. "Take them into you and protect what is left. They have lost enough."

Crash bowed its huge head in acknowledgement and walked to each small pool, scooping up the remains with its long tongue and absorbing it into its larger body. Morian turned to look up as Zoran, Mandra, and Creon's dragons flew through the opening above her. Her heart swelled with pride as she watched the three dragons circle around before landing next to her and shifting.

"It is done," Zoran said, watching as his mother's symbiot scanned the area for any of the gold remains that it might have missed. "We need to find your mate."

Morian nodded. "Crash," she called out before looking at her sons. "Your symbiots know the way. They will take each of you to a different entrance so that we can prevent Raffvin from escaping. He has much to answer for," she added heavily, looking up at the night sky.

"He won't escape this time," Trelon growled out. "We'll make sure of that."

Morian nodded before she looked at her youngest son. "Creon, have you heard from the others?" She asked, unable to completely hide her fear for her other two sons.

Creon smiled and brushed his hand down her cheek, wiping a smear of dirt away. "Mandra and Kelan are fine. I think they are having far too much fun. Vox and Ha'ven were complaining they were not leaving any of the Marastin Dow for them to play with."

Morian gave a slight shake of her head and rolled her eyes. "Men! I swear you never grow up," she chuckled before a painful gasp left her lips and her eyes widened.

"What is it?" Zoran asked, reaching out to steady her when she swayed.

"Paul…. The Queen…. They are in danger," she whispered before turning and shifting.

Morian took off without another word. She would have to trust that Zoran, Trelon and Creon's symbiots would guide them. Crash flashed in front of her, moving faster than she could through the tunnels.

*Can you lead us back,* she asked her dragon in a tone that spoke of the urgency of the situation.

*No problem,* her dragon bit out swerving around a corner and down a long narrow shaft.

A flash of pain that Morian knew didn't come from any injury to her, her dragon, or her symbiot swept through her again as she rounded another corner. She could feel the pain radiating from her mate. The bitter taste of fear filled her mouth at the thought that they might arrive too late. She had to let him know that she and the others were almost there.

Reaching out, she touched Paul's mind using the symbiot on him. *We are almost there! Don't make me have to whip your ass! You get up and do what you have to until we get there,* she demanded fiercely.

*This bastard is pissing me off!* He responded tersely. *Where is he fucking getting his strength?*

*It is the symbiot,* Morian responded with a sudden insight. *That is why his eyes are black. It took me a little while to figure it out. He must have it inside him.*

She didn't say anything else for fear of distracting her mate as he fought for not only his life, but the life of all their people. Her dragon rounded the last corner and burst through into the cavern where her mate and Raffvin were locked in battle. Crash was swooping down over him, reaching for the ruby crystal he had worn around his neck.

Her gaze flew to the tortured figure of the Hive Queen as the black bands of Raffvin's symbiot surrounded her. She flew towards her mate even as the room began to fill with a golden glow as the other symbiots began raining red crystals around the other statues, pulling the dark energy away.

She circled once before gliding to land behind her mate who had shifted back into his two-legged form to confront Raffvin. She rose up tall and proud behind him. He was a fierce figure in either form and her love for him and his determination to protect the people he had adopted showed in his stance.

She shifted as Raffvin stared up at them in disbelief. Walking up behind Paul, she ran her hand along his lower back for strength before stepping forward to look down at Raffvin with disdain. Raising her chin, she began speaking not as *Dola,* not as Morian, but as the Priestess to the Hive. It was her responsibility to administer justice for the savage betrayal to their people and for the harm done to the Hive.

As she spoke, the madness in Raffvin's eyes grew. His low rumble sounded just a split second before he struck out. He was no longer in the form of his two-legged self nor that of the gaunt, gray dragon. Now, a smaller but deadlier dragon formed. One made of the black energy that he had slowly replaced his royal blood with.

Morian screamed out in warning even as Paul pushed her behind him. Zoran, Trelon, and Creon's dragons roared out in rage as Raffvin attacked. Everything seemed to slow as Paul shifted into his golden dragon, meeting Raffvin head-on.

## Chapter 22

Paul saw the look in Raffvin's eyes change and the way he moved his right foot into position. It was the one he liked to favor when he was about to attack. Paul was already reaching for Morian when Raffvin shifted.

Thrusting her behind him, he shifted and charged down the steps as Raffvin moved upwards. Their bodies crashed with a resounding thud, gold against black. Muscles bulged as they gripped each other in the age old battle of good vs evil.

Paul pushed into the slightly smaller dragon, forcing him back far enough that he could swing his spiked tail up between them. The razor sharp tips sliced through the missing scales on Raffvin's thigh, burying deeply into the main artery there. He grimaced as Raffvin's talons sank into his shoulders, but he didn't release him as he swung his tail again and again.

It wasn't until the third blow that he caught a glimpse of red mist flickering as he swung his tail around. Zoran and Creon's symbiots were flying above him, dropping small crystals onto the platform behind him. Every time his tail swung backwards, it would rake up more crystals along the spikes at the end. With each cut, he was pulling the negative energy out of Raffvin who was beginning to wither in his arms more than fight against him.

"The crystals!" Paul yelled out as he struggled to keep his grip on the black dragon that was fighting like the hounds of hell were tearing him apart. "I need Ariel's pendant!" He called out hoarsely referring to the crystal Ariel had been given.

Aikaterina approached where he held the black dragon. She removed the necklace from around her neck and with a wave of her hand, it appeared around Raffvin's neck. Paul thrust the smaller dragon away from him as it began screeching and smoking. Long wisps of black pulled from its body, twisting and melting into the crystal around its neck. Every time the dragon tried to claw the necklace away from its body, piercing roars of pain filled the cavern as the crystal sucked more energy from it.

Raffvin shifted back to his two-legged form and collapsed to the floor in agony. "No!" He screamed. "The Hive was mine to control!"

Morian slowly walked down the steps to rest her hand on the huge golden dragon that stood over Raffvin's tortured figure. "Raffvin, you are condemned to imprisonment for treason against the people of Valdier and for the attack on the Hive. Your sentence is to be confined within the crystal, neither alive nor dead, for eternity. May the Gods have no mercy on your soul," she said dispassionately as he reached out to her with one hand that began to dissolve and flow into the crystal.

Zoran, Trelon, and Creon flew down to stand as guards as they all watched Raffvin slowly dissolve into the crystal. Only when the crystal slowly faded back to its normal color did Morian look up at her mate. Tears glimmered in her eyes as she stared at the man who had come from the stars to her. Raising her hand, she laid it against the golden jaw of her mate.

"It is over," she whispered, staring into the dark brown eyes glowing with flakes of gold. "The terror is finally over. My family is safe."

Paul rubbed his head against her outstretched hand before he shifted and pulled her into his arms. Burying his face in her neck, he just held her tightly against him until both their trembling ceased. Only then did he raise his head to look at the Queen of the Hive.

A small smile curved his lips as he studied her. "I thought you said you couldn't interfere," he said with a raised eyebrow.

An answering smile curved her lips before she shrugged her slender shoulders. "What is the phrase you used? Oh yes - he was pissing me off," she replied, looking about the cavern as it began to glow brightly again.

Paul's eyes followed hers. His eyes dimmed as he saw several of the gold figures standing near the empty pillar of their fallen. Grief welled in him that he had not been able to stop the death of one of the creatures who gave life to this world.

He turned his head and looked at Aikaterina. "I'm sorry I couldn't save your friend," he said quietly.

Aikaterina bowed her head in acknowledgement of their loss. Her eyes followed the other figures as they began to move around the cavern, making soft sounds that woke the symbiots that had hidden during the battle. Her eyes lit with delight as she watched their playful antics as they emerged. They were young and would soon go to a strong warrior. She turned back and smiled at Paul and Morian.

"Do not feel sad," she said to Paul before turning to look past him. "Another has been born to take Aminta's place. You must let her be who she is. It will be difficult for you to accept that at times. She is meant to bring two worlds together," she said looking at Creon.

Morian looked puzzled as she saw Creon stiffen. "Who?" She asked, her voice fading even as she remembered the look in her newest great-daughter's eyes. "Phoenix," she breathed.

Aikaterina bowed her head to Morian in acknowledgement.

"No!" Creon's sharp denial echoed loudly. "She ….." His voice faded as he fell into a defiant silence.

"Has been reborn, warrior," Aikaterina said in a lilting voice. "She is like the Phoenix of her world. She is a warrior. It is her destiny to lead with a warrior who is as strong and fierce as her. Let her discover her powers. Be there to guide her and accept her," she advised before she raised her hands and clapped them together. "Till we meet again, warriors," she said before turning and ascending the steps of the platform again. When she reached the top, a doorway appeared. Through the open door, thousands of star systems swirled.

Paul started as he heard twin giggles as Arilla and Arosa came up to him and Morian. "We will be checking up on you and your family," they both said at the same time.

"I knew he was the one for you," Arosa said with a sigh as she looked at Paul with amused eyes. "I just didn't realize he would take so long to be born."

"Nonsense, sister," Arilla growled playfully. "I was the one who saw him first," she said with a twinkle in her eye. "We will be back soon."

"Where are you going?" Paul asked with a frown as they started up the staircase to follow the other figures.

Arilla laughed and shook her head. "There are many star systems out there that still need to be explored," she replied with a raised eyebrow.

"But this one will always be our home," Arosa added before she and her sister faded into the shape of twin dragons and flew through the opened doorway.

* * *

As soon as the last figure left, the cavern began to dim again. Morian looked around before she released a sigh as Crash came up to brush against her. It was time to return home. She looked around the cavern one last time knowing that the Hive would not be here once they left. It would move to another location. Crash would take her to the new location when it was time for her to know.

*Perhaps when it was Phoenix's turn to learn the ways of their people and the Hive,* she thought with a warm glow.

"I want to go home," Morian murmured, turning to look up into Paul's eyes. "To my hidden home where I can have you all to myself," she added with a smile.

"But....," Zoran started to say before Paul shot him a dark look.

"Unless you want me to open a can of whoop-ass," Paul muttered darkly. "The answer better be 'have fun'."

Trelon started chuckling. "I personally have enough on my hands! Between Cara and the twins, I get my ass whipped every damn day!" He laughed. "Have fun, Paul. *Dola*, I love you and will see you when you return." He leaned forward, slapped Paul on the shoulder, kissed Morian on the cheek and shifted into his dragon. He had a wife and two daughters to try to catch.

Zoran cleared his throat and looked at Paul before holding out his hand. Paul looked at it before he grasped it and pulled Zoran into a brief bear hug. No other words were needed, though, Zoran did mutter a quick 'have fun' under his breath before he shifted and flew off as well in search of his own wife and son.

Creon stared at the platform where Aikaterina and the others had disappeared. A worried frown still creased his brow. He started when Morian laid her hand against his cheek to bring his gaze down to her.

"She will be fine," Morian promised her youngest son. "Just love and accept her for who she is and guide her in who she is to become."

Creon drew in a shuddering breath before he nodded. "I fear she will be like her mother," he admitted.

Paul stepped up and placed his hand on Creon's shoulder. "If she is," he said. "Then you have nothing to worry about."

Creon smiled as he looked into the eyes of the man who knew his mate better than anyone other than himself. He nodded his gratitude to Paul. Before he turned to look at his mother. She was glowing with beauty. His eyes softened as he stared down into her eyes. Emotion choked him for a moment and he pulled her into his arms, holding her tightly.

"I love you, *Dola*," he admitted softly in her ear. "You have given me strength. I know you will help guide my daughter," he whispered before pulling back and brushing a kiss across her cheek. "Have fun," he said before he stepped back and shifted.

Morian drew in a shuddering breath and impatiently brushed the stray tear that escaped down her cheek. "Damn!" She laughed, embarrassed. "Why is it when your child says thank you or tells you that they love you that it tears you up?"

Paul laughed and pulled her into his arms. "It doesn't matter which world you are on, they all have the power to do that. But, you know something?" He asked teasingly.

"What?" She asked huskily.

Paul put his hand under her chin to raise it so he could look her in the eye and brushed a kiss across her lips. "They all said to have fun. What do you think?"

Morian giggled and pulled back. "I think you need to teach me about what it is like to be tagged," she said before she shifted into her dragon and rose into the air.

"Oh baby," Paul said as he gave the small, delicate white and gold dragon a slight head start. "I can't wait to tag your ass," he growled out in a low voice before he started running.

Jumping onto a low rock, he shifted into the larger gold dragon and took off after his mate. This was one pursuit he was looking forward to, because when he tagged her, he was making damn sure he never let her go – ever!

## Chapter 23

Paul shook his head as he stared at Trelon. Morian looked horrified at her son. She opened her mouth, but close it again because she didn't know what to say at first.

They arrived back at the palace after taking a three month 'honeymoon' as Paul called it. She hadn't known what a honeymoon was at first, but decided she wouldn't mind being on one for the rest of her life. It had only been the frantic pleas for help from her sons that forced them away from her hidden mountain home. Now, they were standing at the entrance to Trelon and Cara's living quarters wondering what had happened.

Morian looked at Trelon again. She reached out to touch the side of his head where his hair was a little shorter than the other before reaching up to touch a part that looked like it had been burnt. She shook her head before looking at him with a combination of exasperation and horror.

"What happened to you?" She asked, fighting back laughter. "You look like you've been in a battle."

"I have," he growled as he tried to run his fingers through his damaged hair.

"With who?" Paul asked, sliding his arm around Morian's waist needing to touch her.

He knew he was being irrational, but he had thoroughly enjoyed their three months of seclusion and he missed having her in his arms. He pressed a kiss to the top of her head as she leaned back. His eyes taking in the evidence. His lips twitched even as Trelon shot him a murderous glare.

"Amber and Jade," he admitted. "Cara went to fix them some food this morning and put them in bed with me. Amber had already gotten into some of the Gumtree sap. It wouldn't come out so I had to cut it out," he said in a disgruntled voice as he stepped back to usher them in. "The only way she could have gotten into it was if she had help or….." his voice faded as he shook his head. "She must have had some help."

"Are you telling me two infants did this to you?" Morian asked in disbelief.

"Infants! I… they…. I….," Trelon threw his head back and roared in frustration. "Before my mate, I was in control of my life. I could fight any warrior and defeat them," he muttered hoarsely. "Now, I cannot even keep up with two younglings in diapers!" He growled, walking further into his living quarters just as a small head peeked out from under the coffee table.

"I think you mean dragonlings," Morian said with a delighted laugh as she walked forward and knelt down next to the low table.

"Dragonlings?" Paul asked, puzzled.

A moment later, his confusion was cleared up as a brilliant red and pink dragon about the size of an eighteen pound butterball turkey crawled out from under the table into Morian's lap.

"Dragonlings!" Trelon whispered faintly as he stared wide-eyed at his daughter.

Paul wondered which twin had learned to shift. His question was answered a moment later when a tiny purple and pink dragon crawled into the room dragging Trelon's empty sword sheath in her mouth while furiously growling.

Trelon fell onto the couch in stunned silence as Paul walked over to pick up the tiny bundle, leather sheath and all. He held the squirming dragonling in his arms for a moment before she let out a loud sneeze, dropping the sheath and blowing sparks. Fortunately, he was holding her wrapped in his arms with her back against his chest otherwise he would have the same scorched hair as Trelon.

"Oh Gods," Trelon groaned as he touched the section of his ruined hair and looked at his mother. "What am I supposed to do now?" He asked in bewilderment.

"Paul…. Morian, I didn't know you were here!" Cara said excitedly as she walked in carrying a plate with sliced fruit on it. She stopped with her mouth hanging open when she saw Paul holding a small purple and pink dragon. Her eyes moved to where Morian was sitting on the floor with a red and pink one on her lap. "What…. Where…. Oh. My. God!" She giggled as she quickly set the tray on the low table and turned to reach for the tiny dragon in Paul's arms.

"Trelon, aren't they adorable?" Cara asked as she swung the little dragonling in her arms with a laugh. "You are so beautiful!" She told the tiny dragonling.

"Beautiful!" Trelon said with a grin, sitting back and shaking his head. "I think this answers the question as to how my hair got fried this morning when I was still sleeping," he add drily watching as Amber climbed out of his mother's lap and headed for the plate of fruit.

She shifted back into her two-legged form so she could pull herself up. She babbled as she reached for a piece of the fruit that resembled an apple. She fell back onto her butt and laughed up at her daddy. Jade opened her mouth and whimpered as she saw her sister eating.

Cara set the tiny dragon down next to her sister and watched as she tried to reach the plate without shifting. She snorted angrily and began whimpering again in frustration. A small symbiot the size of a large mouse shifted into a bird and flew over to the plate. It picked up a piece of the fruit in its mouth before hopping over to the edge of the table and dropping it into Jade's open one.

Trelon shook his head and leaned his head back against the back of the couch. "Now you know why we called you," he said with a grateful grin. "I had no idea they could shift already."

"Our young develop very quickly, but I don't remember any of you ever shifting this early," Morian mused as she watched Amber tackle her sister who was opening her mouth for more fruit. "Normally, younglings don't shift until they are around two or three years of age."

"It must have something to do with the fact Cara does everything at hyper speed," Trelon joked as he looked at his tiny wife who made a face at him.

"Hey, don't blame this one on me. I'm not the species that could shift," Cara laughed as she leaned over to give him a peck on the cheek. "And I don't do *everything* at hyper speed," she whispered in his ear.

"Maybe I need a reminder," Trelon growled back before he jerked Cara down onto his lap. Her squeal of surprise and delight attracted the attention of Amber and Jade, who had been wrestling on the floor together, both now back in their dragon forms. Within moments, the two tiny dragons were trying to get to their parents. "I give up!" Trelon laughed out as they both grabbed a pant leg and began pulling as Cara started tickling him.

Paul reached down and helped Morian stand up. "I think they will be fine," he murmured as Trelon slid off the couch onto the floor where all three girls could pile on him. "Let's go check on the others. I want to finish the visits so I can get you to myself," he whispered, pressing a kiss to her neck before leading her to the door with a promise to return later. The four on the floor never heard them leave, there was too much laughter and squealing going on for them to hear the door closing.

* * *

Morian giggled and shook her head as they made their way to their next stop. Abby ushered them in and led them to the small dining table set up near the windows. Zoran and Zohar were wrestling on the floor while Abby was working on a sketch for a new stained glass mobile that she was making for Zohar's bedroom. She offered them some tea that she had just made as she talked about how Zohar was doing better about not waking up as much at night anymore.

"We have it much easier than Trelon and Cara or Creon and Carmen," Abby admitted with a grin. "Zohar is just a sweetheart. He loves watching things, and of course," she said with a shake of her head at the two figures crawling around on the floor growling at each other, "wrestling. I think he learned that if he was going to survive Amber and Jade's attacks he was going to have to get better at it," she added with a laugh.

"Especially now," Paul murmured.

"What's happened now?" Abby asked curiously as she poured more tea for her and Morian.

"The girls have discovered their inner-dragon," Morian replied with a grin. "Trelon was wondering why his hair was a little scorched this morning when he woke up."

Abby's hand went to her throat as her gaze went to her son. "You mean…. Will Zohar be able to….," she turned to look back at Paul and Morian. "This early?" She whispered.

"Abby!" Zoran's excited yell drew her attention back to the where her mate and son were playing. "Look!"

"Yes," Morian laughed with delight. "This early," she said looking at a proud dark brown and copper dragon sitting on his father's lower back, his tiny teeth pulling on Zoran's long hair.

"Just be careful if he has to sneeze," Paul warned just as Zohar leaned back and let go of a loud one. Sparks flew over Zoran's head. "They sneeze sparks," he added dryly.

"Oh my," Abby said in a faded whisper before rising to walk over and kneel by her mate who had rolled onto his back with Zohar sitting on his belly. She reached out and touched the tiny dragonling's head. A soft purr escaped as Zohar looked up at his mother. "You are so beautiful. I'm going to have to change the design I was working on," she laughed in a shaky voice.

Zoran reached over and grabbed Abby's hand, pulling her down next to him. Reaching up, he closed his lips over hers in a brief hard kiss. "Thank you so much for this," he muttered, unable to look at his *Dola* and Paul at the moment as emotion overwhelmed him.

Morian pulled on Paul's hand. He nodded as they both stood and quietly left. This was a special moment for her sons. They had thought they needed help but they didn't realize they would never be alone again.

*They have their mates now,* she thought, not realizing she had whispered the words out loud.

"As I have mine," Paul said, pulling Morian into an alcove and kissing her deeply. "You fill my life, Morian."

Morian wrapped her arms around his neck and pulled him down to her. "Let's make the last two visits then I want to go to my – our atrium. I know of this great place where we can be alone," she murmured.

Paul's eyes darkened as he remembered the room where he had first made love to her. "Soon," he promised, pulling her reluctantly out of their temporary hiding place.

They walked in silence, holding each other's hand as they moved to visit with Trisha and Kelan. Paul's throat tightened as Kelan opened the door at their knock. This was the man who had not only healed his baby girl, but made her dreams come true. They looked at each other in silent understanding for several seconds before he heard Trisha's voice asking who was there.

"Hey, baby girl," Paul said, walking into their living area.

"Daddy!" Trisha cried out in delight. "Look Bálint! It's Pops!" She said lifting the small figure sitting on the floor surrounded by toys.

Bálint giggled as his mommy lifted him into her arms. He babbled when he saw his dad. Leaning forward, he opened his arms and lunged for Kelan. Kelan scooped him out of Trisha's arms with a broad grin.

"He has grown so much," Paul observed quietly as he held his large hand out to the baby. Bálint looked at it for a moment before he reached out and grabbed Paul's fingers, trying to draw them into his mouth.

"He's teething," Trisha said as she wrapped her arm around Kelan's waist. "He has been fussy lately too."

Morian leaned forward and whispered in Trisha's ear what was happening with the other younglings. Trisha gasped and looked at Bálint before looking with wide-eyes at Kelan. A soft giggled followed as she shook her head.

"Oh man, do I feel sorry for Trelon," Trisha said with a slow shake of her head.

"Why do you feel sorry for Trelon?" Kelan demanded as he thought of his younger brother. He and Trelon were the closest of the brothers, almost like twins. "What is wrong with him? Has something happened that he hasn't told me about?"

Paul slapped Kelan on the shoulder. "Nothing he can't handle," he responded.

"Amber, Jade, and Zohar have shifted into their dragonling," Morian clarified as she tickled Bálint on the bottom of his foot drawing giggles from him.

"We were about to go visit with Mandra and Ariel," Trisha said, biting her lip. "Ariel was having minor labor pains earlier this morning. Mandra wouldn't let her stay at their mountain home to deliver. The doctor Kor brought back was with her a little while ago.

"How is Kor doing?" Paul asked curiously.

Kelan grimaced before he looked at Trisha who rolled her eyes. "Let's just say, he is careful before he agrees to anything his mate suggests," he said as he ran his hand over the front of his pants.

"Why?" Morian asked as she pulled Bálint into her arms when he held his arms out to her.

"She offered to give him a vasectomy," Trisha replied dryly as she bent to pick up the bag she had by the door. "He was all for it until she described in explicit detail what it involved and why it was given. Personally, I think she made some of it up," she added as she opened the door and waited for the others to walk by.

"He told me what she said," Kelan admitted with a disgusted shudder. "I am never getting one."

"Until you go through labor, I would be careful what you say never to," Trisha replied with a teasing laugh.

"Gods yes," Morian chuckled as she walked through the door. "But I love holding a little one," she said with an envious look.

Paul's eyes darkened as he watched Morian carrying the infant in her arms. A pang of longing pulling at him as he remembered the joys of having Trisha in his arms. He wondered if it was even possible for him and Morian to have a child together or if she would even want one.

Morian turned and looked at him with a warm glow in her dark golden eyes. "Yes," she whispered as if she could read his mind.

Paul nodded quietly to her before focusing on what Kelan was telling him. He was giving him updates on the battle with the Marastin Dow the night Raffvin was defeated. Kelan laughed as he told how Vox and Ha'ven cursed him and Mandra for not leaving them much to do after they came all this way to help out. Vox had to leave almost immediately after to return to Sarafin as Riley had gone into labor and threatened to kill his ass if he wasn't there for the birth of their son. Paul asked about Ha'ven and was surprised when Kelan grew quiet.

"He returned to his world," Kelan said hesitantly looking at Paul with a strange look.

"What's wrong?" Paul asked bluntly.

"I know how protective you are about the human females that were taken," Kelan began.

He looked at Trisha who was talking animatedly with his mother as they walked just ahead of them down the long corridor to Ariel and Mandra's living quarters. He knew she had been upset about Ha'ven's behavior. He had already promised his mate that he would have a word with Ha'ven about what happened.

"And…." Paul pushed.

Kelan released a sigh and ran his hand over the back of his neck. "He took one of the females with him," he said heavily. "From the looks of her living quarters, there was a struggle before she was taken," he added looking at Paul. "He will not harm her."

Paul's jaw clenched in anger. "Which one did he take?" He asked harshly. "You admit there was a struggle. How can you be sure he will not harm her?"

Kelan looked at his infant son who was watching him intently, as if sensing his daddy was upset about something. Kelan gave Bálint a reassuring smile before he answered Paul's questions. He knew he would have to convince Paul that no harm would come to the female.

"He swore that if she still resisted after six months with him that he would return her," Kelan replied. "She is the one that was injured and rescued when Carmen and Creon were on Earth. She is the one who does not speak."

"And Ha'ven thinks kidnapping her - traumatizing her more - will help her how?" Paul asked in disbelief.

Kelan put his hand on Paul's arm, stopping him in the corridor. "I swear on my life that Ha'ven will do everything in his power to help the female. She is his mate," he explained in a low, deep voice. "He needs her."

Paul's jaw twitched as a protest rose before he nodded. These were good men. Kelan would not have made such a vow or let the woman go if he felt she would be in danger. He needed to trust his son-in-law's judgement that the woman would be kept safe.

"Six months?" Paul asked.

Kelan's eyes darkened, but he nodded. "He has three months left," he replied. "I will personally go retrieve her at the end of the three months if she desires it."

Paul nodded before he turned to follow the women. "I'll hold you to that," he said.

"So will Trisha," Kelan muttered under his breath, drawing an amused look from Paul.

A moment later, they were knocking on the door to Mandra and Ariel's living quarters. A harried Mandra opened the door, his face sinking in disappointment when he saw them. He opened his mouth only to close it as Creon came up behind him.

"Come in," Creon said with a relieved grin. "Carmen is with Ariel. We thought you might be the human doctor. Kor insisted she get something to eat. She was not happy with him as she wanted to stay with Ariel and Carmen."

Mandra ran his hands through his hair. "I'm going to kill that piece of Valdier dragon dung. He just wanted time alone with his mate! What about my Ariel? She is in pain!" He moaned out.

"She is in labor," Ariel replied dryly as she held her huge stomach with one hand. "She is not dying."

Mandra swirled around with a dark scowl on his face. "What are you doing up?" He demanded harshly, striding toward her.

"I had to go to the bathroom and walking is supposed to be good," she said before she bent over with a grimace and began panting. A low moan escaped her. "Don't!" She bit out painfully when Mandra reached to pick her up. "Just…. Wait," she panted holding onto his arm with one hand.

"I think the walking made a difference," Carmen said, wrapping her arm around Ariel when she nodded to her. "Let's get you back to bed now."

Mandra was about to follow them when another knock on the door drew his attention. Creon opened it and Kor and the human doctor walked in followed by two of the Valdier healers. "You should not have taken the human healer," Mandra bit out harshly, glaring at Kor menacingly.

"Take a breath, big guy," the female doctor said walking around him toward the bedroom. "You are going to need it so you don't pass out. Let's go see how your wife is doing."

Mandra glared at Kor again before following the dark-haired female healer into his and Ariel's sleeping quarters along with the two older Valdier healers.

Creon looked at Kor, Kelan, Morian and Paul with a grin. "If you hear a big boom that is Mandra hitting the floor," he joked.

Morian looked at her youngest son with a raised eyebrow. "He wouldn't be the only son I have had that did that," she remarked, deciding Ariel had enough support without her being there as well.

She walked over and looked down at the golden symbiot carriage that was in the middle of the room. Spring and Phoenix were curled up, sound asleep. Each had their tiny arms around a smaller symbiot in the shape of a teddy bear. Morian reached down and gently caressed each one of the little girls. Her eyes blurring with tears as she remembered Aikaterina's words about Phoenix.

"She will be alright won't she, *Dola*?" Creon asked, coming up beside her to stare down at his tiny, dark haired daughter.

Morian glanced at Creon before turning her gaze back to the little girl sleeping peacefully. "She will be fine, Creon, how could she not be," she responded softly. "She has two of the best parents to guide her and an older sister who will balance her."

Creon nodded, still looking worried. "I just want to keep them safe," he said. "They are already scooting around. I can't wait until they can crawl," he added before looking at her with a frown. "Have you seen Trelon? He said the twins were very fussy lately. I hope they are not getting sick," he pondered looking worriedly down at his own two daughters.

"They are not sick," Morian chuckled. "They have learned to shift. Poor Trelon looks like a wreck."

Creon blanched at the news. "Already?"

"Already what?" Carmen asked as she came into the room with a huge grin on her face. "Ariel and the baby are fine. Mandra is being revived by the two Valdier healers."

A low chuckle echoed through the room as Paul, Creon, Kor, and Morian enjoyed the news of the new birth and fall of another warrior. Paul and Morian spent time with the others and visited with a tired Ariel and newborn son, Jabir, who was being checked over by Precious, Mandra's golden symbiot and the human doctor. After almost an hour, Paul had enough of family responsibilities. He loved all of the girls, their mates, and his new grandkids, but most of all he loved his mate and wanted to get her alone.

"Now it is my turn," he grumbled as he swept her up into his arms as soon as they were outside the doors.

Morian's laughter echoed down the corridor as her mate walked with a determined look on his face.

Not one guard stopped him, not one servant could stop the grins from spreading across their face, and not one person could turn their gaze away from the beautiful woman he held in his arms as he took the stairs two at a time. Paul gave a swift command to Crash who had been enjoying the return to the palace by sunning in the atrium.

*Make sure we are not disturbed*, Paul ordered as he headed for the staircase to Morian's private rooms upstairs.

## Epilogue

Paul gently set Morian down on her feet in the center of the room and stepped back. His eyes glittered with the gold of his dragon. They both wanted their mate. They had been totally selfish over the last three months, but Paul felt like he had a lifetime of emptiness to make up for. He reached out and touched Morian's soft cheek, letting the back of his fingers skim down it to run along her jaw.

"You are so beautiful," he murmured quietly, his eyes following his fingers as he traced her slightly parted lips. "So damn beautiful," he said.

Morian slipped her tongue out and touched his fingers as they moved across. A sense of feminine power filled her at his swiftly indrawn breath. She parted her lips further, inviting him to touch them again. When he brushed his thumb across her bottom lip, she quickly pulled it into her mouth and wound her tongue around it. His eyes darkened until only the tiny flakes of gold showed in their depths.

She tilted her head, releasing his thumb and smiled up at him. "I never thought I would find you," she admitted in a husky tone filled with desire.

She ran her hands up his chest to the buttons of his shirt. Slowly unbuttoning them, she paused to run her fingers between the soft material and his warm skin. She loved the feel of the coarse hair on his chest as it brushed against her bare skin. She was so focused on what she was feeling that it wasn't until she got to the last button, running her fingers across his taut stomach, that she felt his trembling.

Paul captured her hands in his and drew them up to his lips. "If you go any further, this is going to be over before I want it to be," he said with a dark grin. "My turn," he said, pulling her closer and bending down to kiss her neck on one of the many marks he had given her over the past three months.

Paul breathed in her delicate scent, rubbing his lips across her pounding pulse. *How about a little help here, buddy? I think another mark or two or three are in order. What do you think?* Paul asked his dragon.

*YES!* His dragon roared in delight. *I get Crash to help a little?*

Paul's lips curved into a devious smile. *Why not,* he replied, hoping he didn't come in his pants at just the thought of the fun they were about to have. *Oh, to hell with it! Yes!* He hissed as his cock swelled painfully.

*Crash!* His dragon called out. *Send some re-enforcements.*

Paul groaned as his teeth lengthened and the dragon's fire built at the images filling his mind. Wrapping his arms tightly around Morian's slender form, he bent her back over his arm and bit down breathing the fire that was scorching him. Waves of intense desire, ignited by the fire inside him flowed into her body.

Her gasp, followed by a long moan and grasping fingers pulled at him. He reached up and gripped her shirt tightly in one hand. The sound of material ripping was drowned by the heavy pants and loud moans. His hand moved to her freed breast, searching for the taut nipple he knew would be ready for his mouth.

He reluctantly pulled back as the last of the fire swirled into her blood stream. With a swipe of his tongue, the wound was healed and a new mark formed. He ran his hand down her bare back as his lips moved over her collarbone to the top of her right breast.

"So delicious," he groaned out as he pressed hot kisses against her flesh. "So perfect."

"Paul," Morian hissed out as she pulled back far enough to thrust her distended nipple into his mouth. "Oh yes!" She cried out as liquid heat filled her making her hot and wet.

"I'll never get enough of you," he growled out sliding down to his knees and taking her skirt and the silky panties with him. "Just the way I like you," he said when he saw the glistening of her soft dark curls.

He ran his fingers over the silky hair that covered her mound and tugged on it just enough to let her know that he was in command of her body. Her heavy breathing told him she was beyond excited. His eyes turned to the gold that was winding around her wrists. With a flicker of his eyes to the metal piping running overhead, she was stretched out for him.

"Paul," she whispered in a trembling breath as the combination of the heated desire in his eyes and the scorching fire from his dragon made her body ultra sensitive. "Please, give me the relief I need."

"I will, baby," he promised as he spread the slick, swollen lips. He ran his tongue along her swollen nub loving the way she squirmed and tried to clench her thighs. "Mm, sweet ambrosia."

Morian cried out again as he continued to tease her. Each swipe of his tongue was followed by his thick fingers sliding up inside her. He worked her over and over until she was sobbing.

Her hands twisting on the fine ropes that Crash had sent. He pulled deeply on her, watching her face as he grew slightly rougher in his urgency to make her come. He wanted to taste her sweet orgasm as it washed over his tongue. He nipped her swollen nub while he stroked her hot vagina with three of his thick fingers, stretching her.

The combination of his mouth and fingers and watching him brought her such pleasure that it was too much for the slender hold on her control. Shaking uncontrollably, she shattered. Wrapping one leg over his shoulder, she threw her head back and cried out as she came.

Paul drank deeply as he watched her face. Her eyes were closed and her mouth was parted. Her cheeks blossomed into a soft rose color that shimmered in the waning light of the late afternoon. His eyes moved down to the rounded mounds of her breasts. He pulled back slowly and rose until he stood in front of her.

Her head fell to the side, braced by her extended arms. "I love you," she whispered looking at the shimmer of her essence on his lips.

He ran his hands up over her hips and across her stomach until he could cup her breasts in both his hands. Running his thumbs back and forth over her nipples, he smiled savagely.

"Show me how much," he demanded.

He released her breasts and stood back so he could undo the button and zipper on his jeans. He kicked off his shoes before he pushed his jeans down over his hips. He hissed as his cock sprang free, straining with desire. He was so turned on by her responsiveness that he was about to explode.

Morian's eyelashes swept down to cover the look in her eyes as she ran them down over his powerful body. She licked her lips when her gaze reached his straining cock. His deep groan echoed this time in the room as his body responded to that seductive lick.

Morian touched the gold holding her wrists. *I think he deserves a little payback. What do you think?*

Her dragon purred in agreement, even as the gold bands dissolved, releasing her. She ran her fingers over his shoulders as she pulled him toward the bed she knew he had ordered installed during their absence in replacement of the divan she had kept before. She turned with him until he was the one backing up to the bed.

She dragged her nails down over his chest, scraping his nipples as she went. His breathing deepened as she moved lower. His hands reached out and grabbed her hips, forcing her forward until he could rub his hard, throbbing length against her belly.

"I'm not going to last long if you keep playing," he said harshly, his voice thick with desire. "I want you now," he growled out.

"I know," she whispered as she ran her hands over his. "But payback can be hell according to the girls."

"What...." He started to say before he felt the golden bands on his arms.

Before he could say another word, Morian flicked her wrists to the headboard of the bed. Paul found himself falling backwards as the bands lengthened and wound around the posts on each side. With another flick, he found his legs in the same position, bound to the bottom it.

"Now, it is my turn," she said with a delicious grin. "I think a little dragon's fire of my own will help make sure you last a long, long time."

Paul looked up at the ceiling and strained as he fought the bindings knowing what happened whenever they both breathed the dragon's fire. They practically burnt her mountain home down with the scorching passion. His body arched as he felt her long hair fall loose from the bun she had put it in.

The silky strands fell over his thighs as she bent forward, pressing tiny kisses up his inner thigh. He trembled, knowing what was about to happen. Winding his hands around the gold ropes, his knuckles turned white as he raised his head and forced himself to keep his eyes open so he could watch her. The anticipation was almost worse than the knowing. His body hummed in preparation for the uncontrollable pleasure he was about to feel.

Morian looked at him with eyes the color of molten gold. She licked the spot on his thigh twice before she let her canines elongate. "Please!" He hissed as she ran her tongue over her teeth. "Please, Morian," he begged in a strangled voice.

His balls were so hard and full he hurt. His cock throbbed with pre-cum seeping from the head, weeping in need. He drew his legs up as far as the golden ropes around his ankles would allow but there was no relief except for what she could give him.

"Damn it, please," he panted as he strained, shaking with need.

"I love you, Paul Grove," Morian whispered before turning and sinking her teeth into his thigh, breathing every bit of the love that she had burning inside her for him.

"Oh God!" Paul gasped as he watched and felt the flaming waves rushing through him. His body jerked as his balls drew up impossibly harder before exploding. "Oh God!" He groaned out as his seed shot out coating her shoulder, neck and back.

He would have been embarrassed, if not for the waves of heat filling his balls again. The heady rush of desire was building up, making him continue to throb. His eyes blurred as emotion choked him. He needed to be inside her. He needed to bury himself so deep there was no way to tell where he ended and she began. He groaned loudly when she pulled away and licked the blazing mark of the dragon that she had left on the inside of his thick thigh.

Brushing her lips along his length, she crawled up his body. With a thought, the gold bands dissolved releasing him from his imprisonment. Paul wrapped his hands around her waist and lifted her until she was straddling him.

With one powerful thrust, he lowered her over his thick, swollen length drawing a long groan from both of them. He raised her up again, pulling back just far enough to pull his bulbous head to the entrance of her slick channel before he thrust up at the same time he pulled her down over him again. Over and over he forced her to ride him until he thought he would go mad with the pleasure.

Flipping her over so he was above her, he let the waves of heat coursing through him drive him with a primitive need to claim, possess, and cover her with his essence. He wanted to draw her into him. His body rocked in and out of her. Her fingers clawed at his shoulders and arms as she wrapped her legs around his waist.

"Yes!" She cried out huskily as her body clamped down on his, breaking apart as she came. The waves of fire burning her as she shattered once again. Her cry grew louder as he grunted and stilled above her, his body jerking as he came heavily inside her.

He groaned as his arms trembled at the effort to hold himself up so he wouldn't crush her. "Damn!" He hissed as he closed his eyes and clenched his jaw as the waves continued to pulse out of him.

He fell over to the side, pulling her close to him after several long moments. He held her head against his chest as the aftermath of such an intense orgasm shook him to the core of his being. It didn't matter how many times they came together, each time just kept getting better. His body melted down into the soft comforter.

He drew in a deep breath before he released it slowly. "Wow!" He said, staring up at the ceiling with unseeing eyes. "That was…. Wow," he repeated.

Morian tilted her head to look at him. "That was just the beginning," she grinned. "Just give us a couple of minutes. The dragon's fire has just started," she giggled as she ran her bare leg over his.

Paul shook his head and grinned like an idiot. "I think I have died and gone to heaven," he chuckled.

Morian rolled until she was looking down at him with a serious expression. "Do you think of this as your heaven?" She asked, biting her lip. "I have talked to Abby about this place. Do you think you will miss your world?" She asked, feeling a small blossom of fear blooming inside her.

Paul brushed her dark hair back from her face with a slightly unsteady hand. "You are my world," he said, looking deeply into her eyes. "You said you would like to go to the stars once. I'd like to take you to my world to show you the ranch I have there, but if I never saw it again I wouldn't miss it. I have found everything I thought I would never have again. I have you and a wonderful family," he admitted with a soft smile.

Morian smiled back before her eyes widened as an intense wave of heat brushed against her insides. Paul's smile turned devilish as he felt the answering wave inside him. The dragon's fire was ready for round two – or three – he had lost count. He pulled her down to capture her lips as they both went up in flames again.

* * *

Several hours later, Paul stood on the balcony that curved around their living quarters. He needed to remember to take extra sheets and leave them in the atrium. He was forever destroying Morian's clothing and having to wrap her up in the coverings from the bed. He had carried her back to their rooms a little over an hour ago where they had bathed together before falling into bed again. Even as sated as his body was, he knew there was one more thing he needed to do before he could give in to the exhaustion pulling at him.

He had carefully unwound his body from Morian and pulled on a pair of loose fitting sweatpants that hung low on his hips. He moved on silent feet as he quietly slipped outside so he could look up at the stars glittering in the clear night sky. He breathed in deeply as he felt the sad emptiness that he had carried since Evelyn's death melt away. His eyes moved from star to star until he thought he had found the perfect one.

"Hi honey," he whispered, staring up at it. "I want you to know I'll always love you. You gave me a beautiful baby girl and helped me protect her as she grew into a beautiful young woman," he said before he looked down at where his hands grasped the thick stone of the balcony railing. He looked up again at the twinkling star with a sad smile. "I know you will always be looking over Trisha. She gave us a gorgeous grandson. You would have loved holding him. He is going to be a strong warrior one day, just like his mom and you." He paused for a minute before he continued in a voice gruff with emotion. "I wanted to tell you goodbye and to…. and to thank you for being there all these years. I don't think I would have made it without knowing you were there looking down on us. I've met the most amazing woman. She'll never take your place, but she fills my heart and my soul until I feel like I'm going to burst from all the love I have for her. She is my future now and I'm going to do everything I can to make her happy." His voice faded as he felt a slender hand slip around his waist. He turned to look down at the tear-filled eyes of his true mate. He pressed a kiss to her forehead. "I'd like to introduce you to someone," he muttered in a slightly embarrassed voice.

He pointed up to the star he had chosen. "That's Evelyn. I was just…. I was just…." He couldn't continue as the tears blocked his throat.

Morian looked up where he pointed and smiled. "Hi Evelyn. Thank you so much for taking such good care of Paul and Trisha," she answered softly. "I want you to know I can take over now and care and protect them for you if you would like," she said hesitantly, not sure how Paul would feel about her offering to take over.

Paul trembled as he tried to hold back the tears he couldn't shed when he was a boy of twenty-one. He nodded. "I'd…. We'd like that," he choked out hoarsely.

He turned with Morian standing in front of him, his arms wrapped around her waist and her holding him close. They both stared up at the star in silence for a long time.

"Goodbye Evelyn," Paul whispered.

"Jalo, watch over her for us," Morian whispered at the same time. "She deserves it."

They both watched as the star appeared to glimmer brightly before it flashed. Before their eyes, a second star appeared near it. A deep sigh of contentment echoed in the fragrant night air as the Gods heard their quiet wish and granted it. It would appear even stars had true mates.

To be continued…

### Author's Note:

I hope everyone enjoyed Paul's Pursuit. The story of Paul and Morian might bring the end of the fight for power between the Dragon Lords and their uncle, but it is not the end of the stories of the Valdier dragons, their warriors or their symbiots. The warriors have a different battle now, helping the women they have brought from Earth come to understand and accept them. Some of the women have encountered great hardship and it is hard for them to learn to trust. This is the case for Melina, Cree, and Calo. The stories continue with **Twin Dragons: Dragon Lords of Valdier Book 7**.

## Preview of *Twin Dragons*
## (Dragon Lords of Valdier: Book 7)
## Synopsis

Melina Franklin was barely sixteen when she and her grandfather were kidnapped from their small farm in Georgia by an alien trader and sold to an Antrox mining asteroid in deep space. Mistaken for a young boy, she lives in fear of being found out and sold. Her only companionship for the next four years is her grandfather and the Pactors, the large creatures used for hauling the mining ore, that she takes care of. She dreams of the day when she and her grandfather will somehow escape and return home to the rolling green hills of their farm.

Calo and Cree Aryeh have been secured as the personal guards for Creon Reykill's mate, Carmen Walker. The twin brothers are a rare species of dragon known for their fierceness in battle. Born to the mystic dragon clan of the Northern Mountains, they have given their allegiance to the Dragon Lords vowing to serve and protect the royal family and their new true mates. The brothers know they will never be able to have a true mate of their own. Never in the history of their clan have twin dragons been able to find a mate capable of handling two male dragons. They can only hope that they die in battle so they are not destined to be caged when the loneliness eventually drives their dragons insane.

The twin dragons are confused when two humans are discovered on an abandoned asteroid mine. The old man and his grandson appear normal enough, but their dragons and their symbiots are driving them crazy, insisting the boy is their true mate. Neither knows how to handle the other two parts of themselves or their need to remain close to the boy. On top of that, the young human male refuses to have anything to do with either of them. He hides and avoids them every time they get near him.

Things become clearer when they discover Mel is really Melina. Unfortunately, finding out their true mate is really a woman does little to change her feelings toward them. She is even more determined to return to her world.

When her wish comes true, the brothers know they have no choice but to kidnap her and hide her away. Can they convince her to give them a chance at happiness or will she seek protection from the royal family they have vowed to serve? If that is not bad enough, there is another who has his eye on their mate and will do whatever is necessary to keep her –

including killing the twin dragons who have claimed her first.

## Characters Relationships:

Jalo Reykill, Ruler of Valdier – Deceased, **mated to** Morain Reykill, Prietess to the Hive

### Five sons:

Zoran Reykill, Leader of the Valdier **mated to** Abby Tanner: one son: Zohar

Mandra Reykill, Commander of the warship *D'stroyer* **mated to** Ariel Hamm: one son: Jabir

Kelan Reykill, Commander of the warship *V'ager* **mated to** Trisha Grove: one son: Bálint

Trelon Reykill, Systems and security specialist **mated to** Cara Truman: twin daughters: Amber and Jade

Creon Reykill, Spy/Operative **mated to** Carmen Walker: twin daughters: Spring and Phoenix

Paul Grove Rancher, Scout, Wilderness Survival Trainer **married to** Evelyn Grove – Deceased, **true mate** to Morian Reykill

Raffvin Reykill: Older brother to Jalo.

Vox d'Rojah: King of the Sarafin Warriors **mated to** Riley St. Claire

Ha'ven Ha'darra, Crown Prince of the Curizan **mated to** Emma Watson

If you loved this story by me (S.E. Smith) please leave a review. You can also take a look at additional books and sign up for my newsletter at **http://sesmithfl.com** to hear about my latest releases or keep in touch using the following links:

Website:    http://sesmithfl.com
Newsletter:  http://sesmithfl.com/?s=newsletter
Facebook:   https://www.facebook.com/se.smith.5
Twitter:     https://twitter.com/sesmithfl
Pinterest:   http://www.pinterest.com/sesmithfl/
Blog:       http://sesmithfl.com/blog/
Forum:     http://www.sesmithromance.com/forum/

## Excerpts of S.E. Smith Books

If you would like to read more S.E. Smith stories, she recommends Haven's Song, the first in her Curizan Warriors series. Or if you prefer a Paranormal or Western with a twist, you can check out Lily's Cowboys or Indiana Wild…

## Additional Books by S.E. Smith

### Short Stories and Novellas
    *For the Love of Tia*
        (Dragon Lords of Valdier Book 4.1)
    *A Dragonling's Easter*
        (Dragonlings of Valdier Book 1.1)
    *A Dragonling's Haunted Halloween*
        (Dragonlings of Valdier Book 1.2)

*A Dragonling's Magical Christmas*
  (Dragonlings of Valdier Book 1.3)
*A Warrior's Heart*
  (Marastin Dow Warriors Book 1.1)
*Rescuing Mattie*
  (Lords of Kassis: Book 3.1)

## Science Fiction/Paranormal Novels

### Cosmos' Gateway Series

*Tink's Neverland* (Cosmos' Gateway: Book 1)
*Hannah's Warrior* (Cosmos' Gateway: Book 2)
*Tansy's Titan* (Cosmos' Gateway: Book 3)
*Cosmos' Promise* (Cosmos' Gateway: Book 4)
*Merrick's Maiden* (Cosmos' Gateway Book 5)

### Curizan Warrior

*Ha'ven's Song* (Curizan Warrior: Book 1)

### Dragon Lords of Valdier

*Abducting Abby* (Dragon Lords of Valdier: Book 1)
*Capturing Cara* (Dragon Lords of Valdier: Book 2)
*Tracking Trisha* (Dragon Lords of Valdier: Book 3)
*Ambushing Ariel* (Dragon Lords of Valdier: Book 4)
*Cornering Carmen* (Dragon Lords of Valdier: Book 5)
*Paul's Pursuit* (Dragon Lords of Valdier: Book 6)
*Twin Dragons* (Dragon Lords of Valdier: Book 7)

### Lords of Kassis Series

*River's Run* (Lords of Kassis: Book 1)
*Star's Storm* (Lords of Kassis: Book 2)
*Jo's Journey* (Lords of Kassis: Book 3)
*Ristéard's Unwilling Empress* (Lords of Kassis: Book 4)

### Magic, New Mexico Series

*Touch of Frost* (Magic, New Mexico Book 1)
*Taking on Tory* (Magic, New Mexico Book 2)

### Sarafin Warriors

*Choosing Riley* (Sarafin Warriors: Book 1)

*Viper's Defiant Mate* (Sarafin Warriors Book 2)
**The Alliance Series**
*Hunter's Claim* (The Alliance: Book 1)
*Razor's Traitorous Heart* (The Alliance: Book 2)
*Dagger's Hope* (The Alliance: Book 3)
**Zion Warriors Series**
*Gracie's Touch* (Zion Warriors: Book 1)
*Krac's Firebrand* (Zion Warriors: Book 2)

# Paranormal and Time Travel Novels
**Spirit Pass Series**
*Indiana Wild* (Spirit Pass: Book 1)
*Spirit Warrior* (Spirit Pass Book 2)
**Second Chance Series**
*Lily's Cowboys* (Second Chance: Book 1)
*Touching Rune* (Second Chance: Book 2)

# Young Adult Novels
**Breaking Free Series**
*Voyage of the Defiance* (Breaking Free: Book 1)

# Recommended Reading Order Lists:
http://sesmithfl.com/reading-list-by-events/
http://sesmithfl.com/reading-list-by-series/

## About S.E. Smith

S.E. Smith is a *New York Times, USA TODAY, International, and Award-Winning* Bestselling author of science fiction, fantasy, paranormal, and contemporary works for adults, young adults, and children. She enjoys writing a wide variety of genres that pull her readers into worlds that take them away.